I0825410

POINT SAUVIGNON BLANC

BLOOD, WINE, MAGIC
BOOK THREE

JUSTIN GODEY

Point Sauvignon Blanc - Blood, Wine, Magic: Book 3 by Justin Godey

This book is dedicated to anyone who has ever made a mistake that they soon regretted. There is no fixing the past, only trying to improve the future.

Oh, and my family, everyone judges if you don't dedicate these things to your family.

I should dedicate this book to coffee as well. Thank you, coffee; I wouldn't be the person I am today without you. Spoiler alert: I really like coffee. Miles's experiences with coffee in this book are largely drawn from my own struggles with caffeine addiction.

And finally, I'd like to dedicate this book to Gentianales Rubiaceae Coffea C. Arabica. Yes, I know that's just the taxonomy of the Arabica coffee plant. I don't intend to offend Robusta; I'll drink it in a pinch, but I prefer the Arabica bean, preferably grown in rocky highland soil. Maybe a bold Peruvian blend. Medium roast. Just a dash of cream and sweetener. Dammit, now I want a cup of coffee...

"Heist movies tend to be a bit superficial, glamorous, and fun. They don't tend to be emotionally engaging."
Christopher Nolan

"Any time you take a chance you better be sure the rewards are worth the risk because they can put you away just as fast for a ten dollar heist as they can for a million dollar job."
Stanley Kubrick

PROLOGUE

ONCE AGAIN, I find myself sitting in bed awake. I check the clock. It's three fifteen in the morning. The clock read seven after three last time I checked, which felt like five hours ago. My body wants to sleep, but my mind is racing. For some years, thoughts of money raced through my mind to keep me awake at night. How was I going to pay rent? Curse the rising prices of coffee—that sort of thing.

Since I got the Syzmek building job, money has always appeared right when things got desperate. A contract with a winery here, someone's estate to be warded there. More recently, Redbrook paid me a lot of cash to betray her, so money isn't what is eating away at me tonight.

Tonight, I'm catastrophizing—I think that's what it's called. What is Hale up to? Is Jeff going to be okay? Is whatever has been going on with him my fault? Am I dragging my friends into a world of misery and hardship? What about Genevieve? Is this going to work out? Is she going to end up seeing me for the phony I am? What does she see in me, anyway?

She is gently snoring next to me. I feel more jittery and agitated; I don't want to wake her up, so I slip out of bed. I slide my jeans on in the dark, a far less graceful endeavor than I'd like. After three tries to put my leg through the pocket, I successfully get them on backward once. Eventually, I manage half-clothed. I retrieve my phone from the bedside table where it is charging and slide it into my pocket, then skulk out her bedroom door and close it carefully behind me.

I'm standing in her living room. Her house is small, perfect for one person, maybe a couple, but you could never raise kids here. It has a simple floor plan, a single large room with a vaulted ceiling, and a split level in which a single one-foot rise separates the kitchen/dining room from the living room. It is all one open floorplan; the only separate rooms are a bedroom and the bathroom. Her kitchen features a large free-standing range with an overhead vent, an inobtrusive sink, and a small refrigerator. The cabinets are well camouflaged on the walls and beneath the counters.

Next to the kitchen is a small dining area with a hardwood table that might seat four in a pinch but is ideally sized for one or two people. Her living room features a large cushy couch, a love seat, and a matching coffee table, perfectly decorated with coffee table books and everything. The whole space is done up in a bright pastel theme. It looks like a quaint weekend cottage in an interior design magazine.

The lone bathroom in the house is next to the single bedroom. I slide in and do not flip the light switch. I know from experience that the vent fan here sounds like an airliner taking off. I relieve myself by the subtle illumination of a night-light. I wash my hands and stare at my reflection in the mirror above the sink. It is just a matter of shadow, but in the faint glow of the nightlight, I look gaunt and skeletal.

The mirror is also a medicine cabinet. I am bored and curious. What does Genevieve store in her cabinet? I open it quietly. I don't remember my mother very well, but my father would often quote her, "Don't be curious if you are afraid of what you'll find."

The cabinet is filled with all sorts of first aid and hygiene products, but the two translucent amber bottles come to the forefront of my attention—prescription medications. To look or not to look? I debate back and forth for an instant. But if I weren't going to snoop, I wouldn't have opened the medicine cabinet in the first place. I strain my ears but hear only silence and the distant hum of the refrigerator. I carefully take the bottles down and turn their labels up in the soft LED glow.

Both bottles are labeled venlafaxine. The dosage says two 75mg tablets a day. To be taken with food. I'm not familiar with this medication. I put it back on the shelf. It takes only a moment on my phone to discover that it is a powerful antidepressant, with 150 mg being a fairly sizeable dose. It shouldn't be mixed with alcohol and can have pretty crazy interactions, which probably explains why she seems so out of control when she drinks.

She's never mentioned depression or being on medication. I've never seen her take any. Maybe it is an old prescription. I should close the medicine cabinet and let it be, but I don't. I pull the medication back out and look at the prescription dates. It is current.

This isn't helping my racing mind. Now, I am curious to know why she's on medication. I don't want to judge her for it. I know I shouldn't. Deep down, I know some part of me does. Our culture has a very unhealthy and stigmatizing relationship with such things. Intellectually, I know this. But it is also the culture I was raised in. Hate it as much as I do, the programming is there. Mostly, though, I think I am hurt that she hasn't mentioned it. Not judgment, I tell myself, curiosity. I can't help being curious. Anyone would be. I can't ask her directly without telling her I snooped around her house while she was asleep. Why did I do that?

What were my intentions when looking through her cabinets? I don't feel like I had any. It was something I just did. I regret it now. Do my intentions matter, or is it my actions?

There is an expression that the road to hell is paved with good intentions. This would imply that intent is not a factor at all but that, ultimately, we are judged only by the outcome of our actions.

That is not right, though; intention must be a factor; otherwise, the universe is just a random series of devolving events, so why bother trying? I've always tried to do the right thing, though rarely has the result been so black and white as I might hope. Have I always tried to do the right thing? Or is that something I tell myself? Like with Redbrook. The antediluvian, cannibalistic, enslaving nightmare that she was.

Lorelei Redbrook was ultimately stopped. Murdered, to be more precise. I didn't do that myself, though I played my part. Is being an unwitting accessory to murder as bad as being a willing one?

Some might dismiss Redbrook's end, saying that she was a monster. But monsters, by and large, started as people. They just let themselves go down that slippery moral slope, justifying their transgressions against others, themselves, against humanity, against morality. This one little thing was okay because it served a greater good or because the victim themselves was a monster. Maybe Redbrook started being a monster by snooping through people's medicine cabinets.

I see where that spiraling logic leads; my unslept mind wanders off the path and down avenues and alleys perhaps best avoided. Snooping in Genevieve's medicine cabinet was the wrong decision. But it is not always so clear-cut. I have also been in too many situations with no clear 'right' answer to a problem. The scenario where to aid the many, you have to harm the few. It's the famous Trolley Problem.

However, the Trolley Problem is foolish. It puts the burden of action on the shoulders of a single individual while creating a scenario with many individuals. Group action could avoid the moral dilemma altogether. While I understand that it is a thought exercise, it misses the key strength of the human species: community.

Am I, like the Trolley Problem, foolish? How often have I taken that burden onto my shoulders when I could seek help? Why would I keep acting out the scenario if I understood the flaw? Is it some deep-rooted megalomania? Do I believe I am unique in my ability to handle these situations? Is my ego the root of my problems? Is my ego why I am snooping through Genevieve's stuff in the middle of the night? Am I asking myself questions, or are they answers that I frame this way to soften the blow of the truth?

If I could face the answers without leaving them hanging as questions, perhaps my brain could relax and let my body rest. Maybe I'd stop doing stupid things like rifling through my girlfriend's medicine cabinet in the middle of the night. If raindrops were lemonade and gumdrops, the world would be very sticky and disgusting.

I decide to forget the amber bottles in the medicine cabinet. Maybe, if I forget about it, ethically, it will be like it never happened. I creep into Genevieve's kitchen to see if I can muster a cup of coffee.

CHAPTER 1

"This is the place," Genevieve says as she parallel parks on the narrow residential street. It's a typical cool, grey, overcast Portland morning. This is an older neighborhood on top of a hill. Several large Victorian homes have been braced in by smaller mid-century homes and further boxed in by even smaller homes built in recent years as Portland's urban boundaries have necessitated subdivision.

She indicates a large, slate-grey Victorian with white trim. It has a two-foot high wrought iron fence around it, giving it the look of a funerary plot. A XenCar is parked and charging in the driveway. The electric charging apparatus looks strangely anachronistic next to the looming cupolas of the old house. Once, this house was probably the only one on a large estate, but now its yard is only ten feet or so wide on each side, with six-foot wooden fences separating it from the neighbors.

As we leave the car and cross the street, I have an overwhelming sense of déjà vu. At first, I glance around to see if Magdalena is nearby, but then I shake my head. This is different. This is not the preternatural disorientation I get when the young lady distorts time around me. I know this place, but I have no idea how that is possible. This is my first time in Portland, Oregon, at least that I am aware of.

We walk through an opening in the tiny wrought iron fence and up the path. The door is painted a slightly lighter shade of grey than the rest of the building. The color scheme is uninspiringly monochromatic.

"So, you are writing a piece on this very welcoming building?" I ask. I look pointedly around the front stoop. Three wireless video cameras are mounted so that there is no approach to the front of the house that won't be recorded. A large sign on the door reads 'No solicitors' with a handwritten note below that says 'If you weren't invited, go away.' Genevieve said she had some work to do here but was very light on the details.

"Not exactly; it isn't really work. It's more like helping a friend."

I narrow my eyes at her. She definitely said this was work when we left.

"Portia and I went to college together," she says.

At that instant, almost as if they had planned it, Portia swings the door open. She is wearing a sleeveless top and yoga pants. I would describe her as a commercially attractive woman, probably in her late thirties. Her blond hair is intentionally touseled and wind-blown. Her makeup is light and subtle. This is someone who has spent a lot of time trying to make it look like she just finished modeling a workout shoot.

"Genevieve!" Portia says as she swings the door open. She and Genevieve exchange a weird pantomimed hug where they intentionally don't touch and blow air kisses at each other's cheeks. "And this must be your ghost hunter!"

This exchange has a predatory energy that reminds me of two lions circling each other before they start to fight. I can't help but think Genevieve may have left the 'enemy' suffix off when she said Portia was a friend.

I look at Genevieve with an eyebrow raised. "Ghost hunter?" I mouth at her.

She gives me an innocent little shrug that says, "Oopsie."

"I'm Miles," I say, holding out my hand for a shake, "I'm an apotropaist, not a ghost hunter."

She goes to shake my hand, but I start moving it up and down when she's just a couple of inches away, imitating their weird, not touching hug-kiss-kiss routine.

Judging by the contorted facial expressions, neither seems to understand my joke. I shrug and then shake her hand.

"Come in, come in!" She says, ushering us into the house. As we step through the portal, I once more have a strange recollection of this house—the lines of the hallway, the narrow stairwell up. I don't recognize the art on the walls or the shoes in the shoe rack by the door, but I recognize the house.

I follow the two ladies who are having a catch-up. I am not paying attention to what they are saying. I am too busy being confused, examining the lines and layout of this house. I feel like I have spent time in this building.

Portia leads us down a hall and through a door into a dining room. It isn't very big, there is just enough room for a table for six and a sideboard. Somehow, I know that all the rooms in this house are small, but there are many. We sit down at the table, and the ladies are still chatting.

"Miles!" Genevieve says, breaking me out of my reverie.

"Yeah?" I say, shaking my head. Apparently, they started talking to me.

"You okay?" Genevieve asks, concerned, "You seem distracted. Portia was asking you your favorite question."

"It's just that window there," I say, pointing at the big bay window next to the table we are seated at, "It's supposed to be stained glass, isn't it? Like a raven or something?"

The window seems wrong to me. I feel like I've seen it a thousand times, and it was stained glass, but this is just a standard, old-fashioned, single-paned window.

"Oh," Portia says, annoyed, "Yeah, they just hung that up for the show."

"The show?" Genevieve asks.

And now I know why this house is so familiar.

"Craven's Gate," Portia and I both say simultaneously.

Portia scrunches her face like she smells something unpleasant and nods, "Your boyfriend is a Gater."

Gaters are obsessive fanatics of the shows, people who post on forums, write racey fan fiction and stand in lines at conventions. My interest in the show is purely professional.

"Not a Gater," I mutter defensively.

Genevieve looks confused.

"It's a TV show," I say, "This is Sophiana Craven's house! Like half the series is set here."

"This is my house," Portia says, with a put-out tone, "And like half the series was filmed here. Which at the time was great. It helped to pay off my mortgage and some of the remodel. But then Gaters, that's what fans call themselves, stop by from time to time and want a tour. Or to rent it, or god, I don't want to know what else they want to do in my home."

Genevieve looks puzzled, "I've never heard of it."

"It was only on the Soliloquy Streaming Network," I say.

"Don't they only air daytime dramas?" Genevieve asks.

"No!" I protest.

"Yes." Portia corrects.

"Okay, yes, but I only watched it for professional purposes," I say. It's not true, but I am a little embarrassed. It was the trashiest sort of daytime drama you could find but also very engaging.

"Professional purposes?" Genevieve asks skeptically.

"It was about a coven of witches, their romantic entanglements, and the weird twists and turns of their lives. How Sophiana's new beau turns out to be her long lost brother, but then in season three, it's actually the spirit of her great-great-grandmother possessing her brother to reclaim the family estate," I begin, then realize I am not selling my professional interest, "Anyway! All the magic depicted in it was like actual, real magic. It all would have worked if they used real blood instead of stage blood."

Now, it is Portia's turn to raise a skeptical eyebrow.

"This ties well into Portia's question that you ignored, Miles."

I raise an inquisitive eyebrow.

"She asked what an apotropaist is."

I sigh, thankful that Genevieve gave me a path out of this conversational tangent.

"Ah. Right, hence my favorite question. An apotropaist," I say, transitioning into my lecture voice, "Is someone who uses wards and magical protectives to prevent evil or dark magic."

"And that is different than a ghost hunter; how exactly?" Portia asks skeptically.

"Well, it's just like on Craven's Gate!" I say, reflecting once more on exactly how accurate that show was.

"Oh, it was filmed in my house, but I never watched it. When they started filming, I'd leave for three or four weeks and return when it was over. For the first season, I just went to my sisters in Hoboken, but when they filmed the fourth season, I went to Milan," She gets a faraway look in her eyes, "I do miss that part of the show."

"What about for the movie?"

"Nothing, they didn't film the movie here. All the shots of the house were B roll from previous seasons," Portia says bitterly.

"I think we are getting a little off track here," Genevieve says, rolling her eyes, "Tell him about the haunting."

"Yes, the haunting," Portia begins, "Aptro-whatever, ghost buster, I don't care, the point is my house is haunted."

"Ah. It's not, though," I say.

Portia crosses her arms as Genevieve shakes her head mirthfully. Genevieve knows exactly where this is going but seems to be enjoying it anyway.

"You haven't even seen the evidence. How do you know it isn't haunted?"

"Well, if you had watched Craven's Gate, you'd know that hauntings aren't real—at least not in the sense most people mean them."

"Okay," Portia says, "You fight evil magic for a living, and you don't believe in ghosts?"

"You have no idea how often I've done this, but it's never hauntings. The spirits of the dead just don't come back. It's just not a thing. I've seen hexes, curses, compulsions, and thirty-foot-tall demons made of fire and burning cows, but ghosts are not a thing."

Portia quirks an eyebrow, "Then how do you explain that?"

She points over my shoulder. I turn around slowly to see a mirror on a wall behind me. There are smudged red letters on the mirror. It looks like dry-erase marker. The letters read: Murder.

I nod and turn back to face her.

"I could come up with a dozen explanations that don't involve ghosts, and only two of them even involve magic. That's a parlor trick at best. At worst, you wrote that on the mirror, and we didn't notice it when we came in."

Portia glowers at me.

I look her up and down. My first instinct is that I am being had. That this is some prank or gag. It could be a stunt to make me look foolish on the internet. But Portia's eyes are wide, her posture alert. She doesn't seem scared, exactly, but certainly anxious and even confused. She is either a very good actor or not the perpetrator of this gag.

Genevieve stands just behind Portia to one side and mouths at me, "What do you think?"

Or maybe she mouthed, "Want a drink?" But that seems less likely. Though, now that I think of it, I could use some coffee.

"Do you have coffee? Could I get a cup, please? Then you can tell me the whole story from the beginning."

"Oh, yes, of course," Portia says. Her face becomes a placid mask, and despite this conversation being strangely tense from the beginning, I can't tell if she's peeved or relieved.

Portia gets up and leaves Genevieve and me alone in the dining room.

"What the hell, Genevieve?" I whisper to her, "You said this was for your job, not a job for me!"

"I know, Miles. I'm sorry," she whispers back. I just didn't think you'd want to come if I told you it was haunting."

"You thought correctly."

"Portia and I are old friends. I figured if anybody could help her out here, it was you."

"I object less to that than being kept in the dark. This is just like with your mother!" I hiss back at her.

"What about my mother?" She asks, her face scrunching up in confusion.

"How you left Napa and just said you had something to deal with at home and didn't tell me it was with your family, but you told Emily!"

"That's what's been bugging you? Yes, Miles, I told Emily because Emily asked! You just shrugged and said," She puts on a hurtfully goofy face and tone mocking me for the final word of the sentence, "Okay."

I sputter incoherently at her.

"And what about you?" She continues, "I don't know anything about your family. Are your mother and father alive? Do you have siblings? Where did you grow up? What, are you an orphan? Did you hatch out of an egg? You never tell me anything about yourself!"

I cross my arms and sit back, glowering. I am pretty guarded about my life.

"You're right, though this probably isn't the time to have a heart-to-heart. I had a mother, a father, and a brother, but they are all gone. It's not something I like to think about, let alone talk about. And I didn't ask you because I wanted to respect your privacy and figured if it were something you wanted to share, you would tell me."

"Oh," her face softens, "I didn't know about your family."

"How could you?"

"You are right. This probably isn't the time to discuss this, and I should have told you what we were doing here before we came. I'm sorry."

"Me too," I sigh. I'm not sure it's true, but it seems like the best way to get peace now.

"Will you help my friend?" Genevieve asks with an earnest look on her face.

"Will you be honest with me that she's not really your friend?"

Genevieve smirks slightly, "Okay, will you help my frenemy? We've always been like that, one-upping each other. I get a job, she gets a better job, I get engaged, she marries a rich old guy, I get a house, she gets a bigger house."

"You were engaged?" I ask.

Just then, Portia comes in with a large tray of coffee and biscuits.

"A story for later," Genevieve says, terminating our whispered conversation.

"What are you two whispering about?" Portia asks.

"Miles was just telling me how much he likes the painting," Genevieve says, indicating a still life of a vase full of flowers. It's one of the most banal pieces of art I have ever seen. Until this instant, I haven't even given it a second glance.

"Yes, the lines are very...vertical," I observe.

"Eh," Portia says, "One of Pietro Beauneaux's earlier works. It cost me fifty thousand at auction, but it is worth it to say I have one of his pieces on the wall. Good eye, Miles."

"Pietro Beauneaux?" Genevieve inquires.

"Oh, an up-and-coming artist, the next Anselm Kiefer, some say. I frequented his gallery here before he moved back to Paris."

"Yes, Genevieve, the next Anselm Kiefer," I say with a smirk, glancing at Genevieve quizzically. Everything is a humble brag with Portia. I very much want to get this over with.

"Miles does love the art scene," Genevieve says, voice dripping with sarcasm. Portia either doesn't notice or refuses to acknowledge her tone.

"Portia," I say, taking a hot mug of coffee and adding cream and sugar, "your alleged haunting. From the beginning."

"Yes," she sips her coffee, purses her lips, and taps one finger on her pouty lower lip to show that she is thinking.

"When my husband and I got married, we bought the house. It's old—old for Portland, anyway—nothing like the old buildings in Milan. There is this lovely little villa where I spend my summers. The building itself is over a thousand years old. And the view..."

"Portia," Genevieve interrupts.

"Yes, of course," Portia continues. Anyway, nothing remarkable or strange happened for the first ten years I lived here, but over the past year or so, strange things started happening."

"If I might interrupt, does your husband still live with you?"

"Oh, no, he died. Cancer," she says. She seems very matter-of-fact about it, and I don't sense any emotion in her voice. There must be something in my expression because she defensively adds, "It was a long time ago. I've lived here without him for almost nine years. We were only together for a few years, but you never really get over it, true love."

Out of the corner of my eye, I can see Genevieve roll her eyes a little at this last part. Apparently, she doesn't think much of Portia's love for her deceased husband.

"Okay, so over the past year, strange things started happening. What kind of strange?"

"You know, little things. My car keys wouldn't be where I left them. I'd hear footsteps in other parts of the house when I was alone, that sort of thing."

I am doing the math in my head. Craven's Gate had five seasons before it was canceled. The last episodes were released about five years ago if she lived here for ten years before the strange things started happening...

"So Craven's Gate started filming here shortly after you moved in."

She nods, "Yes, my husband was old friends with one of the producers. In fact, that was how we found the house initially."

"So you bought the house specifically to rent it to the production team?"

"Yes, I guess so. Scott, my late husband, managed all that in that first season of filming. But then he got sick, and things changed very fast. But I'm not really interested in your fanboying. I have a real problem here!"

I glower at her.

"I think this is relevant, back to the haunting. Things started getting weird: stuff missing, strange sounds. Probably weird lights in the mirrors, cold spots, electrical problems?"

"Yes, all that at first. Then the messages on the mirror."

I glance back at the mirror that had the word written on it. For the first time in this whole affair, I actually feel a little ill at ease. The smudged red letters are gone. It's as if they had never been there at all. No one has been to that side of the room. This doesn't make it supernatural, but it does add an additional level of premeditation to the act.

"It's always like that. They say stuff like Murder. Betrayal. Lies. Perfidy. I had to look that last one up; it means deceitfulness. Then you turn around, and they are gone."

"Perfidy," I say. I know the word, but only because of a very specific context. "In the final season arc of Craven's Gate, Sofiana believes that Gerald's ghost is haunting her."

They both stare at me blankly.

"You see, Gerald and Sofiana were engaged at the end of season two. But Gerald broke it off in season three when he discovered that Sofiana was sleeping with Zane. Gerald was so distraught that he threw himself off of St. John's Bridge and died. Later, Sarah, Sofiana's maid, discovered that Zane was, in fact, an incubus and that Sofiana was enthralled. Then, Sarah, whom it was hinted at in the first season but they didn't confirm until the movie, was actually Sofiana's half-sister. It turns out that Sofiana's father, Vladimir, had an illegitimate child with Consuela, who was Sofiana's nanny when she was little. Sarah was Vladimir and Consuela's daughter. Anyway,

Sarah broke the spell that had enthralled Sofiana. Sarah was always better at magic than Sofiana, even though Sofiana was made First Witch of the coven in season three and Sarah was still just a maid."

Their blank stares have changed to mildly horrified looks.

"Well, it's interesting because Sarah is the only one who wasn't raised in the Coven, but she's the most powerful sorceress of them all."

"I'm sorry, Miles, you lost us in your fan-boy diatribe," Genevieve says, hiding a smile.

"I'm not a fan-boy. It was a professional interest. The magic was all real!" I say defensively. My face is warm and flushed with embarrassment. I don't like to admit it, but I got pretty into Craven's Gate a few years back. I was going through some stuff.

"Okay, sorry! The point is that Sofiana thinks that Gerald's ghost is haunting her for her infidelity. One of the recurring events is that she keeps seeing the word 'Perfidy' in blood on everything. It's not just mirrors, but curtains, windows, the table, whatever. Here, it looks like dry-erase marker, not blood. But perfidy is not a common word. I'd never heard it until the show."

"So you think there is a link between the show and this haunting?" Genevieve asks.

"It's a good place to start anyway," I say.

"Again, I never watched the show. Is it Gerald's ghost?" Portia asks.

"What? Um, no, it was revealed to be Gerald's twin brother, Marcus. Marcus blames Sofiana for Gerald's death and has summoned a Demoglorbin. It's a dumb name, I know. In the show, it's like a torment demon - an imp maybe? I don't know. Anyway, he summons this Demoglorbin through the gate in Sofiana's basement. You see, in Sofiana's basement, there is a magical portal. The coven can summon supernatural stuff through this gate. The gate is a recurring mechanic for chaos and strife in the show. Her last name is Craven, ergo, Craven's Gate."

They both continue staring at me in mild disbelief and possibly disgust.

"I digress. So Marcus wants to torment Sofiana until she confesses to causing Gerald's death. Eventually, he's found out, and it is revealed that Sofiana was enthralled. Marcus forgives her and calls off the demon, but not before it kills her dog, Fluffy."

I stop for a breath. Genevieve and Portia are both silently looking at me like I am a clown who showed up at a cocktail party.

"I'm man enough to admit, I cried when Fluffy died. The weird part was that they decided to have Sofiana and Marcus get married and have kids at the end of the movie. That never made sense to me." My mouth keeps talking even though my brain keeps telling it to shut up.

"Miles, this show sounds like absolute trash."

"Anyway," I say, trying to change the topic quickly, "Portia, does the house have a basement?"

The basement in Craven's Gate is a sprawling labyrinth full of dungeon cells, rooms with stone altars, weird alchemical labs, and the like. Secretly, I hope this house has all of that. I suspect that all it has is a furnace and some storage space.

"No," Portia says, surprising me.

"No?" I ask, disappointed.

"Well, not really. There is like a root cellar sort of thing."

"Close enough, can we see it? I'm getting an inkling of what's going on."

"Yeah, I guess," Portia says, standing up. I take a biscuit and my mug of coffee with me.

"I'm going to hang back here," Genevieve says, "If you don't mind?"

I give her a thumbs up.

"Um, yeah, I guess, if you're sure," Portia says suspiciously.

Genevieve nods, and Portia reluctantly leads me down the hallway. We go through another hall to a back door and, from there, out onto a veranda.

"The entrance is outside of the house?"

"Yes," she says, walking down the stairs and into a little garden in the backyard. The minute we are out of sight of Genevieve, Portia starts walking uncomfortably close to me. She smells like flowers with a faint musky undertone.

There is a low wall of stacked and mortared river stone, and a pair of storm doors are set in the middle. "I don't use the cellar. I think the house originally had an exterior kitchen building here, and they used this as a root cellar and pantry. My husband had some tools stored down here when we first moved in, but I don't do anything with it. You can't access it from within the house."

We each grab a door and yank it open. A set of rough stone stairs descends into the darkness below us. She makes a dramatic sweeping motion with her arms, indicating that I should go first.

"There is a light at the bottom of the stairs. Hopefully, the bulb still works."

I descend down the stairs carefully. Portia starts descending right behind me.

"Oops!" She exclaims as she stumbles on a step, grabbing my arm to stabilize herself. Her hair brushes across my neck as she rights herself. The odor of flowers and musk fills my nose. She squeezes my bicep, "Oh, do you work out?"

Oh, boy.

"Nope, I'm just naturally this flaccid," I say, stepping

quickly to the bottom step and away from her. I see a pull string hanging from the ceiling. I yank it. An exposed bulb flicks on above my head. It is very bright. I glance up and see that it is a modern, high-efficiency LED.

"Were LED bulbs a thing when you were last down here?" I ask.

"Huh?" Portia grunts. She seems annoyed that I brushed off her cheap advance.

"This bulb looks new," I observe, "Someone has been down here more recently than you."

"That's weird," she says.

The walls and ceiling are more mortared river stone. The ceiling has a sort of vaulted look, where the stone has been laid in a row of arches so that it will support the weight of the dirt above. Thick timbers have been placed haphazardly as supports. Newer boards have been nailed in over the years to bolster these supports. The space is long and relatively narrow, extending under the house itself. Ten feet ahead, I see another drawstring.

As I walk slowly forward, a smell hits my nose. It's an unpleasant smell that overpowers Portia's overwrought perfume. It's a smell I wish I were less familiar with. It's the smell of rotting animal carcasses. I get to the next pull string, and before I pull it, I say over my shoulder to Portia, "I think we are going to find something putrid down here."

"Is that smell what I think it is?"

"Probably," I say as I pull the string to turn on the light. Another bright LED flicks on over my head and illuminates the rest of the root cellar.

There, in the bright, harsh light of the exposed bulb, I see the exact scene I expected to see. It is an almost perfect recreation of the gate altar from Craven's Gate, surrounded by an inclusive circle. Floating above the altar is a weird black form.

I can't tell if it is two-dimensional or three-dimensional, as no matter how I move my head, it looks like a flat, colorless disc. One would most easily describe its color as black, but that word does not do it justice. It is abyssal, not only an absence of light but almost as if it is consuming the light itself. It reminds me of the fleeting shadows that formed around Circe when she shadow jumped, but it is a stationary, unmoving shape about two feet across. Looking at it gives me a weird sensation deep in my stomach, Something between vertigo and existential terror. Its very presence triggers a primeval sense of wrongness in my brain.

The ground around it is littered with the tiny, bloody little bodies of white mice. The kind of mice one would buy in a pet store to feed to a python, I think they call them feeder mice. I feel bile in the back of my throat as I look at the smears of blood in a circle of sigils around the altar.

Portia screams a high, shrill scream of terror. I turn to try to calm her, but her scream is cut short by the sound of the storm doors to the outside slamming shut. The air suddenly gets chilled, and the light bulbs start to flicker. The flickering light seems wrong, casting shadows that are too deep and too long.

Then the lights go out, and we are plunged into darkness.

Portia screams some more.

I consider trying to calm her down, trying to say something or do something. But she couldn't hear me over her own screaming if I did. I fumble in my pocket for my cell phone so that I can use it as a flashlight. It takes me a few tries before I realize that it, too, isn't going to work.

Then I hear something; it is faint at first. Slowly, it is getting louder—a strange rhythmic chittering. Portia stops screaming.

"What is that?" She asks, her voice trembling with fear.

"It's the Demoglorbin. This is exactly like a scene from

Craven's Gate," I say, my voice calm. Somewhere deep in the back of my mind is a little part that wants to scream and panic and run. But I know from personal experience and from watching the show that panic is the worst thing I could do right now.

"You said it was made up for the show. How can it be here?" Portia's shaky voice asks in the darkness.

"It can't. I mean, it can, sort of. It's complicated. This isn't really my area of expertise. But I think my friend Russ would say something like," I say and then begin my best imitation of Russ, "So um, like dude, man, dude, see, like any time you think of something, it exists somewhere in the universe and the more people that think about it, the more um, like gravity it gets and the closer to like reality. So if you are in like the right, dude, bro, man, place and time and like remind the universe of that thought, it is like easy to summon something from the like zeitgeist of the universe, dude, man, dude, bro, amigo, peace dude."

"What?" Portia says.

"Sorry, it was funny if you know Russ. I think the idea is that when we imagine a thing, now that thing is in the universe. Somewhere. If it's just us imagining it, the thing is small, light, and distant. So things that lots of people think about and imagine are nearer and can more easily be summoned."

I pause to see if she has any questions, but she remains silent, her breath ragged, on the verge of panic.

"It's much easier to summon an idea like this if you have ways of reminding the universe about the thought and giving the universe context. So we are in the basement of the house where the show was filmed. Someone has recreated the summoning circle from the show. You couldn't get a much better setup for summoning a spirit made up from the show.

The universe doesn't have a hard time figuring out what you are looking for. Summoning the Demoglorbin in a shopping mall would be almost impossible. No one ever imagined it there. Here, not too tough."

"I'm sorry," Portia says. I can feel her hands grab my arm in the dark, and she pulls herself uncomfortably close, "That didn't make any sense. Is it a thought, or is it a spirit?"

I shrug and try to get some distance from her. I'm not really looking to get groped by Genevieve's frenemy in the dark.

"What's the difference?" I ask.

"How," she mewls, "are you so calm?"

"This doesn't even make the top ten list of weird."

"I..." She starts, but then she is interrupted as the weird rhythmic chittering sound comes again, closer than before. Portia's hands bite into the muscle of my arm, and I can hear her inhale abruptly. "What is that?"

"It's still the Demoglorbin, but don't worry, it can't harm you directly. It's malevolent, but it can't touch the living. Or at least it couldn't in the show, so this one should have to follow the same rules. But don't go running around in the dark. In the show, it moved things around in the dark to lay traps. That was how Carrie-Anne got killed off for the third time."

"So what do we do?"

"Well, we need to find our way out of here or undo the circle. Once the circle is gone, it should go away after a while."

"How do we do that? I can't see a thing," she asks. The chittering sound starts again right in my ear. I start and almost move. I can feel Portia flinch, and I put my hand on top of hers to keep her from running.

"Don't move. That's what it wants. It's trying to herd us into danger," I say. I wish I had known this was going to be a supernatural trip. I would have brought my bag with me. I have a few tools that would be handy right now. "You aren't a smoker, are you?"

"No, why?"

"I was hoping you'd have a lighter."

"What about my phone?" She whispers.

"Try it, but I don't think it is going to work. Mine went dead with the lights."

I can hear something dragging over the dirt floor a few feet away. I can hear Portia's ragged breath, and I can tell she is barely containing her panic as she fumbles around in the dark for her phone. The smell of dead mice is thick and nauseating in my nose, with a whiff of Portia's heady perfume hiding within it. The combination is not better than the sum of its parts.

I can hear a thud and the sound of something metal being struck.

"Shit, my phone, I dropped it. It was like something knocked it from my hand! But it didn't work anyway," Portia mutters in the darkness, her voice high and reedy.

"Again, that's just like in the show. We should try to make our way slowly and carefully to the door," I say, "make sure to use your foot to feel in front of you before you step. Like I said, in the show, this thing set traps."

She wraps an arm around my waist. I put my arm over her shoulder like we are in a three-legged race. I start to take a step toward the door, and Portia pulls against me.

"No, I am pretty sure the door is this way," she whispers, pulling me in a different direction.

"It's your house, lead the way," I say back. I am not sure why she is whispering.

Slowly, we fumble through the darkened cellar. Inch by inch, feeling the way forward. She keeps using me to support her weight, which isn't uncomfortable. I come to a place where my foot strikes something hard, and I stop to feel around with my foot. I think it is a rake that's been left out. Portia finds a hole that's been dug in the ground. Some sharpened sticks jutting up just beyond it for someone that trips to fall upon.

There is that strange chittering and the sound of something moving in the darkness the whole time, but nothing ever touches us. It seems like hours we've been creeping slowly through the blackness, clinging to each other. Then, I see a tiny shaft of light. It must be filtering in through the edge of the storm door. Without references to judge distance from, it seems miles away.

Suddenly, the storm doors fly violently open. A figure stands at the top, silhouetted by the light behind it, like a triumphant Valkyrie beckoning us to Valhalla.

"What the hell are you two doing?"

Genevieve is staring down the stairs at us. My arm draped over Portia's shoulder, and her arms wrapped tightly around my waist.

"It's not what it looks like!" I blurt out, taking my arm off of Portia. She doesn't let go of my waist, though.

"No? Because it looks like you got yourselves trapped in the storm cellar in the dark and were trying to feel your way to the door. If that isn't it, then what is it?" Genevieve says, crossing her arms and smirking.

"I stand corrected. It is exactly what it looks like!" I wriggle free of Portia and start up the stairs. Portia follows on my heels.

Once we are back in the sunlight, we sit down.

"I know what is going on," I say.

"And I know who is doing it," Genevieve says.

I quirk an eyebrow curiously at her.

"You first," she says.

"Like I said before, in addition to the complex and intricate storylines and the dramatic character interplay, the really interesting thing about Craven's Gate was that all the magic portrayed in it was real and could really work if you used real blood."

Genevieve nods. Portia is just sitting there, staring blankly and nodding. I think she was truly terrified.

"Anyway," I continue, "Someone has recreated the summoning from season five and used it to summon this Demoglorbin. I assume all of this was to torment Portia. If we follow the plotline from the show, this would be because they believe she is actually responsible for her husband's death."

"And that is where I come in because that isn't why they are tormenting you, Portia," Genevieve says, "I took the liberty of going through Portia's office while you were looking in the cellar."

"You what?" Portia says, suddenly snapping out of her funk.

"I knew you wouldn't let me if I asked," Genevieve replies, "Anyway, you have a big stack of unread Craven's Gate fan mail."

Portia still looks pissed, but suddenly her interest is piqued, "Yeah, a couple of years ago, some jackass figured out the address where most of the show was filmed and posted it on some internet fan forum. Now I get mail all the time—people who want to tour or take photos, rent it, or even buy it. I have people randomly stop by and ask to look around. It's been an absolute pain in the ass. I put up the sign, the cameras, all because of that."

"But it looks like you haven't read the mail in a while," Genevieve says.

"Yeah, it's all the same crap, and I don't really want anything to do with it."

"Then why do you keep it?" I ask out of curiosity.

Portia shrugs.

"Anyway, I skimmed through them, starting with the unopened ones. Most are just requests to tour it or ask if you can rent it on AwayFromHome. But there is one guy who has sent you seven different letters in the past two years," Genevieve says, holding up a small stack of opened envelopes. "They are all requests to buy your house, but check out this last one."

She pulls a letter out of one of the envelopes and unfolds it. In large hand-drawn letters, it says:

STOP GHOSTING ME, OR I'LL GHOST YOU.

"It sounds like we have a culprit. Good work, Genevieve!" I say.

"This one isn't signed and doesn't have a return address, but the handwriting and postmark are the same as all these increasingly desperate attempts to buy the house," Genevieve says, holding up the rest of the stack. "The show's biggest fan! It would be his life's dream! He'll pay anything! Yadda yadda."

"What's his name?" Portia says quietly.

"Shawn Casey is what he signed the letters asking you to sell."

"I've never heard of him," Portia says.

"I bet you've met him, though. He's probably come to your door, at least. He sounds obsessive," Genevieve says, "You should call the police."

Genevieve hands Portia the stack of letters.

"What do we do about the...Demoglorbin, was it?" Portia asks.

"Well, if the police arrest this guy and that circle sits long enough, it will just go away when the spell fails, which will be when the blood dries. I think. Down there in the dank cellar, that could be a few days. Or if you have a garden hose, I can take care of it right now.

Portia points to a concrete pedestal a dozen feet away with

a spigot and hose attached. From the top of the stairs, it only takes me a few minutes with a sprayer to wash the bloody sigils away enough to end the spell. Almost immediately, the lights flicker back on.

"I am going to check it out," I say, propping the storm doors open with some loose rocks from the garden. "Watch my back?"

Genevieve nods. Portia is red-eyed and shaking, arms wrapped around her chest. Apparently, she was not prepared for being locked in the dark with a TV show monster.

I descend back into the root cellar and march across the floor toward the altar again. I didn't have much time to examine it earlier before we were plunged into darkness. Things have been strewn along the floor as obstacles in the dark. A rake here, loose rocks there. Divots have been dug all over, and now sticks have been broken off and placed facing up like spikes in the earthen floor. In the light, it looks like a child was playing down here, but it was much more ominous in the darkness.

I am impressed with how much the altar looks like the one from the movie—a concrete pillar almost my height, surrounded by a low pool filled with a viscous reddish-black substance. The gate is still open. Hovering, there is that strange black disk or orb that makes it feel like my soul is being sucked into it. That concerns me. As I get close, that palpable sense of dread begins to build inside me again. It is a gate into the Dreamtime, a hole in reality that leads into the infinity beyond. Why is it still open?

I should know more about this gate. The Phantasmigoricon discusses this phenomenon at length. I keep intending to read that. I have copies on my phone. The whole thing is so convoluted and wildly organized, though; it's an intimidating read. I should start reading it tomorrow. Of course, that's what I told myself yesterday.

The smell is terrible, and as I often do, I pull my shirt up over my face to mask the odor. It doesn't really help. It never does. It feels better to do it anyway. Maybe just knowing I made the effort is important.

"How did someone get this much concrete down here and build this altar without Portia noticing?" I ask myself as I reach out and lightly touch the altar's surface. My question is immediately answered. It looks like concrete, but it isn't. It's painted styrofoam. It's just a foam prop.

My attention is suddenly drawn to the stone ceiling of this cellar by a chittering sound. I glance up, and there, clinging to the wall, is the Demoglorbin. About the size of a large raccoon, its body roughly resembles a bald, black-skinned cat, but where paws should be, it has little human-like hands. Its face is a nightmare of features. If you began with a mummified cat's head, made its mouth open sideways, and added diagonal fangs into the four corners of its mouth, you would have a good start on what this thing looks like. Its eyes are strange, with square, goat-like pupils, yellow irises, and red sclera. It moves in a weird, almost semi-mechanical way as it hisses a weird clicking hiss at me.

I stagger back a couple of steps at the sight of it. It crouches as if it is ready to leap and attack. I shield my face with my forearms as it leaps. However, halfway through its flight toward me, it changes direction mid-air. Like a tissue sucked into a vacuum cleaner, it careens through the air and into the little black hole and vanishes without a sound. The gate narrows and blips out of existence like a closing eyelid. Instantly, the palpable sense of dread and wrongness lifts like a weighted blanket taken from my shoulders.

I blink and exhale a long sigh of relief, then turn my attention back to the altar. Everything about it, from the details of the altar itself down to the bloody sigils on the ground, is an exact recreation of a scene in the show's final season. It turns out there may be a bigger fan out there than me.

When I get back to the surface, Genevieve is still waiting for me, but Portia is not there.

"She went into the house to call the police," Genevieve clarifies when she sees me scanning the garden.

"You don't even like her, do you?" I ask.

Genevieve shrugs.

"Why did you help her?" I ask.

"When she called, I thought, "What would Miles do in this situation?" She says, then after a quiet moment, she adds, "Besides, I am going have this on her forever."

"Very mature," I say.

"What can I say? I am young at heart."

We wait around with Portia for a while. She isn't quite the same now; the humble bragging and uninvited flirting have stopped. She seems in shock after our encounter with the Demoglorbin. Eventually, two police officers come by to get a statement from Portia.

We detail what we discovered and Genevieve's theory on the culprit. I don't mention the Demoglorbin, just the obsessive recreation of details from the show. It takes longer than I'd like, but we leave Portia's before dark. Genevieve insists we stay until Portia is packed up and leaving to stay with a family member, at least until her supernatural stalker has been arrested.

As we drive away, I look back at Craven's Manor looming in the setting sun, and I can't wait to get home.

CHAPTER 2

I'M NOT a huge fan of air travel, so even the uneventful, boring, and very short flight from PDX to SFO is a white-knuckled exercise in barely controlled panic. Staring down an imp that crawled out of a tear in reality? No problem. Put me in a metal tube rocketing through the sky? Terror time. By the time we make it back to my apartment, I am exhausted.

"Hey, Hank!" Genevieve says as she plops her suitcase on my bed.

Hank, the mannequin, stands inert in the corner; he's wearing the same jeans and t-shirt I left him in when we departed for Portland. Hank is my simulacrum, a magical effigy of me meant to confuse and divert hexes and curses away from myself.

"Well, hello there, pretty lady!" Hank replies in a more flirty tone than I am comfortable with. Hank talks, but apparently, only I can hear him. I'm unsure if this is common for a simulacrum, but I have no one else to ask about it, so I assume it is.

"Don't make it weird," I mutter.

"Yeah, it's me that's making this weird."

I toss my jacket over his head.

"You need to get a real office. That way, you have space to do stuff in your apartment that's not in your bed."

"I like doing stuff in my bed. Sorry, that came out wrong."

"Did it?" She says coyly.

"Well, maybe not. But you're right. I should probably try to get some work-life separation. The problem is commercial real-estate prices around here are insane!" I exclaim.

"Yeah, it's a growing problem in many places."

"I hope if my Ward-in-a-Box thing works, I can find a better apartment and get an actual office space."

"What's holding you up?"

"Money, expertise, marketing know-how, pretty much the whole business side of it."

"I could give you a personal loan," Genevieve says cautiously.

I immediately know that I am going to say no to this, but I give it a minute to think it over anyway. Mostly because it's a very sweet and generous offer, and I don't want her to think I am just shutting her down. After a minute, I reply.

"I'm concerned that making a personal relationship into a business relationship might complicate both. I'd feel more comfortable tackling it myself. It is kind of you to offer, though. Thank you."

"I had the same concern, but I still wanted to offer. I understand."

I nod, suddenly feeling awkward.

"And thank you for pretending to consider it before answering," she says, smiling, "in the meantime, since the only place to do anything in your apartment is in your bed..."

She takes both my hands and starts pulling me toward the bed. I follow her, grinning like an idiot.

We are interrupted by a knock at the door.

"Ugh!" I exclaim.

"You get it. I'll go freshen up and meet you there?"

"Sounds like a plan!" I say, bounding to the door.

I am about to throw the door open, then I remember: check the peephole. I look through it. Magdalena, my youthful, time-bending assassin of a neighbor, is standing there looking impatient. She's wearing an intentionally tattered t-shirt and a black newsie cap.

"No solicitors!" I call through the door.

"Fuck off, Miles, open the goddamn door."

I open the door, "Language, young lady."

"Fuck yourself, old dude."

"Well, you came, you insulted, you left. Good to see you again, Magdalena," I say as I start to close the door. Magdalena sticks a foot in it.

"Sorry, I thought we were doing banter. I have a business proposition for you."

"Considering your line of work, I will say no to the business proposition."

"This is a side job I picked up. No wet work, I promise," she says, holding her fingers up and crossing her index finger over the middle of both hands.

"I don't think that hand gesture means what you think it means."

She looks at her hands, unfolds her fingers, and puts her hands at her hips, "Whatever. Can I come in?"

"This is really not a good time. I'm entertaining," I say. My face feels warm.

"You're enter...oh...ewww. Why'd you answer the door?"

Shoe firmly on the other foot, my face feels like it's on fire, and the back of my neck is prickly.

"Good afternoon," I say and start to push the door again.

"Okay, come by when you're finished...you know...old people sexing...eww."

"I won't be coming by! And we aren't old!" I call after her as she retreats to her apartment.

"You will, and you are!" She hollers back as she closes her apartment door behind her.

"Who was that?" Genevieve asks from my bedroom doorframe.

I glance back, and she's put on a black negligee. I think it's called a negligee, anyway.

"It was, um. You know what? It doesn't matter. We can talk about that later. Right now, I feel like we have other business to attend to."

"Damn right, we do."

CHAPTER 3

We are laying under the covers of my bed. I'm sleepy and half-napping at this point. I'm warm with Genevieve's body snuggled up beside me.

"Who was at the door earlier?" Genevieve asks, snapping me out of my drowsy, mindless post-coital torpor. My brief conversation with Magdalena is now on my mind; my bliss is lost.

"It was Magdalena," I say, exasperated. I don't really want to talk about my nosy, time-bending assassin neighbor right now.

"What did she want?"

"She had a business proposition or something. I told her I wasn't interested."

"Weren't you just complaining about money?" Genevieve asks.

"Yeah, but I mean, she's Hizarin. She does bad things for money. I don't want any work she'd pitch my way, right?"

"If she wants you to kill people, then no, but I think she's got that under control. If she wants your help, it's probably just warding something, right?"

"Do you think she's eavesdropping on me? We were talking about my money problems, and then she shows up at the door with a job." I ask.

"I wouldn't put it past her based on what you've told me. It's possible, but she might have just been waiting for you to get home all week."

Genevieve shrugs next to me and then tousles my hair.

"Maybe."

"You should see what she has to say. I mean, what can it hurt?" Genevieve asks. "Definitely not your bank account."

"Well, last time I helped her out, half of Napa burned to the ground."

I can still see the fire demon that Magdalena summoned by 'accident.' Its body composed of burning cows, as it lumbered toward me. It wasn't ten days ago, but it seems like something that happened to someone else. It's like I saw a very graphic video a long time ago, but I won't ever forget it. No matter how much I try.

"That's a huge exaggeration, and you know it. Besides, think about what might have happened if you didn't help her?" Genevieve says.

I sigh a big sigh.

"Bah! You're right! I should at least hear what she has to say so that I can stop her, if nothing else."

"That's the spirit!" Genevieve says.

"You mind if I shower and just go get this over with?" I ask.

"I'm satisfied," she says coyly, "for now."

I jump up and walk naked to the shower.

"I hate seeing you leave, but I love watching you go!" Genevieve says after me.

"You sound like Hank."

"Hank talks to you that way?" She says, quirking a skeptical eyebrow.

"No, I mean he talks about..." I sputter, "... never mind."

I climb into the shower, and Genevieve keeps calling from the bedroom.

"Oh, he talks about me like that? I am glad you left the jacket over his head then."

"I am all-seeing! Hey, Genevieve, watch the hands! Boundaries!" Hank calls out from the other room. I can't see him, but I ignore him. I know he's just trying to get a reaction out of me.

After a quick shower, I throw on some clothes.

"I'll be right back," I say, giving Genevieve a quick kiss before she climbs in the shower.

"All right! Don't agree to any jobs that I wouldn't do!"

"That's not much of a prohibition!" I say. It's meant in jest, but I immediately realize it could be taken the wrong way. I feel awkward and uncomfortable, but only for a moment.

"Oh," Genevieve says in a very suggestive tone, "You have no idea..."

Touché, Genevieve. I think that I'm blushing as I knock on Magdalena's door.

"Wow," Magdalena says as she opens her door, "You have a certain glow about you...eww."

Now I know that I am blushing.

"What do you want, Magdalena?" I ask.

She motions me into her apartment. I follow her in, looking around cautiously as I do. I've never been in the abode of a sorcerer-assassin before.

Her apartment has basically the same layout as mine. A short hallway opens out into the living room area. The kitchen is through an opening in the hallway to my left. There is another hallway, for lack of a better term, on the other side of the living room where the kitchen connects back into the bedroom and bathroom. The whole layout is basically a small, cramped circle.

Magdalena leads me into the living room and motions me to sit down.

"Can I get you anything?" She asks.

"No, thanks. Can we get down to business?"

I look around the living room. I have this set up as an office in my apartment. Magdalena has more traditional furnishings. A large sectional couch wraps around one wall. Facing it is a huge wall-mounted television. There is a classy-looking coffee table but little other furniture. The walls are decorated with paintings of animals, and the stuffed head of a large African deer is on one wall. Tribal spears cross over a wooden shield on the opposite wall, making it look like a colonial hunter's game room.

Magdalena sees me eyeing her decor and points to the stuffed deer's head.

"Shot him at a half mile with a crosswind. One shot through the heart. We ate bushmeat for days."

"You're a big game hunter?" I ask, wondering if this is an endangered species.

"No, I'm just messing with you. I got it at an estate sale."

This leaves me a little bewildered.

"Okay," I say, sitting down on her sectional. "What do you want?"

"Wow, Mr. Cranky much? Everything is not as good in the bedroom as...you know what? Nevermind. I've picked up a little side hustle, and we need someone with your skill set. Four days, starting tomorrow. It's a percentage payout, but I can promise you two-fifty as a floor."

I crinkle my nose at her and make a face. I'm not saying I

couldn't use two hundred and fifty extra dollars, but I'm slightly insulted. Do I really come off as that desperate?

She sees my facial expression and bursts out into peels of laughter.

“Two hundred and fifty thousand. I don’t get out of bed for less than six figures.”

I blink. That’s a lot of money. I could definitely get my business started with that kind of money. However, I’m also sure that this isn’t going to be strictly legal.

“That’s a good chunk of change,” I say, trying to sound cool and detached, “What’s the catch?”

“Until you’re signed on, I can’t give you the details. But in overview, there is a very bad man with some very stolen goods that we will steal back from him for a profit.”

“I’m not a thief,” I say, “and I’m not a killer.”

“I know, you fancy yourself the good guy. I wouldn’t come to you with something you’d have a problem with. I swear, Miles. Sign on, get the full details, and you will be on board with this.”

“What if I sign on and then change my mind?”

She squirms uncomfortably, “Personally, I don’t really care, but I’m just a contractor here too. I don’t think the guy in charge would love that.”

“The guy in charge?”

“Yeah, like I said, this isn’t my job. I’m just hired help. But I was asked to find a spellbreaker for the job. You’re the best there is,” she says.

“I’m not the best there is,” I say.

She shrugs, “Since you’re the only one I’ve met who’s still alive, I will beg to differ.”

Well, that sounded ominous.

“So it pays big, and you think I’ll be on board with this, but if I back out, things could get ugly?”

She nods, “Two-fifty, that’s the base."

"American dollars?"

She rolls her eyes. "Yeah, and there’s potential for more.”

“Potential? What does that mean?”

“You will have to hear the details from the guy in charge, but each player gets a cut of the end take,” she says.

“Can I think about it?” I ask.

“Sure, but I’ll need an answer by tomorrow evening. That’s when we are meeting.”

Ambivalence is often used to mean indecisive, but its meaning is more nuanced. It means to be of two minds, to hold two contradictory thoughts or opinions simultaneously. I am ambivalent.

On the one hand, I could use the money. And Genevieve is correct; if Magdalena is going to kill someone, she probably doesn't need my help. Based on my brief time with her, she has proven stunningly efficient in that department. She has some understanding of my boundaries, and it's unlikely that she would ask me to do something I wouldn't want to do, knowing that I would refuse to follow through.

On the other hand, this is very short notice. It feels like someone is trying to sell me on a timeshare in Des Moines. The carrot being dangled in front of me is almost too enticing. This smells a little like a con job.

“What if I say no?”

“If we can’t find a competent spellbreaker, he'll probably just change the plan,” she says flippantly. She's trying to bait me, and I know it.

“That sounds ominous,” I say through gritted teeth. Why do I always take the bait?

“It is. I know this guy doesn't like messy, but he isn't afraid of it. Please say yes, Miles,” she smiles an overly toothy smile at me.

“I’ll think about it and get back to you by tomorrow.”

I get up and walk to her door.

“See you later,” I say.

“Looking forward to working with you!” She says as she closes the door behind me.

"Are we doing a heist now?" Hank says as the deadbolt clicks shut on Magdalena's door. It sounds like he's standing right behind me.

I used to hear Hank only if I was near the simulacrum, but since I rebuilt him, he doesn't seem as bound to the mannequin. I hear him all over the place now. I didn't hear him in Portland, but if I am anywhere in Napa, he has started speaking up with increasing frequency.

"What is it that lets you follow me when I leave the apartment now?" I murmur over my shoulder.

"Love," he says in a sarcastically drippy tone.

"Fuck you."

"Woah, slow down there, buddy, not that kind of love."

I flip him off over my shoulder, then realize he isn't actually there, and I hope Magdalena isn't looking out the peephole in her door right now, or it would look like I am giving her the old bird.

I head back into my apartment to tell Genevieve what Magdalena had to say.

“I THINK YOU SHOULD DO IT,” Genevieve says after I explain my conversation with Magdalena.

“Why? It’s almost certainly criminal. It’s definitely dangerous.”

“It sounds lucrative. I don’t think Magdalena would ask you to help if she thought you’d object.” Genevieve says.

“I don’t know.”

I see a look in Genevieve's eyes, one I have started to become familiar with. She's excited. I really like Genevieve. She's fun and adventurous. I don't feel judged by her. But those same traits have another side. She gets very excited by danger and breaking the law. While I don't like getting on a plane, Genevieve wonders why we aren't jumping out of it.

"Listen, Miles," Genevieve says, "It sounds like this job is going down one way or the other. If you are involved, you get paid and can help mitigate damage. If you pass, you get nothing, and probably people get hurt."

"I could just report it to the police."

"Right, 'A teenage magic assassin told me she and some other people are going to steal something from someone somewhere, and it is probably sometime this week.' That's your plan? Do you think the police can stop Magdalena?"

I think back to when Magdalena assassinated the mayor in front of the whole town, complete with video cameras. I think back to Magdalena driving across the entire state at felonious speeds without being pulled over. I remember Magdalena picking me up and throwing me like a rag doll to save me from a fire demon. A fire demon that she summoned.

"Dammit," I say, "Fine, I'll do it."

"See if they need another set of hands, I want in!" Genevieve says. Her tone sounds joking, but I know she's not.

"I don't think that's a great idea," I start to say.

"It's a heist, Miles, it's a magical heist, you know it is, it has to be. They have a time-bending assassin and an apotropaist! They are building their team of specialists! I've always wanted in on a heist ever since that movie about the casino!" Her voice trails off into a pleading moan of vocal fry.

"Okay! I'll ask!" I say exasperated.

"Please! I have to be in Atlanta for a convention all of next week, but before that and after that, I am totally open. You said four days starting tomorrow. It was meant to be! Please!"

"I'll ask!"

Now that I've said I'll do it, I feel bound by my word. I probably shouldn't have said yes. Nothing about this feels smart, or safe, or right.

Once, when I was fourteen, my dad and I briefly lived in a town outside of Albuquerque that was a boring little speck on the map. I started hanging around with a group of kids whose local pastime was hanging half-full soda cans on fishing lines off the highway overpass, making cars hit them. Nothing about it was amusing to me. It didn't feel smart, or safe, or right. But I went along anyway because I wanted to fit in.

One night, I ended up spending three hours hiding in a dumpster while an angry guy with a baseball bat and a mullet prowled around in his pickup truck hunting for me. I got home smelling like sour milk and rotten fish to impress some kids whose names I couldn't remember now if I wanted to.

Am I letting my ethics be bought here? Am I that desperate to impress Genevieve? Though, I didn't get paid a quarter of a million dollars to hide in a dumpster. That kind of money buys a lot of moral ambiguity.

CHAPTER 4

GENEVIEVE and I follow Magdalena as we drive Up Valley. After our trip to Oregon, I'll never get in a car with Magdalena driving again. I am driving a cheap sedan that my insurance company rented for me while they figure out the claim for having my car explode in a wildfire. It's taking a lot longer to figure out than I expected.

Magdalena pulls into Enchanté. When people name-drop their favorite winery in the Valley, I rarely know where they are talking about. There are hundreds of wineries; only a handful are big and famous enough to be household names. But I've heard of this one before. The prestige of their wine is exceeded only by the prestige of their clientele. Renowned for completely off-the-hook parties, they throw the kind of parties that A-list celebrities don't turn down invites to and where I am not pretty enough to serve canapés.

I do not belong at Enchanté.

A large pergola stands over the drive, with hops interwoven between the wooden slats. To the left and right of the drive, an immense hedge cuts off view of the winery from the road. As we pull around the circular drive, it feels like we are pulling into an exclusive resort.

We pass by a parking lot to our right. I can feel my crappy rental car cringe in shame at the thought of being parked next to the cars in that parking lot. Any one of these cars costs more than my total net worth. Of course, I haven't looked at my finances in a while. A forty-ounce malt liquor might cost more than my total net worth.

I follow Magdalena around to a valet stand. We park our cars and get out.

Magdalena leaves the keys in her tiny sports car, casually slides out, and saunters toward the front door. I note that Magdalena's car fits right in with the other vehicles in the parking lot.

“Excuse me, miss,” the valet addresses her. I suspect her very young appearance throws him off. But she off-handedly tosses a bill at him as she walks past without ever actually looking at him.

I get out of my rental car as the other valet opens the door for Genevieve.

“Sorry about that,” I say apologetically. I hand him a twenty. He looks nonplussed by it.

“That your kid?” The valet asks.

I am about to object, but Genevieve cuts me off.

“Yeah, kids these days, it’s so hard to teach them manners,” she declares as she drags me by the hand into the winery.

The valet eyeballs our car judgmentally.

"The Lambo is in the shop," I say sheepishly as Genevieve drags me through the front door. The valet doesn't look impressed.

We leave the valets behind to park our cars.

If the outside of the winery looked like a resort, the inside supports that impression. Beautiful, elegant, and simple in design. There is only a little decor. A plant here. A painting there. A long, simple oaken bar runs down one side of the room with bottles and bottles of wine in a large rack behind it. Everything in this front room is minimalistic, emphasizing the natural beauty of the stone and wood it is constructed from.

A faint murmur of calm, classical violin music echoes from hidden speakers. While I think it is supposed to be relaxing, everything about this room makes me feel like an outsider, like someone who doesn't belong or deserve this place.

"Do you have reservations?" A Maître d' standing by the door asks.

Before Genevieve or I can say anything, Magdalena chimes in.

"Burlesque room. Don't show me. I know the way," she says, shoving another bill into his hand as she brushes past him. The Maître d' shrugs at us.

"Sorry," I mutter pitifully as we move past him.

We catch up to Magdalena as she turns down a hall and goes out of the main room. The hall is dark. The music has become a ballroom jazz sound, echoing from more speakers cleverly concealed in the ceiling. The walls are covered with a burgundy fabric or carpet of some sort and otherwise unadorned. The covering has the effect of muffling sound. Despite the fact that we are walking on bare concrete floors, there is no echo at all.

"So," Magdalena begins as we walk down the hallway, "He's agreed that Genevieve is in, but only because I said Miles was out otherwise. You get to split your cut. No using real names. He will assign you monikers inside."

"Monikers?" Genevieve says, her voice is almost a giggle as she does.

"He always does it. I've worked with him before. I think he thinks it's cool."

"Anything else we should know?" I ask.

"Yeah, you know that thing where you get nervous and say stupid stuff?" Magdalena says, looking at me.

"Yes."

"No," I say, glaring at the point over my shoulder where I hear Hank's voice. "I mean, I know sometimes I over-explain or put on a funny accent or whatever. I mean, maybe I talk too much, but I don't know that I ever say stupid stuff."

"Yeah, that right there, and everything you just said, don't do that," Magdalena says as she opens the strangely carpeted door at the end of the hall.

We enter the Burlesque Room. I feel like the name is underselling it. In the center of the room is a large octagonal stage. In the center of the stage, a three-inch diameter brass pole extends up into the darkness above. The ceiling is black and gives a sense of unguessable height. The stage itself is a dark stained wood with brass trim around the edges. In a circle around the stage are a number of overstuffed burgundy couches.

A half dozen high-top wooden tables are spread out over the rest of the room. Another half dozen coffee tables are spaced with plush high-backed chairs next to them. A long bar with a brass pole at the base runs along the back of the room.

The walls are a dark hardwood paneling draped with lush burgundy curtains tied back with gold ropes. They give the room a feeling of additional space, as if you could pull the curtains back and walk through. Large cages hang at the ceiling height around the top of the room. Inside the cages are featureless flat white mannequins in an assortment of burlesque outfits, frozen mid-strip-tease.

"Hot damn! This is my kinda party!"

The whole room feels like a bordello if Disney Imagineers designed it. I wonder if there is a switch somewhere that will cause the animatronic mannequins to continue their burlesque show.

Beyond one row of curtains, I can see a long, dark wooden table with chairs around it. There are people seated there. Magdalena walks toward the table without hesitation. Genevieve and I follow her more slowly, taking in the gaudy and ostentatious room as we go.

A distinguished-looking man in a black suit stands at the head of the table. He has salt-and-pepper hair and a well-trimmed beard to match. He has a wry smile, and his dark eyes take us in with some humor as we push our way past the curtain. He motions us toward a table, pointing us each to our assigned seat.

There are already two other people at the table. Directly opposite me is a middle-aged man with stubble and a green trucker cap with the now-familiar Knights of Saint George logo on it. I blink as I look at him. I recognize this man, Allen, I think his name is. He accosted me outside of the Lantern a few months back, trying to recruit me to help the Knights take out Lorelei Redbrook.

I don't recognize the other man. He is younger, portly, and balding with glasses. He's wearing a polo shirt and has a laptop in front of him. His face is large, and round, and soft-looking.

I notice that there are cards propped up in little stands in front of seven of the seats.

I sit down at my indicated seat and see that the card before me is one of the Major Arcana from the Tarot: The Magician. I glance at the others. Allen's card is The Wheel of Fortune. The portly man has The Hermit before him. At the head of the table, the well-dressed man has The Hierophant in front of him. In front of Genevieve is The Tower card, and Magdalena has The Fool in front of her. I suppress a chuckle when I see this.

Magdalena sits down, looks at the card, snorts, picks it up, and throws it at The Hierophant. A familiar sense of déjà vu washes over me as the card embeds itself in the plush cushion of the seat he is standing behind. He glowers at her.

One card is left in front of an empty seat—The World.

"Miles!" When he sees me, Allen says, "We finally get to work together!"

He has a fake-looking smile. I can't tell if he's excited about this or disgruntled because I didn't help him before.

"No names!" The Hierophant says sternly.

"Well, that's silly. I know half the people in this room!" Allen says.

"I agree with Vanna here. There are a shocking number of familiar faces," I say.

"Vanna?" Magdalena scrunches her face up at me.

"Wheel of Fortune? No? Nothing?" I say as Magdalena looks blankly at me, "Never mind."

"I get it," Allen says, "It's funny, heck yeah."

His grin seems more authentic.

"I'm afraid that I am very insistent that we use the pseudonyms that I have provided, some plausible level of anonymity," The Hierophant says. His face is placid, but his voice has a tone of mild irritation.

I look at the cards and ponder. I grew up with Tarot, so I have a pretty good idea of what each is getting at. He's clearly trying to tell a narrative with the cards he has selected. The art on these cards is not any traditional Tarot art I've seen before. He has clearly had them custom-made—a surprising and specific detail for him to add.

The Fool, a blindfolded young woman, runs toward a cliff and is chased by a wolf.

A more traditional Tarot card might depict a young male walking jovially toward a cliff, with his dog barking warning; the version of the card on the table is far more aggressive and menacing. I can't help but shake the story of Little Red Riding Hood from my head when I see this card. I wonder what this man knows about Magdalena that I don't.

These cards are actually a test.

The Fool card was placed upside down in the stand before she stuck it in a cushion. Inverted like that, it represents youth and impulsive or reckless action. That works for Magdalena.

The Magician. The more traditional version I am familiar with is a robed man with an infinity symbol above his head. He usually holds a wand aloft and is surrounded by books and paraphernalia. The version before me is clearly meant to be me. It depicts a man sitting at a table with a book before him. He has sigils tattooed on his arms and chest, including an ouroboros. While I have no such tattoo, it is clearly a callback to the traditional infinity sign. The Magician figure has a dazed expression on his face. He looks lost.

The card is upright. Thus, it represents resourcefulness and power. Reversed, it could be poor planning or being manipulated. Again, this is not a coincidental assignment.

The Tower. I'm more accustomed to an image of a large tower being struck by lightning, with people flying from it to their doom. Calamity. The version before Genevieve is not dissimilar, except it seems obvious that the two figures falling from the tower are Genevieve and I. It seems like a personal threat.

The card is upright. It represents sudden change, upheaval, and disaster. I'm guessing he doesn't like that she forced herself into being a last-minute addition to his crew.

The Wheel of Fortune. I'd expect to see a wheel with symbols guarded by a Sphinx and looked upon by angels. The one on the table before Allen is a wheel with a dead dragon draped over the top. There are no angels. Something about the wheel's depiction is bugging me, but I can't place it.

The card is upright. It represents good luck, fortune, life cycle, or a turning point. I've met Allen once briefly in passing. I know he's good at blending in. However, I don't know him well enough to guess what this means.

The Hierophant. More commonly, an ecclesiastical figure with a scepter in one hand and a headdress. Other figures often lay prostrate before The Hierophant. The card on the table before our host is similar but more modern. A man in a business suit sits in a board room before an array of other suits prostrating themselves. The card is reversed, representing freedom, personal belief, and challenging authority. I feel like he's telling us something about his motivations for this caper.

The Hermit. The version I am familiar with depicts a lone-robed, bearded man standing at night. He'd lean heavily on his staff and hold a lantern up to ward away the darkness. The card on the table shows a man with glasses holding up a more modern-looking electric lantern. From the lantern, light extends out in rays, but the rays split and meet other rays, forming an almost web-like pattern across the card. The lines are precise and meticulously rendered.

This card is upright. It represents introspection, guidance, and being alone. I do not know what this might mean regarding the bespectacled man at the table.

Finally, the empty seat. The World. The cards you'd buy in a bookstore might depict a nude woman wrapped in a scarf or maybe her own hair. She'd hold two batons and be encircled by a wreath with animals in the corners. This version is a stout nude woman standing before a globe with a swish of wind around it. The lines are suggestive of the traditional card, but the imagery is completely different. There is also something about the card that is very familiar, but I can't quite put my finger on it.

Upright, this card represents completion, accomplishment, or travel.

Ah. I understand.

"Not too complicated then."

"Shut up," I whisper. I get a sharp look from The Hierophant, but no one else notices.

If I compare what I know about myself, Magdalena, and Genevieve to the cards we received, they clearly communicate his expectations of each of us. I do not believe that these cards were assigned randomly. I have to assume that this means the cards for the people I don't know also have meaning. Let's test it out.

"Your driver is late," I say flatly, motioning toward The World card with my head.

The Hierophant grimaces but nods and sits down. Suspicion confirmed. The cards are not only intentional but related to our roles in whatever this job is. The World, this is the last person to touch the job. It indicates travel. This is the person that gets us out at the end. This is the driver.

"A very astute observation. I'm afraid we cannot afford to wait. We will begin without her," he says.

He produces a small beige remote control from his pocket and presses a button. A screen descends from the ceiling on the side of the room opposite the occupied chairs.

"The individual you see before you is Jim Devora." He says.

A familiar image of a sixty-something man appears on the screen. It takes a second for all the connections in my brain to complete. I'm left a little confused.

"Jim Devora, the movie producer?" I ask.

"Duh," Magdalena says. I see Genevieve smirk at this. As always, I feel like I am the last one to the party.

"He, um, started his career as a director. He considers movie producing to be his, um, retirement career, according to the um, internet," the man with The Hermit card in front of him mumbles. He has an odd cadence to his speech.

The Hierophant nods and continues.

"Devora has a large, private, and secured estate on the east side of the Napa Valley. A good portion of the estate burned in a recent and unexpected fire. Most of the security systems are non-functional until repairs are completed."

Genevieve quirks an eyebrow at me. I, in turn, quirk an eyebrow at Magdalena, who, in turn, gives me an innocent shrug.

"This has created an opportunity for us to access a secret vault below his estate. Devora is a known collector of...antiquities. There are a number of priceless items contained there, but one specific item is of interest to me personally. Additionally, he is said to have a large cache of gold bullion. I have a source giving me visual confirmation of this fact. We will auction off the rest of our haul, other than the item I intend to keep. I will keep half of the proceeds and split the remaining half between the five of you. This will be in addition to the retainer fee that you have already been offered."

He looks pointedly at Genevieve and me to make sure we understand we split my share.

I look over at Magdalena, my eyes wide open. This is not what we talked about. She said I'd be on board with this, and I am not.

"Tell him more about the gold," Magdalena says quickly.

The Hierophant looks irritated but continues.

"You are familiar with the movie producer Jim Devora," he says.

"And the dozens of sexual misconduct allegations against

him," Genevieve chimes in. The Hierophant nods at the interruption.

"That is mostly a matter of public record; this, however," he says, clicking on his remote and changing images, "is not."

There is a black and white drawing. It looks archaic, medieval even.

"This is Herman of Podiazice, or Herman the Recluse. Alleged author of the Codex Gigas."

"The devil's bible," I chime in.

"That is correct. It is said that walled into his cell, he sold his soul to the devil to write this book in a single night. Less well known is the legend that in doing so, he was cursed to walk the earth forever. This is not exactly correct."

"How, exactly, does this relate to Devora?" Allen asks.

"Or the, um, gold," The Hermit says.

Magdalena blurts out, "He's a Lich. Devora is a Lich, and Pi...err, I mean, The Hierophant is saying that he is Herman the Recluse. He's a centuries-old undead that possesses the bodies of powerful people to continue his legacy and attain more power and wealth."

The Hierophant stares at her, his eyes narrowed, his face contorted. He's annoyed.

"You're making it too dramatic. You got to get to the point, Grandpa," she responds with an eye-roll.

"The Fool," he pauses for dramatic effect. I can't help but wonder if he gave her the handle specifically for these moments, "is fundamentally correct. This is not just some rich and powerful person we are dealing with. This is an ancient and powerful sorcerer who uses people as if they were convenient pieces of attire. The gold in question is a fortune he has collected through the centuries, profiteering off of countless wars and genocides."

The Hierophant takes a moment to look squarely at Allen

and then myself. Clearly, he feels that both of us need more motivation than just the payout. He thinks Devora being an undead necromancer is that motivator. He may be right.

"I suppose you have some evidence of this?" Genevieve asks.

"Yes, Tower, I do," he says snootily, "I will provide you with a USB drive with all the materials you need. You are welcome to verify all of my sources yourself."

"So, if this guy is some ancient evil," Allen says, "We are just gonna steal from him and then move on?"

"That is the scope of this endeavor, yes," The Hierophant says, "there is no profit in his assassination. Our efforts will disadvantage him significantly, and you may feel you have struck a blow, however partial, for justice."

Allen nods and scratches his chin thoughtfully.

"I would warn," The Hierophant interrupts Allen's contemplation, "that dispatching his mortal vessel will only slow him down. He has his soul housed in a Phylactery, from which he will find a new vessel to imbue."

"A Phylactery is a small leather box used to house scrolls with Hebrew prayers on it, used by Jewish people as a reminder of their laws," I correct, "The use of the word to refer to a Soul Jar is cultural appropriation."

The Hierophant, The Hermit, and Allen all stare at me with an expression I can only describe as 'stink-eye.'

"Fine, a Soul Jar then, a far less poetic word, but we will respect the politically correct musings of our Magician."

"Apotropaist."

"Apotropaist is not one of the major Arcana. You are our Magician," The Hierophant says, "May we move on from this prattle and get back to the task at hand?"

"Sure," I say. Allen nods. The Hermit looks impatient.

Genevieve is watching The Hierophant like a raptor, watching its prey. Magdalena seems to be playing a game on her phone.

"I have selected each of you," he pauses and looks at Genevieve, "I have selected 'most' of you for your special skills. I will explain this now. We will need each of you in order for this to work."

He surveys us all, then indicates The Hermit.

"The Hermit is our technologist. He will access the digital security systems and deal with bypassing them."

He turns to Allen.

"The Wheel of Fortune, he is our safe cracker. Once we get to the vault, he will be the one to get us into it physically."

That is what looked familiar about the Wheel on the Wheel of Fortune card. The Wheel also looks like a vault door. It's not a literal representation, but armed with the knowledge of Allen's role, it seems intentionally suggestive.

He turns to the empty place at the table, "The World, if she should arrive, will, as The Magician has adroitly surmised, be our driver. She will get us onto the property and transport our plunder away unnoticed."

He turns and looks at Genevieve.

"The Tower, you will be our lookout. We will position you with a proper view of the estate to apprise us of any complications."

Genevieve stands up, "Lookout? Are you kidding me?"

"I would also request that you lead the research arm so as to assure the more...moralistic of our company that this is indeed a worthy endeavor. I am led to understand that you are talented in this particular area."

"Shit, she's downright famous for it!" Allen announces suddenly.

The Hermit quirks an eyebrow and starts typing on his

computer. Genevieve rolls her eyes with a grunt and sits down, crossing her arms.

"The Magician," The Hierophant turns to look at me, "has perhaps the hardest task. He must eliminate or neutralize the extensive magical protections on the estate. If he fails his charge, I am afraid that we will not only fail at our intended task but also likely perish in that failure."

Great.

"What about The Fool over there?" Allen asks.

"Hopefully, The Fool has no role in this endeavor. The Fool is our fail-safe, if you will. She shall accompany us. If things should diverge from the planned itinerary, she will enact our secondary plan of action. A less elegant prospect, to be sure, a messier plan, but a certain one."

"What does that mean?" The Hermit mumbles. His voice is very nasally and hard to understand as he barely moves his lips.

"He means," Allen chimes in, "That the little girl is gonna shoot shit up. Let god sort 'em out kinda thing."

The Hermit quirks an eyebrow and looks Magdalena over appraisingly. She is still playing a game on her phone and flips him off without looking up.

"I assure you," The Hierophant says, "She is more than capable of performing her portion of this endeavor should the need arise. I rarely work with the same individuals on more than one occasion, but I have worked with she before and would work with she again."

The Hierophant has no notable accent. He sounds like a TV weatherman, but I notice that he has a strange way of speaking. He uses the wrong articles and sometimes puts words in an odd order, almost like he is not a native English speaker.

"Sorry, I'm late!" A woman abruptly barges into the room

and flops in a chair, not the one with the World card in front of it.

"The World is to sit in that chair," The Hierophant declares, pointing at her designated chair.

"The World, I like it!" She says, getting up and moving to her assigned seat.

The World is a hearty-looking woman with a square jaw and the frame of a wrestler. She is wearing khaki pants and a blue buttoned shirt. I notice she is wearing clogs with extra thick soles. I surmise that she works a job that requires a lot of standing. My guess is that she works in a tasting room or some other corner of the hospitality industry.

"What did I miss?" She declares in a loud voice.

The Hierophant sighs a sigh of exasperation. Then, he proceeds to summarize everything we've just covered.

"This is the floor plan," The Hierophant declares, clicking a button on his remote.

A new image flashes onto the screen: a schematic of a house. The house is enormous.

"Here is the main floor. We will be entering through the garage here," he says, shining a red laser light onto the screen, pointing to the garage, "We will all be coming in a shipping truck that is bringing construction materials for repairs on the house. We will disembark from the truck and begin to unload materials."

"It is a World Wide Delivery truck," I blurt out as it strikes me, "She works for World Wide Delivery!"

"He's smart, I like him!" The World declares. I try to play it cool, but I am proud that I figured this out and said it before anyone else.

The Hierophant stares me down momentarily, "Most astute, but not a detail we need to discuss now."

I look over and see Allen and The Hermit looking at me expectantly.

"The card, the earth with the swish around it? It looked familiar. It's the World Wide Delivery logo, you know, without the WWD bit across it," I say, then finish by singing the jingle, "World Wide Delivery, we ship things. Foooor youuuuuuuuu!"

"Oh, yeah! I see it now!" Allen declares. The Hermit nods sagely and starts typing on his laptop.

"The vault is in the basement, through these stairs," The Hierophant indicates a stairway on the first floor, "However, the security is operated out of an outbuilding, here," the image changes to a satellite photo of the estate. He indicates a building some distance away with a chain link fence around it.

"Two security guards are stationed on the estate at all times. Due to damage from the fire, gas and water are currently shut off to the location. Devora and the rest of the staff have taken leave of the estate. The Hermit will need access to the security office to disable security systems on the main house."

"We have a plan for the security guards?" Allen asks curiously.

"We believe that many of the cameras were damaged in the fire, giving access through here," he indicates a path behind the house and to the back of the security office. It isn't a direct path and is fairly circuitous, probably to stay in the blind spots where cameras were damaged.

"The Hermit and The Fool will go to the security office. The Fool will incapacitate the guards," he pauses and looks specifically at me, "with non-lethal ordinance. Then, The Hermit will disable the security systems. Once that is complete, The Magician, The Wheel of Fortune, and I will go to the vault. The Magician will need to be prepared to circumvent the magical security as we go. They will be extensive."

"Do we have an idea of the breadth and scope of what I am working with here?" I ask, "Anything specific?"

"I am afraid," the Hierophant says, "that we have the least intelligence on this aspect of the security. It is my hope that in the short time we have before our delivery, you can perform some reconnaissance independently to better prepare for these measures. Otherwise, you will have to improvise. Something I am told you excel at."

"Okay," I grunt. I'm not a fan of this whole plan. But Devora sounded like an absolute piece of crap when he wasn't an undead sorcerer that possessed other people's bodies for his own immortality. Gaining some financial stability while taking him down a notch seems like a win-win.

"Once we have made our way to the vault and The Magician has bypassed the magical security there, The Wheel of Fortune will need to get us into the vault. I will provide you with the specifications of the vault at the end of this meeting."

"Heck yeah," Allen says enthusiastically.

"Where will I be through all of this?" Genevieve asks.

"We have identified a spot here," The Hierophant says, indicating a hill just off the estate. "This location will give you the optimal view of the estate, the front drive, and the road approaching it. From there, you will be able to keep us informed if there are any unexpected visitors that might interrupt our...operation."

"I get to sit on a hill with binoculars?" Genevieve says, disappointed.

"You will also be issued a radio to stay in communication. Your role is to observe and report," The Hierophant asks.

"Yay," Genevieve says sarcastically.

"If Devora or anyone else unexpectedly arrives, it will be your place to call for an evacuation. You must be prepared to provide us with optimal escape routes, should that need arise."

Genevieve sits back sullenly.

"I hope you understand I had previously arranged for someone else to fulfill this role, but I have changed my plans. I do not like changing my plans. I am generally unwilling to do this," The Hierophant gives Genevieve a monotone lecture. Genevieve and The Hierophant glower at each other, leaving the room in an uncomfortable silence that seems to draw out forever. Finally, The Hierophant breaks eye contact and continues.

“Once the vault is open, The Wheel of Fortune and The Magician will transport the goods up the stairs and into the freight elevator here,” he indicates a space next to the vault, “then we will load it into the truck back at the garage. The Hermit and The Fool will meet us as we pull the truck out the front, and we will simply drive out as if we have just finished a delivery.”

“It sounds too simple,” I say. I see Allen and Genevieve nod in agreement.

“Simplicity is an illusion created by our ignorance. Your task, Magician, is filled with unknowns and uncertainties. I am certain, though, that the hexes and protections wrought upon this building will test the limits of your abilities.” He pauses and looks us all over for dramatic effect.

“Devora has been wielding magic in this way for centuries. A single slip in disabling the security guards or security systems will end in our imminent arrest. The vault is state-of-the-art and custom-made. This plan would be impossible if not for the breaches and opportunities provided by recent events. Please do not mistake simplicity for ease.”

There is a long silence as everyone at the table seems to be contemplating something.

“Are there any questions?” The Hierophant looks our motley crew over.

Magdalena raises her hand, and The Hierophant sighs, "Yes?"

"I'm hungry. You spent all this money on getting us a fancy room to plan in, and you couldn't even get it catered? Could we get a couple of bottles of wine up in here? I mean..."

The Hierophant glowers at her crossly.

"I have data on your respective roles in this plan to give to you. I suggest that you review the files tonight, and we meet here at this time tomorrow to discuss the plan in greater detail," he pauses, looks at Magdalena, and then continues, "I will provide a repast tomorrow, but I ask that we refrain from consuming drugs or alcohol while working on an operation like this, there is little enough room for error as it is."

Magdalena rolls her eyes.

"What is the timeline you are working on here?" Genevieve asks.

"We will be executing on Saturday," The Hierophant says flatly.

"You mean in three days?" Allen asks incredulously.

"Precisely."

"That's not a lot of time," Genevieve observes.

"We have a small window of opportunity. I believe that this window will be closed by Monday when repairs begin. We strike when the opportunity presents itself. Please prepare yourselves," The Hierophant says conclusively.

The Hierophant walks around the table and hands us all USB drives. Each is in a polished copper casing with the image of our Tarot card engraved into it, except for Genevieves, which has a grey plastic casing and the word "Tower" written on the side in permanent marker. The script is neat and blocky.

"Until tomorrow," he says and walks out the room's back door, leaving the rest of us sitting at a table, staring at each other awkwardly.

Allen breaks the silence with aplomb.

"Well, heck yeah!" He declares, "This is gonna be a barn burner."

"That's what I'm afraid of," I mutter.

"M...Magician, The Magician has a history with burning barns," Genevieve chimes in.

The World quirks an eyebrow at me thoughtfully.

"You're Genevieve Gale. You're, um, a journalist and an author. You have a blog. It's about magic." The Hermit says.

Genevieve quirks a single eyebrow at him quizzically.

"I ran a reverse image search on your, uh, photo," The Hermit says.

"You're Howard Rasmussen," Genevieve says flatly in response.

Genevieve shrugs enigmatically. Howard Rasmussen, aka The Hermit, looks taken aback.

"Oh, I love this game. Who am I? Who am I?" The World asks over-enthusiastically.

"Elizabeth Barnes, you, uh, work for World Wide Delivery as a driver. You make forty-three dollars an hour. You were interviewed for the World Wide Delivery, um, quarterly publication. You said that you loved working for World Wide Delivery, hmm, because of the people you got to meet," Howard continues in his soft voice.

"I didn't actually say that. It's just what the marketing person said they were going to write. I actually said that you meet a lot of odd ducks in this job," Elizabeth responds.

"Who am I?" Magdalena asks, leaning forward in a challenge like she's daring Howard to come up with something.

"I don't know. You don't exist," Howard says very softly, seeming to recoil away from her into his chair.

"Damn right, I don't," Magdalena whispers at him.

"All right, all right, y'all. This is getting a little weird," Allen says. Why don't we keep this all professional and stick to our respective nomes des gar-res?"

Howard, The Hermit, nods enthusiastically.

"See you all tomorrow," I say and get up from my chair.

"Would it be possible for you to, hmm, give me a ride?" Howard asks almost inaudibly. He is staring at me.

I look around the room at the other faces. He's clearly intimidated by everyone else. He looks lost and scared. I had initially taken his silence throughout the meeting to be disinterest. Now, I think he doesn't manage social situations well.

"Sure," I say, "but just out of curiosity, how did you get here?"

"Rideshare app."

Genevieve gives me an inquisitive look. I give her a little shrug.

Genevieve, Howard, and I leave. Magdalena is a few steps behind us. Allen and Elizabeth stay seated silently at the table. I don't know if they plan to have a private conversation or if they want distance while departing.

When we return to the valet station, Magdalena's car is already there. She tips the valet again and all but leaps into her car. She tosses us a v-sign with her right fore and middle finger. It quickly morphs into just the middle finger as she roars off at unreasonable speed. She vanishes behind the hedge surrounding the property, and the screech of brakes and chorus of car horns promptly serenades us. I get a dizzying wave of déjà vu.

"Not that I need it, but remind me never to ride with her again," I mutter.

"She seems to drive very recklessly," Howard contributes.

"You have no idea," I say.

The valet pulls my rental car around, and Genevieve and I climb into the front seats, with Howard in the back.

"Where are you heading to?" I ask as we start to drive.

"The Wellmonte, um, resort and spa, The Hierophant got me a room there. It is nice." Howard says.

"So, Howard," Genevieve starts.

"Should I call you Genevieve or, um, The Tower or, um, Ms. Gale?" Howard asks.

"Genevieve is fine, except I guess on the job, then it's The Tower, but I hate that, so let's avoid it unless Mr. Hierophant is around."

"What card would you have preferred?" I ask.

Genevieve thinks for a moment, putting one finger to her upper lip.

"The Chariot, I guess," she responds, then returns to her previous inquiry, "Anyway, Howard, you're a computer security expert. You seem to do well enough financially. Why are you doing this job? If you don't mind my asking."

"Mr. Devora, um, is not a nice man, hmm. I am not doing this for the, uh, money. He has taken something, um, from me, and I want to see him, um, punished for it. This is, um, hmm, personal."

Genevieve nods and looks pensive, "Do you mind if I ask what he has of yours?"

"Um, yes," Howard says and falls silent.

After a beat, I decide to fill the awkward silence, "The Hierophant, it's an odd choice, isn't it? I mean, he's clearly telling stories with his choices of cards. They all mean something. I'd expect the guy organizing to choose a card like The Emperor for himself. Or I don't know Justice. The Hierophant reversed. It's about personal freedom and bucking the system. It's not profit, revenge, or justice...I don't know, it's weird, right?"

"Yeah," Genevieve says. She's looking out the window, and her tone is distracted.

“The cards all mean something?” Howard asks.

“Yeah, they are major arcana of the Tarot. They all have meanings. In Tarot, the meanings are all contextual. Really, one card alone doesn’t mean much without the context of the others. And even so, the major arcana don’t mean much without minor arcana mixed in. But that said, he is telling a kind of story," I say, then I think I have a metaphor that Howard might get, "like if he assigned us specific characters from a video game.”

“If you aren’t reading too much into it,” Genevieve says, “he might just think it sounds more badass than Mr. Pink and Mr. Blonde.”

“Maybe.”

We chat with Howard more. He’s an odd guy, nice enough, but I think he spends more time with machines than people. Howard managed to take everyone's photos and run image-matching software on them while we were meeting. He knows quite a bit about everyone now. Everyone except Magdalena and The Hierophant, both of whom it seems are ghosts. He considers this legwork to be his due diligence.

Howard spends a lot of time asking me about my work and about magic in general. He seems fascinated by it, like a child being told a particularly fantastical fairy tale. However, he clearly has no background in or understanding of the topic.

Finally, we deliver Howard to the Wellmonte.

The Wellmonte is a huge resort, almost a small town in and of itself. It has shops, three restaurants and two bars. It has multiple swimming pools and a spa larger than my apartment building. It’s the sort of place that costs thousands of dollars a night for a room, and all the amenities cost extra. It's a place that caters to a demographic that doesn’t stop to consider that the price per night is more than I pay for a month in my apartment.

We bid Howard good night and agree to pick him up and give him a ride tomorrow. Howard does not have a driver's license.

Genevieve and I drive back to my apartment in contemplative silence.

I notice that Magdalena's car is in her parking spot in our shared apartment building. Genevieve and I walk up to the second floor, and I knock on Magdalena's door as we pass by. There is no answer. We wait a moment, and she doesn't answer the door, so we continue on to my apartment.

I let myself in, and I walk into my office space. I am startled to find Magdalena sitting on my desk, staring at her phone.

"So what'd you think?" Magdalena asks.

"What the hell?" I say, "personal space, Magdalena."

She shrugs.

Genevieve smirks and, with a small chuckle, sits in my office chair.

While I am annoyed at Magdalena for letting herself into my apartment, it does answer a question that has been nagging at me. Circe couldn't, or wouldn't, enter my apartment. She was always very careful to stay just outside of my wards. Maybe the magical barrier wouldn't allow her in, or maybe it would weaken her or reveal something about her she didn't want revealed. I don't know.

But I had wondered if whatever prevented Circe from entering would also prevent Magdalena. Apparently not.

"She was totally looking through your junk!" I hear Hank calling from the other room.

"Were you looking through my stuff?" I ask Magdalena.

"What?" She scoffs, "No."

She has a slightly guilty look in her eye. She was looking through my stuff.

"Hmmph," I say.

"But," she says, "it is pretty weird that you had your dummy made anatomically correct. Right?"

"Okay, she was looking at my junk."

"What the hell!" I exclaim, my ears feel hot, and the back of my neck feels prickly.

"Oh, come on, I was curious. You'd be curious, too. And it's weird," she turns to look at Genevieve, "Right? It's weird?"

"Oh, leave me out of this!" Genevieve says.

Then she puts a hand covering her mouth and stage whispers, "But, yeah, it's a little weird."

"Okay, this isn't about me. I didn't break into anyone's apartment and ogle their simulacrum."

"Oh! It's a simulacrum. Cool. I read about those! It makes a lot more sense," Magdalena chimes in.

"Why are you here?" I demand of Magdalena.

"Why are any of us here? That age-old question. Sorry though, I never really got too into philosophy," Magdalena quips.

"Enough games," Genevieve finally speaks up. Her voice is firm and unrelenting.

"Fine, I wanted to touch base after that meeting. See what you thought."

"You live next door. Why'd you have to let yourself into my place?"

Magdalena shrugs, "I don't know. It seemed like a good idea at the time."

"Well, it wasn't, so please don't do it again."

It occurs to me that I need to bring more carrot to this conversation since, with Magdalena, I don't really have a stick.

"All right, all right. Like I said, it seemed like a good idea at the time, but now that you have your panties all in a twist, I'm not sure why I thought that," she says, holding her hands up defensively, "I mean, I know how sensitive you are by now."

I let the dig slide.

"You know The Hierophant, you almost slipped his name," Genevieve says.

"Yes, or a name at least. It's probably also fake. But I'm not going to tell it to you. We have a standing professional relationship. He hired Circe and Morgan for a job I tagged along on, and he's hired me for some non-Hizarin side hustles.

"Isn't that a problem for the Hizarin?" Genevieve asks.

"As long as it's not an elimination contract, the Hizarin does not care. I can get involved in all the multi-level marketing schemes I want."

I quirk an eyebrow at her.

"I just mean if he wants to hire me to parachute into the jungles of Colombia, steal an ancient gold idol from a lost temple while dodging poisoned darts, spike pits, and giant rolling boulders, evading hexes and curses, and narrowly escaping in a stolen boat...the Hizarin doesn't consider it Hizarin business."

Genevieve looks wide-eyed with excitement, "Have you actually done that?"

Magdalena shrugs and waggles her eyebrows.

"No," I say, "she's just trying to get us worked up."

Magdalena smiles one of those infuriating teenager smiles. Undeservedly smug. I'm worried Genevieve is going to try to slap her.

"What do you think of this gig?" I ask Magdalena, trying to change the topic.

"I'm concerned; honestly, it sounds like this one is personal for him. I have had bad experiences when a job gets personal."

"How so?" I ask.

"Well, Morgan made it personal with you. See how that ended up for her?"

Genevieve scoffs, "Yeah, but didn't you kill her?"

“I’m tired of defending myself on this,” Magdalena says, “But I was literally in a kill-or-be-killed situation, and that was my best opportunity. She knew it, I knew it, Circe knew it. But if Morgan had done the job she was hired to do and hadn’t made it personal, she’d still be alive, and I’d still be an apprentice, like a dog on a leash, awaiting my moment to strike.”

“I see. So, do you think we should not take the job?”

“No, I think we should, but don’t make it personal,” Magdalena says, “But moreover, working this one with, um, The Hierophant...you need to keep your eyes open and adjust if the personal nature makes him start making bad decisions.”

“Do you think that is likely?” Genevieve asks.

Magdalena shrugs, “Yesterday, I’d have said no. He’s always been a pro when I’ve worked with him in the past. But I don’t know. He was different today. I could kind of see it. He’s got a grudge.”

I think back to the Hierophant. He seemed aloof, methodical, and anything but emotional, but of course, I don’t know the guy.

“What’s your take on the rest of the team?” Genevieve asks.

“The Hermit guy, whatever, he’ll get the job done.”

“It’s personal for him, too. He said as much in the car,” I add.

“Hmm,” Magdalena responds.

“He seems like a decent guy, though, a little socially awkward, but fine,” I add.

“I have a lot on him,” Genevieve chimes in. I find myself staring at her questioningly.

“I sent photos of everyone to my assistant to see what she could dig up,” Genevieve says defensively.

“You have an assistant?” I ask.

“Yeah, just someone who does little errands and research for me, keeps my calendar. You know, she does my shopping and occasionally picks up my mail when I'm out of town. Her name is Gail."

"Genevieve Gale's assistant is named Gail?" Magdalena asks, laughing, "Is her last name Genevieve?"

"No, it's Genecitas," Genevieve says flatly.

I can't help but smirk at this. Magdalena bursts into peels of laughter.

"Seriously?" Magdalena finally gasps out between laughs.

"No, it's Brown," Genevieve says.

"Ah," Magdalena says, pulling herself together, "well, that is disappointing."

"Seriously, how did I not know you have an assistant?" I ask.

"It's like a part-time thing. She has two other clients. Between us, it's a full-time gig for her. She makes good money doing it. She calls herself a concierge, but saying 'my concierge' sounds weird, so I say assistant. I could call her My Girl Friday," Genevieve explains, air-quoting the phrase 'my concierge' with her fingers.

"So, the Wheel of Fortune guy, he's a pro. He's got that aura to me," Magdalena says suddenly, pointedly changing the topic.

"He's a member of the Knights of Saint George. I've run into him before, but I don't really know anything about him. He was undercover in Redbrook's gambling racket," I add. Maybe I have some internal bias based on his dress and demeanor, but Allen never struck me as a pro. I wonder if there is something that Magdalena sees there that I don't.

"So you are cool with this job then?" Magdalena asks.

Am I cool with this job? It is a moral quandary. On one hand, stealing is wrong, it's bad. That is a premise of our social contract. On the other hand, the Robin Hood principle says that sometimes stealing from those with too much and giving to those with too little is okay.

This was how my father justified most of his life. He only swindled those who could afford it. I will say he was known, on the rare occasion that he had the resources, to help those less well-off than himself. I never knew my father to turn away someone who was hungry. I never knew him not to stop to help a stranger on the side of the road. As many problems as I had with him as a parent, I always respected that about him.

Devora is, by all accounts in the media, a grade-A scumbag. He and half of his ilk had their evils dragged into the light a few years ago. Some of it was unthinkably awful, but aside from being 'canceled,' there seems to have been no legal or financial impact on Devora at all.

What being canceled seems to have meant for Jim Devora is that he still gets to make box-office movies. It's just that half of the population won't admit to watching them.

If we add in that he's allegedly an ancient, undead, body-snatching monk, now he seems like an even bigger monster than Redbrook. Somewhere deep down inside me, I have this urge, this compulsion to do whatever I can to thwart him, to undermine him. To impotently and ineffectively lash out in any way I can.

"This is definitely not someone manipulating you," Hank chimes in a helpful footnote to my inner thoughts.

"Yes, obviously, but that doesn't mean it isn't the right thing to do," I whisper. Magdalena looks at me with a raised eyebrow, but Genevieve doesn't even seem to notice when I talk to Hank anymore.

Do I think this heist is the best or wisest way to do this? No. If I were going to come up with a way to lash out, this would not be it. However, now I have been assured that if I don't help, they are going to do it a messier way. Probably normal people, guards, police, and the like will get hurt, and Jim Devora will still only be financially inconvenienced.

If I take the sum total of good done by participating and subtract the sum total of bad, it still seems like a positive total. If I take the sum total good done by not participating and subtract the sum total of bad, it then seems like a negative total.

I look up, and Magdalena and Genevieve are both staring at me patiently, waiting for me to answer.

"I'm going to do the job," I say, "But honestly? I'm not excited about it."

"Yay!" Magdalena says, jumping up out of my chair.

"What about you, Genevieve?" I ask, "How are you feeling about it?"

"Oh, I love the idea of stealing from that piece of shit," she says, "and you know I don't mind bending some laws..."

"Breaking," I interrupt.

"Okay, breaking some laws for truth and justice," she says unironically, "and who knows, maybe I'll find something interesting to write about!"

"Well, I should probably get researching the wards. It sounds like we have a very small window," I say.

"The...um...Hierophant always operates in short windows; he doesn't want too much time to get close to the other players, and he doesn't want to give anybody time to rethink and work a side hustle or something," Magdalena explains.

"You seem to know our Hierophant pretty well," Genevieve says, quirking an eyebrow suggestively and judgmentally.

"Eww, no, not like that," Magdalena says, "He's, like, older than you. He could be like my grandpa. Eww. We've worked together a handful of times, and he's always treated me like a professional, which I don't get a lot, looking like a kid. He's a straight shooter."

Magdalena looks at us both, a moment of apparent vulnerability.

"Listen, Morgan basically raised me. Everything with her was plans within schemes within a double cross. She would lay out who the target was and what the plan was, but there was always something she wasn't telling me. There was always a twist, a hidden agenda, another plan that only she knew about. It usually put me into dangerous places I had to get myself out of. It's never like with The Hierophant. He's always read every one in on all the pieces. When he's hiding something, he tells you, and he tells you why it is crucial that he does so."

"Okay," Genevieve says. I just sort of nod.

"I'm not saying he's like this saint or anything. I've done jobs for him, well, let's say, ones I wouldn't ask either of you to help out with. Especially you, Miles," Magdalena says, but in a way that makes me sound like a boring stick-in-the-mud, "But he knows that secrets are what makes a job go sideways. He's all about communication."

"Understood," I say.

"To that end, though, you're right. We should do our homework," Magdalena says.

Genevieve nods and starts to get her laptop and the USB drive The Hierophant gave us.

Magdalena gets up and struts out the door without another word.

"She's an enigma," Genevieve says, "I feel like she's a different person every sentence."

"Yeah, she might be. I feel bad for her."

"Why's that?"

"She was taken away from her home as a child and raised to be an assassin. She's had zero positive role modeling, but she's still trying. To top it all off, she's stuck as a teenager. Maybe forever."

"It's just magic. You could figure out how to undo that, right?"

"Yeah," I say hesitantly, "Maybe, but I don't think she is willing to give it up though."

"Why not?"

"This is just hypothesis, mind you," I say, "But she says she lives through failures, one at a time, until she figures out how to succeed, and it sounds like it can take days, or months, or years. So, if she aged, it stands to reason that she would age faster and faster each time she used that spell..ability...I don't know whatever it is. Reversing whatever is keeping her young, she might begin rapidly aging every time she time bends."

"It's a sound hypothesis," Genevieve says, "But it might not be true."

"Maybe. I'll try to talk to her about it if there is a chance."

Genevieve nods, but she has seen something in the files on her computer that has her attention. She has drifted away from the conversation and into her head. This is a behavior pattern that I am getting used to.

I sit down to read the files that the Hierophant sent to me.

An hour later, I stand up, finished and disappointed. There is very little of use in the data I have been given. A map of the house and a bunch of images of runes and sigils about the place. The house was designed with warding in mind. It is aligned with cardinal directions but skewed just enough that I can tell it's aligned magnetically and not cartographically. The layout of the house generally has a certain flow to it.

This flow is a 'know-it-when-I-see-it' thing. It is hard to codify clearly. The hallways are largely exterior on the first floor, giving a clear boundary to ward. The upstairs is the inverse, with all interior hallways and open rooms radiating outward. The floor plan has a rough symmetry, with the subterranean vault being the focal point in the center.

The images I have of the sigils are incomplete. I can't tell the whole structure of the spell; it's just some of the intention. It's like reading a heavily redacted letter; you can infer the missing bits, but it's still mostly guesswork, and the really important contextual clues are lost completely.

That said, the spells laid out around this house are alarming. They are intricate and menacing, and I have no doubt an immense amount of blood was spilled to weave them. The worst part of all, there are no pictures of the vault, no details of the spell laid upon it. I am told that the vault is the most dangerous part, but I see nothing on which to base or refute that assertion.

I go to the kitchen and make two cups of coffee, grab a silver packet of toaster pastries, and toss them into my toaster. A few minutes of grumping to myself later, I bring a cup of coffee and a toaster pastry to Genevieve.

"Considering that he didn't want you on the job, he sure gave you a lot of information," I say, placing the drink and snack next to her.

"Thank you," she says, taking a sip of the coffee, "No, there was just like a map and some information about delivery and security schedules. The Hierophant has provided a file of information on Devora, but I want to do my own research before taking what he says at face value. I started digging into Devora more. There is more than enough material already available about the man."

"Find anything useful?"

"Mmm," she murmurs, "Interesting, yeah, useful? No, probably not. I can find nothing to say he isn't the sleaze he appears to be. If an ancient and evil sorcerer possessed him, it either was a long time ago, or it didn't change his behavior much because it seems like he's always been a creep."

"I am confused by the whole possession thing," I say, "I've never seen any indication that there is a soul or spirit to live on and possess people. As I said back in Portland, I've investigated more hauntings than probably anything, and they have all been more or less bunk."

"There is more in the world than Miles Ward has observed."

"Yeah, I guess."

"What about your files?" Genevieve asks, "Anything in there?"

"Some. I have a general idea of what the protections on the building do, but there is as much missing as there is included. There is nothing about the vault."

"So. What's the general idea?"

"It looks like a lot of summoning symbols, similar to other stuff I've seen. It's akin to the Demoglorbin, actually. It has a similarly aggressive feel to it." I say, and then I pause for a second to make sure Genevieve is following.

She nods for me to continue.

"This, well, I think it has a lethal bent. I get the idea that there is some sort of passkey or device that makes the spell ignore you if you have it on your person. If I could see the whole spell, I could probably forge the passkey. With only the information I have, it would take me weeks, months, maybe."

"So forging this pass-key and just walking past the wards is a no-go."

"Not without quite a bit more information. I see three ways past these protections. One is we get the magical pass-key. It seems likely that the security guards would have them. Devora certainly has one unless it's been infused into his body directly, or else there is a part of the spell I am not seeing that excludes him."

"Maybe getting the pass keys off the guards could work," Genevieve nods, "But it is an extra step in The Hierophant's plan, and he seems like a 'my way or the highway' kind of guy."

"The second is that I could try to counteract the wards, disabling them the 'old-fashioned' way, with a line here and a sigil there."

"But..." Genevieve says, sensing the impending concern.

"But," I say, "From what I see, it's all sort of interwoven. Changing one part of the spell changes the whole context in a way that triggers another part of the spell. It's filled with fail safes. It would be very slow, and a single mistake could mean the end for all of us."

"That seems like a non-starter."

"I agree."

"So what's the third option?" Genevieve asks.

"I get as much of the Acetobacter Magusficedula from Jeff as I can, and I hope it's enough."

"What's the problem with that solution? It seems like the most sure bet."

"Well, there are two complications there," I say.

She stays silent and waits for me to continue.

"Actually, three, but let's start with number one. I haven't talked to Jeff since before the fires. He was getting a little...I don't know, off. So I am not sure if and how much Acetobacter Magusficedula he'll have. Number two, the time for it to work can vary dramatically based on how big the scope of the spell or spells in question. This is big. From what I've seen, this makes what was on the Lantern look like kiddie scribbles. This is on the level of what we put together on the Syzmek building. Only it's all aggressive, where Syzmek was defensive."

"So it might take a while?"

"Yeah, which is the third complication, too. In order to make it go faster, I could put it in an inclusive circle to flow magic into the building, so there is more for the bacteria to feed on."

"Why is that a problem?"

"Um, well, it's going to power everything up. Until the Acetobacter Magusficedula hits a critical mass, all of the spells will be more dangerous and less stable."

"So, in order to make it happen fast enough, it gets riskier?"

"In a nutshell."

We sit and ponder for a minute.

"And!" I say, "That's just the building. I don't even know what we are looking at with the vault. I really need to understand better how the vault is warded."

"But there is no way to see it without physical access, which it seems we won't get until we are on site."

"Yeah. Considering the complexity of these wards and the anecdotal statement that the vault is much more heavily fortified..." I heave a deep and burdened sigh, "I don't know."

"Buck up, you got this!" Genevieve says chirpily, "So you won't be able to walk in and look at the vault. Is there another way we could get that information? Drones or scrying or something?"

"No, scrying is just made up," I start to say. But then I realize that isn't true. "Well, it is sort of made up. There is a Dreamwalking thing that Russ did that was basically like scrying, where he can find people in his sleep."

"You should call Russ!"

"Yeah, I don't think that is going to work, not for a couple of reasons."

Genevieve waits for me expectantly.

"Ah," I say, realizing she wants me to elaborate. "The first reason. I'm just not good at Dreamwalking. Ever since Circe got trapped, I haven't been able to Dreamwalk. Nothing."

"That is weird, why is that?" Genevieve asks.

"I honestly don't know. Russ thinks she was helping me, dragging me along somehow. But, honestly, I think it is more of a mental block. It scared me, I guess. I haven't Dreamwalked in weeks, and I don't miss it," I say.

Genevieve nods and bites her lower lip pensively for a moment.

"Why can't Russ just do it?"

"Something like this needs to be more personal. In order for it to work, he would have to get more involved. I am not sure I want to drag Russ into this thing we are doing."

"Heist!" She says, "It's a heist."

"I think you are a little too excited about that. From what I have seen, I suspect the magical defenses might extend into the Dreamtime. It may be insanely dangerous to tamper with from that angle. I don't feel comfortable asking Russ to get involved."

"So what does that leave in the way of options?" Genevieve asks.

"Figuring something else out or going in blind."

"That doesn't sound like much of a choice."

CHAPTER 5

The Hierophant's plan is all laid out on the thumb drives he's given us. It has been meticulously crafted to include no names, addresses, or other identifying information. Floorplans and schematics have even been simplified to make it hard to identify the target. I can't imagine how much work went into being so specific while still being so vague.

The plan is simple on paper. We drive in, subdue the guards, disable the cameras, blow the vault, and make out with the goods. I guess it makes the most practical sense. My only real exposure to this sort of thing has been movies, so I expected the plan to involve a lot of fake outs, deceptions, phone tapping, misdirections, etc. Which, in reality, doesn't make sense. That many moving parts would fall apart in a second. Even knowing that, I still feel a little disappointed at how simple the plan is.

There is one flaw in the plan: one place where there are a bunch of question marks. That, of course, is my part of the plan. The part where we bypass the magical security measures. It is obvious to me that The Hierophant understands that these are very real and very dangerous protections. However, the fact that he is so glib about it raises questions.

My ego might like to think that he has that much faith in me, but I don't really believe that. He might think this is a lot easier than it is. Possibly, he is working for someone who insists that he take the magical defenses seriously, even though he doesn't really. I could speculate on why he doesn't seem to be taking it as seriously as everything else, but without more information, it is all just that: speculation.

I'm pondering that when my phone rings. I glance at the caller ID, and it says HERMIT in the place of the phone number. On one hand, that is weird. On the other hand, I am pretty sure I know who is calling me.

"Miles Ward speaking, if you're the hermit, then I'll..." I pause midway, my mind suddenly black of potential rhymes, "Um, I'll uh croak like Kermit?"

I hang my head in shame.

"Permit, emit, remit, admit..." Howard's soft voice begins to list.

"Omit, outwitted me. I submit. Good work, Howard," I interrupt him before it starts to really feel shameful.

"I can think of four more rhymes and at least ten near rhymes for hermit," he offers. I think he's trying to be helpful. It is soul-crushing.

"What can I do for you, Howard?"

"I was looking at the plan. You talked in the car about what you do, and it seemed to me that of all of us, your portion of the plan was the least, hmm, well-developed," Howard says in his weird, soft manner.

"I had noticed that too. I would really like to get a better look inside the building. Especially at the vault."

"I think I have an idea there," Howard says.

"Oh? Tell me more."

Howard's plan tells me he has seen a heist film or two. It's much more what I was expecting. Basically, Howard suggests he hacks into the houses' smart home features, causing them to do erratic things. When the staff calls the company for service, Howard has arranged somehow to intercept this call and send me as the technician.

Howard's plan sounds fine on paper, but I don't see how it could work in practice.

"I don't know, Howard, there are a lot of intricacies in that plan," I conclude after he explains.

"If your concern is that I, um, cannot perform my portion of the plan, I have, hmm, already gained access to the Syzmek Abode-Intelligence system that, um, operates the home. I have updated it so that the maintenance phone number, uh, will ring me. I have also rerouted all security alerts from it to my system."

"Wait, you what? How?"

"I used to, um, work in the Abode-Intelligence division of Syzmek. My team implemented its network security features."

"I see," I say skeptically. I can see how that might be a leg up, but that doesn't explain how he got in so quickly and thoroughly unless he was involved enough to put in backdoors.

"Backdoors were, hmm, installed in all the systems to be leveraged by law enforcement. They are very easy to, uh, exploit if you know how they work."

"Still..." I say, biting my lip and thinking.

"Based on your employment history, you should have plenty of technical knowledge in order to pretend to be a service technician," Howard says. It's creepy how much cyberstalking he's been doing.

"Yeah, that isn't my problem," I say.

"You sound, eh, agitated. I am, um, sorry. Did I, hmm, do

something wrong?" He asks, sounding confused, a touch of panic seeping into his voice.

"No, no. I'm just surprised. I need to think this through."

"Okay," he sounds hurt.

"Does The Hierophant know about this plan?" I ask.

"Do you think I should ask what he thinks?"

"Yeah, I think that's for the best," I say. I don't want us to throw the plan off the rails.

"I will, um, present this to him before we execute."

"Okay, great."

"I will call him now," Howard says and hangs up without another word.

I sigh and sit back.

"The Hermit is going to get you in to see the vault?" Genevieve asks.

"Apparently so."

"Great, let's get dinner. I'm famished!" Genevieve says, leaping up out of a chair and grabbing her purse.

"Let me get my keys."

CHAPTER 6

"GET THAT!" Genevieve mutters, elbowing me awake.

My phone is ringing.

"Seriously, don't you know that you can leave it in vibrate mode? You can even...wait for it...turn it off. Really, dude," Hank mutters at me sleepily, *"Who is going to call you that isn't already in this room?"*

I swing my legs out of bed and reach for my phone.

"How the hell do you know about vibrate mode, dummy?" I growl at Hank as I look at the caller ID. Once more, it says HERMIT.

"You better be talking to your mannequin," Genevieve growls in a muffled voice, her head buried beneath a pillow.

"I might be a dummy, but you are the one getting awakened at three a.m. 'cause you don't know how to operate your phone!"

Why does he sound groggy? Does Hank sleep? Can he be awakened? Does he wake up grouchy, or is he always this way? Why have I never pondered these things before?

"What, Howard?" I grumble as I answer the phone.

"It's go time."

"What do you mean 'it's go time'?"

"Mr. Hierophant, um, approved our, hmm, Abode Intelligence plan. They just called and want it fixed immediately. I said we had a, uh, twenty-four-hour technician in the area."

"Howard!" I say, raising my voice. Genevieve grabs another pillow and smashes it into the pile over her head. "The plan wasn't for you to call me at three a.m. for a house call!"

"We are under severe time constraints. I thought that it would be best if you could get in sooner than later."

"Oh my...Jarlsberg! Howard!" I say, standing up.

"Are you, um, angry with me?"

"Yes! No! I don't know. It's three in the morning, and you woke me up..."

"It will be, uh, suspicious if you don't show up at this point."

"Okay, okay," I say, "Let me get some coffee and get dressed. Where should I meet you?"

"Oh, I'm not coming along. I don't, um, do well with stressful social situations. I'm sending your credentials to your phone. Do you have a laptop? You should bring that."

This is not a plan anymore; this is an ambush. Unfortunately, I think Howard has got me over a barrel. He's right. If no technician shows up at this point, it will cause problems that will jeopardize the rest of this job.

"So I just grab my phone and laptop and head there? How am I supposed to actually fix things?"

"Nothing is broken, just disabled. We will stay on the line and you will inform me as you go. I will restore each node to its proper function."

"Uggh!" I say, "Fine. Hold on, I'll be back."

I set the phone down on the bedside table and start rifling around, looking for my headset.

"Genevieve?" I ask while I search, "I am going to sneak into Devora's as a service technician. Do you want to come?"

"Normally, I'd say yes, but I am very comfortable, and it's three in the morning, and you woke me up!" She grumbles at me, head buried in pillows.

"Don't worry, I'll hold down the fort. Just lay me down on the bed, and she will never know you're gone."

I ignore him as I silently dig through my closet for a shirt with a collar and some slacks. I slip out of the bedroom and get dressed in the living room. I make a quick cup of coffee, splash some water on my face, grab my laptop and messenger bag, and bustle out the door.

I put my stuff in the car and then realize I should have some food, so I run back upstairs for a toaster pastry. I'm eating far too many of these lately. I wonder what my doctor would say if I had one. Halfway down the stairs for the second time, I realize I left my phone in the bedroom. I sneak back in for it.

"Having a private moment!" Hank exclaims as I try to open the bedroom door silently.

"Don't you ever quit!" I hiss at Hank between my teeth.

"Are you still here?" Genevieve moans from under her pile of pillows.

"Just on my way out," I whisper. I consider leaning over to give her a goodbye kiss or something. I would never get through her pillow armor, though, so I sneak back out the way I came.

I AM TURNING onto Silverado Trail by the time I'm actually awake.

"What the hell am I doing?" I ask myself.

"You are gathering information for the job," Howard says

over the phone on my headset. I forgot that he was there. I jump in my seat and swerve briefly onto the shoulder. My rental car vibrates jarringly as I hit the rumble strip.

"Sharp cheddar, Howard! You scared the hell out of me. I forgot you were there."

"Do you always use cheeses as, um, a curse?"

"Only when people wake me up in the middle of the night."

"That is very odd."

"Let's not get into that, Howard," I say. Seriously, who does this guy think he is, calling me odd?

"Okay," he says, he sounds dejected again.

"So once I get there, what? I show them this ID you sent me on my phone, and they let me in?"

"Yes. The IDs are all digital. They will take you into the security office, which is separate from the main house. You will, um, tell them there is a problem with one of the peripheral nodes and that you must inspect them physically. They should let you into the main house to look at the cameras, light switches, ovens. Basically, everything in the house is connected to the Abode Intelligence system."

"Even the vault?"

"No, not the vault. That would have simplified this process by a geometric factor. The only smart devices near the vault are the lights in the entryway. The vault and whatever may be inside of it are on their own isolated system."

"And you'll be listening and just turning stuff on as I go?"

"Yes."

We've just finished this little pep talk when I pull up to the front gate of the Devora compound. I am suddenly very self-conscious about the dingy rental car I am driving. However, it probably fits the bill for the late-shift on-call repair technician. There is a security guard waiting at the gate. It opens as I pull up.

I roll down my window and come to a stop.

"Hi!" I say, blinking as he shines a large flashlight in my eyes. "I am from Abode Intelligence. I got a call that your system was acting up."

"Took you long enough," the guard says. Now that the light is not shining in my eyes, I can see him better. He's a middle-aged man with grey hair and a big, bushy 70's mustache. It reminds me of my father. His skin is weathered and worn. This is a man who has spent a lot of time in the sun. His complexion is ruddy, almost like he is perpetually sunburned.

"I'm based out of San Mateo. I made pretty good time, I think."

"Local technician, my ass," he mutters as he nods and waves me through the gate. I roll slowly up the drive until I come to a small lot by a small building. There are two vehicles parked there: an older mid-sized pickup and a crossover SUV. Neither is fancy enough to be Devora's. I assume these are the guards' personal vehicles. The drive continues up to the main house, but the guard shines his flashlight onto an open spot next to the small building. He is clearly indicating that I should park there, so I do.

"How are you doing this evening? Well, morning, I guess," I ask.

He shrugs and beckons me to follow him into the small building. It's pretty, with elegant wooden siding and a quaintly shingled roof. It blends into the stand of trees behind it well and would barely register to someone driving all the way up to the main house.

We walk around the back. Hidden from the drive, the entrance to the security building is protected by a chain link fence with coils of razor wire on the top. Here, he keys a code to get us past the fence and another to get us past the door. I try to look at the codes casually, but he is careful to block the keypads with his body.

Inside, there is another guard. This one is younger and also has a mustache, but it is thin and whispy. He is sitting in a chair at a bank of monitors. He's eating a donut and drinking some coffee. A number of rooms are visible on the consoles, all dark and empty. Many of the screens are powered off and blank, with angry red lights flashing next to them.

"There is the smart home system," the first guard says, motioning me to a housing mounted on the wall.

I walk over to it and look it up and down. I don't know what to do now and can't ask for Howard's help directly.

"Yup," I say, "That is an Abode Intelligence Accel48! Says it right there on the housing!"

The guards look at me askew.

"Sorry," I say, "I'm still waking up. Honestly, we don't get a lot of these emergency calls."

"Yeah, I'm not sure how much of an emergency it is, but our boss freaks if he finds out anything isn't working," the older guard says.

"You want some coffee?" Asks the younger guard.

"Yeah, that'd be great."

"Okay, so you will want to open the housing; there is an LCD monitor inside and a fold-down keyboard," Howard's voice sing-songs in my ear.

"Could I grab a donut with that coffee?" I ask pointedly, indicating a half-empty box of sugary confections nearby.

The older guard looks annoyed, but the younger one says, "Sure, knock yourself out."

I pour myself a paper cup of coffee from the coffee pot in the corner and grab a donut.

I sip the coffee, nibble the donut, then walk casually to the housing and open it. Just as Howard said, there is an LCD display and a fold-down keyboard. I fold down the keyboard and arrange my body so that it is hard to see the screen from the guard station. Both the guards sit down and go back to their duties, apparently unconcerned with me.

"Now you will want to tell them that there are some errors with the peripheral nodes, and you will need to cycle them manually," Howard says.

I tap on the keyboard a bit and fiddle for a moment.

"Looks like there are errors on some of the peripheral nodes. I need to cycle them manually," I say finally, slapping the keyboard back up and closing the housing.

"What does that mean?" The older guard asks.

"It means," the younger guard begins explaining before I can respond, "that he's got to go in the house and turn off and turn back on the smart devices."

"In a nutshell, yes," I confirm.

"Shee-it," the older guard curses, "I don't want to write up that report. The boss is not going to like that."

"We go in, he pushes some buttons, we come out, right?" The younger guard says, giving me a questioning look.

"That's it. Open and shut," I say.

"We don't need to put this in the log. It's nothing," the younger guard says.

The older guard glowers at the younger guard and then looks appraisingly at me. I shrug helplessly.

"I don't know about logs or whatever. I'm only here because I get triple time on these graveyard calls. Log it or don't, I won't say a thing," I say as nonchalantly as possible.

"Yeah, shit. You walk him up there," the older guard says to the younger guard, "And you get to file the report. Your ass if the boss finds out."

The younger guard winks at him, "You got it."

"Here," the older guard says gruffly, tossing me a little wooden amulet on a string.

"What is this?" I say, catching it and holding it up to examine it. The little wooden disk has a series of runes delicately carved into it. It is bound to a little chain.

The older guard pulls one up off his neck and shows it, "Everybody wears one in the house. The owner is very superstitious and very particular."

"You don't have to wear it," the younger guard says.

"The hell he don't. Weird shit happens if you don't wear one. There was this guy, Reiman, who used to work here before your time, kid. He didn't wear one when he went in, and he never came back. Vanished. Wear one!"

The younger guard rolls his eyes and then shrugs helplessly at me.

I shrug, "Whatever. It's fine."

I slip the amulet on. Now I know how some of the magical protectives work. As I suspected, the amulet should prevent the spells on the house from triggering on entry. I will need time to examine the amulet more closely if I want to try to copy it.

On one hand, the younger guard seems less suspicious and more friendly. On the other hand, the older guard seems less technically savvy. I'm not sure which one I'd rather have looking over my shoulder.

"The streamed cameras are all down, but the security system is all closed circuit, not connected to the internet. So you are still being observed and probably recorded," Howard continues, whispering in my ear.

The younger guard leads me out of the security building and onto a stone path that winds its way through a thicket to the back of the main house.

"I'm Todd," the guard says.

"Mi..ke..al," I say, "I'm Michael. It's good to meet you, Todd."

Todd looks curiously at me. He's not a big guy, but the uniform gives him more gravitas. He's got a taser and a pistol on his belt.

"That was Pat back there, he's a bitter old codger. Used to be a cop. Retired. He treats everything like it's something."

"And is it?"

"I've been here for three years. It is dull. The most excitement is handing out candy on Halloween."

"You get a lot of trick-or-treaters?"

"Some, not a lot."

We get to the house. It's an immense structure, three stories high, ten or fifteen thousand square feet in total. It is half-built into the side of a large hill. The first floor is built above ground level, with huge bay doors for entrance into a garage below the house. I know from the schematics that the garage is big enough to park a dozen cars in. It's dark, but I can still see that a section of the back of the house has been damaged by fire. A large swath of blackened shrubs and grass runs the length of the hill behind the house like a giant took a forty-foot wide paint brush and made a big black swath down the hill to the rear corner of the house. I scan the area. I can see a melted electrical junction box and a number of blackened telephone poles. Cables and wires have been spliced onto the house, bypassing the melted junction.

"Got hit pretty hard by that fire. We've been having all sorts of weird problems since. Not surprised the stupid smart home system is on the fritz now," Todd says.

"Yeah, it looks like a close call," I say, looking pointedly up the charred line on the hillside.

Todd leads me up the stairs to the front door of the house. It is wide and made of glass. There are blinds, but they have been raised all the way up, so I can easily see into the house. It is immaculate inside. The decor is clean, simple, and modern. Todd stops at the door, where a keypad is attached to the wall. He keys in a code on the door. It doesn't open.

"Shit," Todd mutters.

"Oh, the doors are hooked up with the Abode Intelligence System," Howard informs me in my ear.

"Hold on," I say, "I'll have to cycle this first."

I move up to the door and get very close to the keypad. I cup my hands around it and hunch my shoulders so that Todd can't see that I am not actually doing anything. I feel very self-conscious as I realize that from behind, it probably looks like I am urinating on the door handle.

"Okay," I say, "The back door lock is power cycled. It should work now."

I step back, and Todd steps forward and puts in the code again. The door whirrs and clicks open.

"How did you do that?" Todd asks, looking incredulously at the handle.

"It's pretty simple. Just insert a reset key into the reset socket and hold down the button for ten seconds."

"You just put a little paper clip in the hole and held it down for ten seconds?" Todd asks. He cranes his neck around, trying to see the fictional reset hole. Thankfully, it is dark enough that a tiny pinhole would be hard to find if it did exist.

"Yeah," I lie, "That's right. It only resets it, forcing it to reinitiate its connection to the primary hub."

"You are good at this," Howard marvels in my ear.

"Do you have to cycle everything individually?" Todd asks. I see his eyes scanning all the light sockets and switches in the small mud room we've entered. If this one small room is any indication of the number of smart devices in this large house, it would take a full day to go to every device and pretend to reset it.

"No, we just need to find the one device malfunctioning and causing a packet storm; reset that, and it should be all set," I say, throwing out an intimidating buzzword I remember from my days in tech support.

"Packet storm? That sounds bad."

"It's not a big deal. It's when one device asks another device for information, and that second device decides to ask all the devices on the network for the information, so they all send out a request asking for the information until they all spend so much time asking that they don't have resources left to answer anyone."

"Oh," Todd says, confused.

"Let's go," I say.

I start through the door, and Todd follows close at my heels.

"Do you know where you are going?" Todd asks.

"I'm just looking for the malfunctioning device," I say.

"How can you tell which device is malfunctioning?"

"I can make a red light flash on many of the devices," Howard says, "Just let me know which one."

"It will have a red light flashing on it."

"Oh."

So I go room to room, with Todd at my heels. I pretend to be looking for flashing red lights, but, really, I am checking out all of the runes and hexes placed on the building. After about half an hour of going room-to-room and investigating all of it, I say, "I don't see the problem device. Is there anywhere I'm missing?"

"Nope," Todd says. "That was it."

He seems uncomfortable. He knows that there is one more area we haven't looked into. The stairwell down to the vault.

"Huh, weird. I guess I could run a full level three diagnostic on the unit," I say, then sigh, "Man, I was hoping to see my kids after school tomorrow."

Todd nods at me, biting his lower lip.

"But on the other hand, who can say no to fifteen or sixteen hours of triple overtime!"

"You know, there is one more place we could look. Really not supposed to go there unless there is a security event there."

"I don't want you to get in trouble, Todd. Don't break the rules on my account."

"We are already breaking the rules," Todd says. "Let's just get this fixed, and no one is the wiser."

"That's the spirit, Todd."

"Whatever works for you," I say out loud, maybe too loudly.

Todd leads me through a series of winding passages and down to the first floor. There, he opens a door in a wall beneath the main staircase. Calling it a secret door is probably an overstatement, but it is certainly a hidden door. It is covered with the same material and painted like the rest of the walls so that it looks like a panel in the wall with a door handle and a keypad. It's not exactly invisible, but it blends in. Todd punches in a code, and the door swings open, revealing a staircase winding its way down inside a concrete tube.

With Todd in the lead, we descend into an area that reminds me of a fallout shelter. The only fallout shelters I've seen are in movies, and this fits the bill pretty well. It's a big concrete box. A vault door is on one end of the box, probably five feet across. The huge steel door is mounted in a solid wall, encircled with runes cast directly into the concrete. The old modify-them-with-a-permanent-marker trick isn't going to work here. I'd need a jackhammer to erase or change these runes. Many of the runes look familiar, but they aren't ones I can immediately place.

"Weird, huh?" Todd asks as he follows my gaze to the runes.

"It looks like something out of a story," I say.

"Yeah, our employer is a bit eccentric. Like Pat said, superstitious."

"Huh," I say, spending as much time as I feel I can studying and trying to memorize the runes.

When I feel I can stall no more, I turn and look at the light fixture. I see it has a flashing red light on the side.

"Good job!" I say, mostly intending this for Howard, "We found the problem unit."

Todd follows my line of sight.

"Cool, now what?"

"Well, I have to cycle it, of course." As I say it, it occurs to me that now he expects me to get up there and do what I did before. But the roof is a good ten feet high. "Do you have a ladder, by chance?"

"Yeah, I know where there is one," Todd says, bustling off.

No sooner do I hear the door at the top of the stairs close than I say, "I can't believe he left me alone in here, Howard."

I am greeted by silence.

"Howard?"

I look at my phone. I have no service here. Not a single bar, no emergency service, nothing. This concrete box is a complete radio dead zone. I scan the room. There are two closed circuit cameras on the ceiling, one aimed at the stairwell coming down and one at the vault door. I calculate that a little area should be out of view of cameras in the far corner, away from the vault. I casually wander over there. Once I think I am unobserved, I use my phone to take photos of the vault and its runes and then of the amulet I am wearing.

I take out a pocket knife and shave the edges of the wooden amulet off into my hand. Then I frantically dig one handed around in my courier bag, trying to find something to store them in. I find a little stoppered glass vial. I have no idea why or even when I put this in here. I store the shavings in the vial and place the stopper in.

I've barely finished when I hear the door at the top of the stairs bang open. I shove the vial into my bag, lean against the wall, and try to look bored. An instant later, Todd comes banging down the stairs with an aluminum ladder, awkwardly slamming and thumping on the stairs.

"Pat is pissed I brought you down here, but don't sweat it. We'll just reset the light and be gone."

As Todd begins setting up the ladder, I start to panic. I can no longer talk to Howard to let him know he should turn the light off since I don't have cell service down here. I don't know how to actually turn the light off without him. I know literally nothing about the system that I am working with.

I climb up the ladder with sweaty palms. I examine the steel housing. Other than the flashing red light, I don't see anything else I can interact with. The reset button I discussed doesn't actually exist. I stand there staring at it for a moment, maybe a moment too long.

"Aren't you going to reset it?" Todd asks.

"Yeah, just a second."

Okay, here goes. I take the glass dome off of the light and hold it out.

"Catch!" I say as I toss it down to Todd. He frantically scrambles to keep it from smashing on the concrete.

"Jesus, Michael!" He cries, "Give a guy a chance here."

I reach up and unscrew the light bulb. I count to two. I screw it back in, I repeat. I unscrew it for five seconds, then screw it back in, then repeat. Then, I do the two seconds twice more. It's

Morse code, but I don't know Morse code. But almost anybody who knows Morse code is a thing knows SOS, and so that is the only message I can do, the good old dot-dot, dash-dash, dot-dot.

"What the hell are you doing?"

"Oh," I say, "These light bulbs work differently. They don't have a reset button. You have to take the bulb out and put it back in a certain way."

"Huh?" He asks. For the first time, I think Todd might be getting suspicious. However, everything is resolved when the red light winks out. Todd hands me the glass cover, and I replace it.

"And done, everything should be back in order," I say, climbing down the ladder.

He folds the ladder up and follows me back up the stairs. We exit the house out the back door, and Todd leaves the ladder against the rear wall of the house while he escorts me back to my car.

"I think you should just go. Pat's pretty pissed. The sooner you're gone, the sooner he can chill out."

Todd takes a radio off of his belt and makes a quick call to Pat. After a couple of moments, standing in silence in the dark, Pat comes back on the radio, indicating that the smart home system is working again.

Todd gives me a thumbs up, "All set, thank you."

"And thank you!" As I climb into my car, I say, "You are going to get a survey in the mail. Make sure you give me a five-star review, anything less than five stars, and it's a black mark on my record. Nobody makes you feel smarter in your home than Abode Intelligence!"

For a moment, I think he is going to let me drive away with the amulet still hanging around my neck. This would be a huge boon. Trying to create copies would be easy with an original to work from. Unfortunately, as I start my car, he waves at me. I roll my window down.

"What's up?"

"I forgot. I am going to need the necklace," he says.

"Right, sorry! Forgot I was even wearing it!"

I nod and take the little wooden token off my neck. I hand the amulet to him out my window.

Todd looks both perplexed and relieved as he opens the gate for me, and I drive out. I'm only a couple of hundred feet down the road when Howard calls me back.

"Oh, thank fromage!" I say as I answer, "I am so glad you got my message."

"What message?" Howard asks.

"The SOS? Dot dot, dash dash, dot dot?"

"SOS is three dots, three dashes, and three dots," he says, judgment in his voice.

"Oh," I say sheepishly, "Right, well, you got the message either way."

"I saw there were errors on that bulb, and I assumed that was you. I did not know we would lose service when you went into the vault. That was my mistake."

"It's okay. I think I got everything I needed. Thank you, Howard!" I say with genuine gratitude.

"That's good," Howard says.

"And you know what's weird?"

"What is weird, Miles?"

"That ID you sent me. They never even asked for it."

"The weakest link in any security system is always the people who have to operate within it."

I sadly have to agree with his assessment.

"Good night, Howard," I say, "I'll see you tomorrow."

"Good night, Miles. I am impressed by your improvisational skills, even if your understanding of Morse Code is faulty."

"You were pretty impressive, too," I say. I don't think he meant to sound so judgy.

With that, Howard disconnects our call.

I drive the rest of the way home in constant rotation between driving exactly the speed limit, getting impatient to get home, speeding up, then getting worried about being pulled over and slowing down. After an interminable drive, I get home just as the sun rises. I skulk in the door so as not to wake Genevieve, but she is already up.

"Good morning!" She says.

"Good morning! After I grab a cup of coffee, I have a story for you!"

CHAPTER 7

We arrive back in the Burlesque room. The table is now set with an impressive spread of food: smoked meats and cheeses, fancy little salads with arugula and endive, trays of olives, and a whole fish. Everything seems to have a drizzle of sauce, foam, or other topping. It all smells mouth-watering.

But then I see the most majestic sight. The apex of man's technological achievement. The grandest gesture that The Hierophant has provided. My heart stops, and my hands shake with giddy excitement.

"Is that the Crugle LavaJava 24K SXR?" I ask enviously.

The Hierophant nods distractedly at me.

"The LavaJava 24 huh?" The World bellows at me.

"The twenty-four-kay SXR," I correct. "It is the world's most advanced automated coffee machine. You can program the grind as low as a hundred microns. You can specify the brewing temperature and length of exposure to the grounds. It has seventy-four froth settings and storage for up to four different milk options. All with a touch of a button! It's such a finely crafted and expensive machine that they all have a twenty-four-karat gold trim. That's where the 24k in the name comes from!"

I am shaking with excitement. I have read about this machine before but have never seen it. I could buy one, but then I wouldn't be able to pay my rent or car payments, buy food or toilet paper, and end up homeless with nowhere to plug it in.

It is clear from the blank and slightly worried expressions on everyone else's faces that this excitement is mine and mine alone.

"You sound like an infomercial," Magdalena snorts.

"Can I?" I ask The Hierophant.

He looks at me like a particularly annoying child, "That is the precise purpose to which this device has been acquired."

I all but dash over and grab a mug. I carefully, reverently place it in the receptacle at the base of the Crugle LavaJava 24k SXR. With as gentle and delicate a touch as I can muster, I program in all the parameters that will make the perfect cup of coffee. I press the button.

The machine hums to life. Lights flash. The display begins with a colorful animation of a mountain as pressure begins to build in it. Then, just as the undulating mountain seems like a balloon about to burst, coffee begins pouring down into my mug in a stream. Synchronized, the animated mountain begins to pour molten rock down its sides so it looks like the coffee is the end of the lava flow.

"Kaboom!" I cheer at the animation.

I triumphantly take my cup of coffee from the machine and turn toward the table.

Everyone is staring open-mouthed at me except for Genevieve, who seems to be pretending she doesn't know me.

"Sorry," I mutter as I skulk my way back to my seat.

I sit down.

Everyone is still staring at me; their awkward expressions are now expectant. After all the drama, they want to see if the coffee lives up to my hype.

I smell it. Nutty and warm, it smells like wrapping yourself in a blanket in front of a fire on a snowy day. It smells like the first rays of sunshine on my face as I stand on a dock overlooking a fishing pond. It smells like a mother's love...

"Okay, you are going to drink it or write a poem about it?"

"Shut up," I mutter as I take my first sip.

I don't spit it back into the cup. I smile and drink it down.

It's terrible.

It's too bitter and not nutty enough. It's thick and muddy and gritty. I think I overdid it on the grind.

I smile at everyone. My teeth feel coated with the thick black coffee. My tongue needs a shave.

"Mmmm! It really puts the lava in the java!" I say and raise my mug of mud up to everyone, "Cheers."

I slump into my seat and drink my terrible cup of coffee in silence. Everyone else serves themselves plates of food. The Hierophant and Genevieve are both fairly reserved in their helpings, but the others all heap huge plates before themselves.

I pick at a few items here and there. The coffee has really spoiled my appetite, though. After all the hype, I feel obligated to drink it, but it isn't pleasant and doesn't blend well with the rest of the repast. When I finish my coffee, it leaves the nerves in my fingers electrified and makes my face buzz like I just ate a half-pound of espresso beans—which maybe I did.

Magdalena eats more than any human I have ever witnessed. I consider that she might make more money in professional eating contests than as a world-class assassin. Probably not, but it would certainly be more morally justifiable.

Just as Magdalena is going for her second heaping plate, while everyone else is just starting on their first, the Hierophant taps his glass with a spoon.

We all turn and look toward him.

“I assume that you have all reviewed the materials I have provided you?”

There is a general murmur of acknowledgment.

“Before we begin to run through the plan, are there any concerns or questions?” The Hierophant asks.

I look around. Everyone seems confident. I raise my hand slowly.

“Magician, yes?”

“There was nothing indicating what spells are on the vault, and what you provided for the house itself was inadequate. So last night, Ho...The Hermit and I did a little digging," I begin.

"What do you mean 'digging'?" The Hierophant asks, his brow knitting in concern.

"Um," I say, confused, "Well, The Hermit said he got your okay."

I look at Howard, who shrugs at me.

"Okay, to what? He asked if it seemed appropriate to make a plan to gather information. I did not assent to the execution of said course of action without my personal review."

"I guess I misunderstood," Howard says, his round face taking on a look of innocence. I scratch my chin. Howard may be more manipulative than I thought.

"What did you do?" The Hierophant asks.

"The Hermit engineered a failure of Devora's smart home system, and I went in as a technician to fix it. I got photos of the vault and the wards protecting it as well as confirmation of how to bypass the magical security on the rest of the house."

The Hierophant looks on the verge of rage. His face gets a slightly red tinge, and his jaw is firmly set. The veins and tendons in his neck bulge out. I don't know this man well, but it seems out of character and inappropriate to the circumstances.

"This could easily jeopardize the job. If Devora hears that crews came on-site without his knowledge, he will get suspicious. Highly suspicious. He may change his course of action," The Hierophant snarls through gritted teeth.

"M..agician was amazing," Howard says, "The guards aren't going to report it to Devora."

"I don't think they will. They don't want to deal with him any more than we do," I add.

The Hierophant seems to be reigning his emotions in from barely contained rage to poorly contained displeasure, "I do hope that you are correct. At least your rogue side operation resulted in useful information, I hope?"

"Getting us past the wards on the house should be no problem. I still need to figure out the spells on the vault itself, but it shouldn't be an issue."

I see Allen give me a subtle thumbs-up from across the table.

I am relieved that I won't have to rely on Acetobacter Magusficedula to devour the wards. I was concerned about breaking that out in front of a large audience. The potential impact on the magical community could be stunning if made public. It would also be revealing the most useful tool in my repertoire to people I don't know well enough to trust.

There is suddenly a palpable sense of relief in the room. A tension I hadn't even registered has suddenly drained from the group. This job is a huge financial windfall for all of these people. I think the ambiguity regarding the magical protections was making everyone nervous.

I see part of the Hierophant's tactic now. He recruits people who are a touch desperate. People who aren't going to ask a lot of questions and who will ignore some obvious red flags. He keeps us on a tight timeline so that we don't have time to adjust and get comfortable. I wonder what that says about me?

"I'll get my part done, easy-peasy-lemon-squeezy," I assure everyone.

"Very well. Let's run through our timeline," The Hierophant says with one last dark glance at Howard and me.

We spend the next three hours discussing timelines, contingencies, and exit strategies. I shake the feeling that the Hierophant keeps staring at me whenever I look away.

"He's testing you."

"Hmm?"

"Come on, Miles, this guy is detail-oriented. He's got everything else planned down to thirty-second intervals. He's got schematics for the custom vault. But he's got almost no details on the magic? No way. But now he seems annoyed that you've worked that out so quickly. It's a test that he hopes you fail."

"It's a good point," I mutter.

"What?" Genevieve whispers at me.

"Nothing, talking to myself," I whisper back.

The Hierophant looks at us curiously but doesn't say anything.

It's late afternoon, and we are on our third run-through of the timeline. The total caper will take about three hours if all goes well. I'm estimating an hour to take down the spellwork on the vault, but that estimate might be shorter once I figure the sigils on it out. Allen estimates an hour for the vault door. That leaves another hour for us to get in, load the van, and get out. I think it sounds unrealistically quick, but no one else seems to share my concern.

"All right, I am going to need to leave," I say.

"I think we should run through this at least once more," The Hierophant says.

“If you want me to get what I need to take those wards and glyphs down, my best window of opportunity to get the materials is in an hour. Your call.”

The Hierophant looks a little peeved at me but huffs, “Fine. Maybe a break could be benefiting us all. We can reconvene first thing in the morning. I should not need to remind you of the tight timeline we work on.”

“Fine,” I say.

Everyone else concedes. Genevieve and I get up and excuse ourselves without fanfare. Thankfully, while Howard rode here with us, Allen agreed to drive him back to his hotel.

Once the valet has returned my rental car to us and we are on the road, Genevieve breaks the silence.

“It’s weird, right?”

“Which part?"

"That he’s got, like, every detail thoroughly analyzed and planned out, except for your part? Then he gets all bent out of shape because you got information on that part.”

I nod, "You aren't the first to make that observation."

“Maybe we should pull out of this,” Genevieve says.

“Yeah, but that's more of his detailed plan. He’s made a scenario where working with him makes more sense. Devora is absolutely unconscionable. Not acting against him feels more like helping him than anything. I can’t just un-know that. If we bail, they will do the heist anyway, but it sounds like it will be more of a smash-and-grab. It will get messy, and anyone who gets in their way is going to get hurt. The Hierophant has said as much. Todd and Pat seemed like decent guys. Who knows what might happen to them?”

"Todd and Pat?"

"Todd and Pat were the two guards at Devora's place."

“Right, but that isn’t your responsibility. Besides, we could inform the police.”

"We could," I say hesitantly, "Though you said it yourself, what are the police going to do if confronted with a fire demon? The Hierophant there clearly has deep pockets. There's also no reason for us to assume that he doesn't have connections. We don't know if he's got magic to bring to the table. Involving the authorities could be so much worse."

"He's definitely a practitioner," Genevieve says, "I looked at his aura. He has spells woven all around himself. A lot of spells."

"There's that. Then, I don't know where Magdalena's loyalty lies. She's terrifying."

Genevieve scrunches up her face, "Really? I mean, I know you said she can, like, loop time or something, and I get it, she's a crack shot."

"Yeah, and she acts like a bratty teenager. But, let's not forget, she summoned a swarm of Rebobs on us. She summoned a fire demon that almost burned the city down. By accident. That is some pretty complicated magic."

"So your concern is as much about keeping Magdalena in check as anything?"

I nod slowly, "Yeah, I guess if I am honest with myself, I feel responsible for her. Hearing even little bits of her life it sounds awful. I do think she's trying to be better than Morgan raised her. I feel like pushing her away will be the bigger evil."

"I think the Hierophant is using that to manipulate you," Genevieve says, "Are you sure Magdalena isn't also?"

I sigh, "No, but I don't think I can live with not trying. Possibly literally, I have no idea what The Hierophant will do if we bail on this caper."

"Well," Genevieve says, "if you're out, I'm out. I'm just the lookout."

"You rhymed."

"I'm a..." Genevieve starts, but I interrupt

"No poet rhymes."

Genevieve blows a raspberry at me, and we both laugh.

"So, where do we have to be in order for you to get the materials you need to spellbreak the Devora house?" Genevieve asks.

"Oh, sorry, I am going to have to drop you off at my place. It's Thursday. Poker night."

Genevieve looks at me, eyebrows raised, a smirk on her lips.

"At Jeff's house," I say pointedly, "It's poker night at Jeff's house."

"Oh," Genevieve says knowingly. I like that she's quick enough that I rarely have to explain my logic to her. By the time I find my way to the end of my thought, she is usually there waiting for me.

CHAPTER 8

Tonight is the first time the guys are getting together to play poker since before the incident at the Lantern. Alistair went out of his way to text me an invite. I originally declined because Genevieve was in town. However, now that I need industrial quantities of Acetobacter Magusficedula by Saturday, I think I am going to make a surprise showing.

I drop Genevieve off at my apartment. She seems sullen and quiet when she gets out and closes the car door without a word. I consider asking her if there is a problem, but the clock is ticking, and she's already halfway up the steps. I'll ask her later.

I drive back across town to Jeff's place off Wine Country Ave. When I get to Jeff's house, I see Alistair and Mike's cars parked on the curb nearby.

I ring the doorbell, and a few moments later, Jeff answers.

"Hey, Miles," he says, there is a lack of enthusiasm in his voice, "Didn't expect you. I thought you had a hot date."

"Genevieve is visiting, but it's the first time you all are

playing in over a month. I figured I'd slip away for a bit to play."

"Oh, okay, come on in," Jeff says. There is an uncomfortable tone to his voice.

He turns and walks down the hall. I follow him, closing the door quietly behind me. We get to his game room, which looks basically the same as last time I was here, except there is one new detail.

There is a stranger sitting in my chair at the poker table. He's wearing slacks and a shirt and tie. He has a matching jacket hanging off the back of his chair. He wears heavy-framed tortoiseshell glasses. Short, well-kept hair and a trim but chaotic salt-and-pepper beard. He's husky, and while he doesn't look like the sort to go to the gym, I'd still describe him as 'beefy.' From the half-empty bottle of wine next to him, I'm also guessing he is used to holding his liquor.

"I'll grab you a chair," Jeff says, wandering off through another doorway.

"Miles!" Alistair exclaims when he sees me, "I thought you couldn't make it."

"I changed my mind."

"Hey, Miles," Mike says, completely non-plussed.

"Mike!" I say.

"This is Chase King, a friend of Jeff's," Alistair makes an introduction. It feels awkward, as everyone is aware that I feel like my place at the table has been filled.

"This is Miles," Alistair says.

"Nice to meet you, Miles," Chase gets up and enthusiastically shakes my hand, "I've heard a lot about you."

"Good to meet you, Chase," I say. I feel even more awkward. I've never heard of him before in my life.

"Chase King, The Snack King of Napa?"

I stare at him blankly.

"Snack King, like Snacking? It's my last name?"

"Yes, it's a good pun," I say, trying to smile, but I feel like I am just making an awkward moment more awkward.

“The Nuthouse? Purveyor of fine snacks? No? Nothing?” He’s grinning like it’s a joke. He doesn’t expect me to know him.

“Sorry,” I mumble.

“No problem!” He says, handing me his card. Apparently, he sells nuts, snacks, and candies.

“Good to meet you...wait, are you the guy Jeff gets all of his snacks from?”

“One and the same!” Chase says. He’s got a big voice and a big personality.

“Oh, well then, I have heard about you. I am a big fan of your nuts.”

"I have very popular nuts," he says, unbelievably straight-faced and without a hint of irony.

"I don't know what to do with that," I say.

He laughs a big, hearty laugh.

“And you are like a magician, right?” Chase asks earnestly.

“Not exactly, but yeah, I guess something like that.”

“Wait,” Mike interrupts, “You aren’t going to lecture him on the whole apotropaist thing? No ‘I’m not a magician. I’m an apotropaist. Don’t know what that is? Here, let me show off my vocabulary?’ And all that?”

I feel my cheeks burning, “No, I guess not.”

"There is an alien here pretending to be Miles!" Mike cups a hand to his mouth and exclaims to the room like he's warning a beach full of swimmers about a shark in the water.

“Give him a break,” Alistair says.

Jeff returns with a chair and puts it down. His energy is lower than I am used to. He is being very taciturn.

“Introductions all done?” Jeff asks.

"Yes, and Miles didn't even lecture Chase about being an apotropaist or about magic or anything!" Mike says incredulously.

"Can we just play some cards? Or are you too worried that I am going to fleece you?" I ask, looking at Mike.

"Oh, since we thought you weren't going to be here, we are doing a little higher buy-in tonight," Alistair says, "Hope it's not a problem."

"No, no problem at all. My financial prospects are looking up."

"Oh? How's that?" Jeff asks.

"I have a big job coming up. Doing some work at Jim Devora's place up in the hills," I say as Alistair deals.

"The movie producer?" Chase asks.

I nod.

Chase grimaces, his jovial manner fading quickly, "That guy is a piece of shit. I've met him a few times at the film festival and other events. Piece of shit."

"I know a guy who works on a crew that landscapes up there. He says Devora is a weird dude. All sorts of creepy stuff going on. Crazy security systems. Guards watching his crew like hawks the whole time, like they are going to try to steal stuff," Mike says.

"Devora doesn't sound like the kind of guy you'd work for," Alistair says.

"Miles worked for Lorelei Redbrook," Jeff muses.

"That's different," I start to say, "Actually, no, it's not different. I wasn't really working for Redbrook, and I'm not working for Devora."

Jeff quirks an eyebrow at me, "What are you up to, Miles?"

"Can we play some cards?" I say, changing the topic. I don't really want to get into all the details of the heist. I realize I've already said too much, and if what we do on Saturday at Devora's gets out, they will know I was involved. I'm hoping that whatever The Hierophant wants from Devora's vault will not be the sort of thing that will get publicized.

"Okay," Alistair says.

And we are playing poker. The stakes are much higher than usual, and after a couple of hands, I am already a hundred dollars in the hole. I miss the days of our nickel ante games.

I'm staring down a hand of three threes, jack high. I'm about to fold when a familiar voice whispers in my ear.

"Nope, stay in."

"Dude!" I say, startled by Hank's sudden appearance.

Everyone looks at me curiously.

"These snacks," I say, covering my exclamation poorly, "Dude, they are delicious!"

Alistair smirks and shakes his head.

"Nobody else has anything," Hank whispers.

I shrug. This is going to hurt if Hank is wrong. I toss another chip on the pile.

Alistair throws his cards down, "Fold."

Mike looks appraisingly at me and also folds.

Jeff and Chase both eye me and then each other. Chase raises another five dollars. Jeff raises another ten. I've already spent way more than I should on this game. I'm going to have to Venmo the winner. I should fold.

"Stay in, trust me."

I sigh a big sigh and call Jeff's bid.

There is a quiet moment, and then Chase folds, grinning like the Cheshire Cat.

I look at Jeff. Jeff looks at me. There is something about his stare that I don't like. He looks mad.

Finally, after a long moment, Jeff throws his cards down. I see he was holding nothing but an ace high.

I lay my cards down and show my three-of-a-kind. I feel

elated. This is my first time winning a hand at our Thursday night poker game. At any poker game, really.

"Woah!" Mike declares like a sports announcer, "And Miles Ward makes a surprising grab for the biggest pot this game has ever seen!"

Alistair and Jeff look at him skeptically.

"By this game, I mean with these four...five people specifically, playing in this room. Today. I know we've played much bigger pots when Miles wasn't here. But this is one for the record books!" Mike clarifies.

We play for another hour. I experiment with listening to Hank as he whispers tips in my head. Every time he gives me advice that I listen to, it pays out. Everyone at the table starts playing more cautiously with me. Alistair, who usually runs the table, seems confused and begins reining his bets in quite a bit.

"I think Miles is stacking the deck," Mike says.

"You always think someone is stacking the deck," Jeff says.

"This time, I agree. Miles, you suddenly got game?" Alistair asks.

"What can I say? It's magic."

Mike scoffs, "He's been doing online poker behind our backs."

Alistair grins and shakes his head.

Jeff, however, is staring at me darkly, curious, like he's wondering if I am using magic to cheat. Which I guess I am.

"I'm kidding!" I say to Jeff, "I think."

"You think?"

"I mean, you know that voice in your head that says do or don't do something? I just finally started listening to it," I say.

"Nice save."

"Mmm..." Jeff grunts.

The game winds down when Chase gets up.

"This has been lovely, gentlemen. Miles, it was good to meet you finally," he says.

"Great to meet you, Chase."

"I am afraid I have an early meeting in the morning. No matter how salty or sweet, deez nuts don't sell themselves."

Mike jumps up right behind him, "I should go too. We've been all hands at work since the fire. Suddenly, everyone is concerned about safety protocols and brush clearing. It'll all be forgotten by the time the next one rolls around."

Mike fist-bumps everyone on his way out.

"Good to have you back, Miles," Mike says as he taps my knuckles with his. I actually think he's sincere.

After Mike has left, I ask, "You guys have been playing without me?"

Jeff shrugs.

Alistair says, "Yeah, we had a couple of slow weeks there. Then the fire happened, and you were out of town, so we just picked it up."

"Chase supplies all the nuts and pretzels for our tasting room," Jeff says. "We were chatting, and the games were a little slow with just three people, so I invited him."

"Oh."

"Miles, it's good to see you," Alistair says, "How have you been? We haven't heard from you much since the fire."

I feel like there is a question and a judgment in his tone.

"Listen, okay, I know every time something bad happens around here, everyone thinks I had something to do with it," I say defensively, "I didn't start the fire. A teenage sorcerer summoned a fire demon, and I helped her banish it. I only helped stop the problem. I didn't have anything to do with starting it."

Both look at me blankly. Alistair's mouth falls slightly open.

"I didn't..." he begins, but I'm on a rambling tear.

"Okay, well, I mean, I guess sort of indirectly I did. She was trying to find Circe and messed up, I guess. While I knew where Circe was, I didn't trap her, and I didn't know that anyone would accidentally - she said it was accidentally, anyway, summon a fire demon in order to find her, or obviously, I would have just said where she is."

"Um," Jeff says.

"Yeah, see Miles, we actually didn't think you had anything to do with that," Alistair begins, "But now, well, obviously... that's less true."

"Okay, but I didn't."

There is an awkward moment where we sit and take turns staring at each other.

"So, you've got a girlfriend?" Alistair breaks the silence.

"Yeah. Um, Genevieve and I have been seeing each other for a few weeks now."

"Do we ever get to meet her?"

"Oh, um. Yeah, of course. You say meet her, and I feel like an ass, but yeah, of course you can. It's not like I am hiding her from my friends or anything. We should do a little dinner party."

Alistair gets a dubious look on his face.

"At your place?" Jeff asks.

"Um," I hadn't really thought that far ahead. I try to envision a party at my place, and it sounds like a catastrophe. "I guess..."

"No, no, no," Jeff says, "We can have a little get-together here. How about Saturday night?"

"Will Emily be joining us?" Alistair asks inquisitively.

"Yeah, how are things with you and Emily? I know it was a little rocky."

"We are in the taking-a-break-but-still-friends state."

"Ah," I say.

I see Alistair nodding sagely and silently. I decide to follow his non-verbal lead.

"Anyway, I'll invite Mike and his family, Alistair, you come, bring Jon and the kids. Miles, bring Genevieve. I'll see if Chase is available. I've got a great recipe for braised short ribs and some wine. We'll make an evening out of roasting Miles for his new lady-friend."

"Well, at least I know the short ribs and beer will be fun," I say sullenly.

"We'll be gentle," Alistair assures me, glowering at Jeff.

"Saturday night it is!" Jeff says.

"Saturday night it is!" I repeat.

"I should get home myself, but I'll see you all Saturday," Alistair says, grabbing his jacket and starting toward the door.

"Hey, Jeff," I say, turning back to him as Alistair leaves, "I was wondering if you could do me a favor?"

Jeff holds up a hand and waits until he can hear the door close as Alistair lets himself out.

"You need more Acetobacter Magusficedula," it's a statement, not a question, "I told Alistair that I wasn't playing around with magic stuff anymore."

He motions me to follow him. He leads me out to the shed behind his house, unlocks it, and lets me in. The laboratory is even more involved and messy than the last time I saw it, which is saying something.

"I got a little carried away for a while there," Jeff says, "Alistair came and talked to me about it and made some good points. So, I'm being more conscientious about how I spend my time. Not mentioning it to Alistair, you know, so he doesn't worry."

"Oh," I say. I don't really like the sound of that.

"So, how much do you need?" Jeff asks. Suddenly, this whole thing feels like a drug deal.

I sigh, "How much can I get by Saturday?"

"Why?" Jeff asks, "What's going on Saturday? I mean, other than my party."

Shit! How did I agree to a party at Jeff's on Saturday when I know we are doing the Devora job on Saturday? I think it through. The schedule has us arriving at noon and being out by three, so we should have plenty of time to make it to Jeff's party.

"Yeah, what could go wrong?"

I glower briefly over my shoulder. Not that I can see Hank there, but I feel like I have to glower somewhere.

"I have that job on Saturday, but it should be wrapped up by three or four. While I can probably manage without the acetobacter, it will be much easier the more of it I have."

"Why? What are you doing?" Jeff asks.

Jeff is my closest friend. If I can't trust Jeff, I might as well give up on trusting anyone or anything.

"Between you and me?"

Jeff nods.

So, I explain the whole heist to him. I use all of the code names that The Hierophant assigned to us instead of actual names. Maybe I gloss over a few details here or there, but I tell him the whole thing.

Jeff whistles.

"That sounds dangerous. Are you sure you want to do this?"

"No," I say, "But I'm not sure at this point that I have a great deal of choice. Overall, it seems like the greatest good will be done by making this quick and painless. Plus, it pays a lot."

Jeff shrugs, "I don't pretend to understand all the nuances

of your world, Miles. Yeah, I've got a pretty big batch cooked up. I've also got something else that might be helpful to you."

Jeff gets a plastic bottle off of a table and holds it up. It contains a mostly clear liquid with a brownish tinge to it.

"This is a suspension of a series of polyphenols in distilled water," Jeff explains.

"I don't know what that means."

"It's chemicals I derived from wine, but these polyphenols coincidentally can also occur in small doses in blood. In higher concentrations in the liver. I hypothesize that when something dies. These are released into the blood in larger concentrations."

"I don't understand."

"It acts like blood for catalyzing magic," Jeff says, "At least when it comes to making the inclusive circles you showed me, I can use it instead of blood, and it works fine. I know you said that for bigger spells, the blood's volume and quality affect the result, so I don't know how it plays out there."

I stare at the bottle.

"Wait," I say, bewildered, "So you made a compound that eats magic from wine and another compound that catalyzes magic from wine?"

Jeff nods, "I'm working on some other stuff. World-changing stuff."

This doesn't make sense. How can Jeff have discovered in a month these properties that no one else ever seems to have discovered? Then, I reflect on the enigmatic tale that Goldsmith told me. Maybe this is what the Blethspa Amah is really all about. I've been mulling over what the dragon told me, and there are a few different ways to interpret it. Maybe these haven't been discovered before because they weren't true before.

"What's this new thing?"

Jeff makes a zipping motion across his mouth, "I'm happy to share the acetobacter and this polyphenol compound with you. Those aren't the money-makers. This next thing, it's so big. It's huge, Miles. As I said, world-changing stuff, I am not telling anyone anything until I've got all my I's dotted and T's crossed."

"Okay," I say. He's suddenly so fired up, not the dour and quiet guy he was through our poker game.

"Here," he says, handing me the plastic bottle of magic catalyst, "Come on, I have a ton of Acetobacter Magusficedula in my cellar."

California homes rarely have true cellars. So when someone around here says cellar, they usually mean a cool or cooled room or closet where they store their wine.

I follow Jeff back into his house, to his kitchen, and through a door in the back of his kitchen. I forget how fancy Jeff's house is sometimes. He has a chef's kitchen with a stove free-standing in the middle of the room. Above the stove is a huge vent hood that could suck a small dog up off the floor—a full house of the most modern appliances and enough counter space to shame an old-fashioned diner. In the back, there is a door painted a dark blue-black color.

I've never been through the door in the back of the kitchen. I guess I always assumed it was a pantry. However, it is not.

Behind the door is a room that once might have been another bedroom. However, now it is essentially a walk-in refrigerator. It is easily the size of any room in my apartment. It isn't as cold as a true walk-in, but it's cool. Racks upon racks of wine bottles line the walls. I don't know enough about wine labels to identify most of them, but I suspect that some of these are pretty covetable vintages.

Glancing around the room, I notice that he has drawn some sigils about the room, making the whole thing an exclusive magical boundary. I presume to prevent magic from building up in the room and causing his wine to spoil.

In the middle of the room is a large plastic carboy. Jeff motions to it.

"Five gallons of Acetobacter Magusficedula, all yours if you like it," Jeff says, "I cooked it up for you back before the fire. It should still be good."

"I see you put up an exclusive boundary to keep magic from building up in here."

"Yeah, I figured it would slow the growth of the aceto-bacter and also keep all my wine safe from spells."

"It's good thinking," I compliment him, "And yeah, I'll take the whole carboy. Do you mind if I pick it up on Saturday morning? I think it will be more stable here."

"Sure, I guess," Jeff says.

"Hey, Jeff?" I ask.

"Yeah?"

"When I got here, I thought you were pissed at me. You seemed, I don't know, grumpy. But you've seemed like you were in a better mood since Alistair left. Is there a problem?"

"Mmm," Jeff grunts and takes a second to think before fully responding, "Alistair thinks I'm getting obsessed with all this."

Jeff motions at the sigils and the acetobacter.

"And like I said, he was right. It was becoming a little bit of a problem. I've got some amazing things in the works. Talking to him, though, I realized this is a marathon, not a sprint. I need to take time for myself, too."

"And that wasn't good enough for Alistair?"

"He thinks I should get a shrink and drop the whole thing altogether. He doesn't think it's healthy. We had a couple of bouts of it, and I'm tired of him trying to run my life. So yeah, it's been a little tense between us."

"I don't think he's trying to run your life. I think he's just trying to help."

"I'm sure that's how he sees it, but he also needs to learn when his help isn't wanted. Or needed."

I nod, "Well, I'm sorry you and he aren't seeing eye to eye, but I'm glad we don't have a problem."

"Me too."

"Do you mind if I ask what's up with you and Emily?"

"It's more of the same. She felt like I was getting obsessed with studying vinomancy, and I felt like she was getting obsessed with Redbrook."

"Vinomancy?" I say, laughing.

"Yeah, that's what she called it, all the playing with wine and magic."

"That's kind of funny."

There is a long, tense pause in the conversation. Jeff seems a little on edge, ready to be insulted or assaulted by any comment.

"Yeah, I guess it is. Just not how she said it. Anyway, we got snippy. We both said some stuff we probably shouldn't have. It's over. It's probably for the best."

"Oh," I say. I have a concern here, but I am unsure how to broach it. Jeff either predicts my concern or can read it on my face because he addresses it without me saying anything.

"Don't worry, it's fine if you still hang out with her. If that's what you are wondering, it's not like a her-or-me sort of thing. We just realized we weren't working. No harm, no foul."

I raise an inquisitive eyebrow.

"Okay, fine, no harm that won't heal in a few weeks and no foul that I can't forgive."

"And Emily is on the same page?"

He shrugs, "I hope so. You shouldn't have to choose between your best friend and your friend that you almost dated. When I say it like that, it sounds like I'm making it a choice. Sorry, that wasn't my intention. I mean, it isn't about you, regardless of what history there might be."

I nod.

"Thanks for this," I say, patting the carboy of Acetobacter Magusficedula, "This is going to make my life much easier and give me some emergency options."

"You're welcome," he says, giving me a goofy half-smile. It looks plastic and foreign on his face.

"I should probably get back to Genevieve. She wasn't excited about being left in my cramped apartment alone for too long."

"Well, if you found someone that will go into that place at all, don't keep her waiting. I look forward to meeting her in a couple of days!"

I give him a double thumbs up, "I'm looking forward to it too!"

He walks me to the front door, and I keep up a jubilant attitude the whole way. Once I am alone in my car, I let out a big sigh and let the anxiety and stress about the next few days overtake me.

"What the fuck did I get myself into?" I ask my steering wheel.

"Just another day in the life of Miles Ward."

"Oh," I say as I start the car, "Just the guy I wanted to talk to."

"You've reached Hank. I'm unavailable right now, but if you leave me your name, number, and a brief message, I'll get back to you at the earliest possible opportunity."

"Cut the shit, dummy."

"Don't call me dummy. I'm not the one that booked a party a couple of hours after I'm planning to rob a Lich's vault."

"How did you know what hands everybody had?"

"I looked," Hank's voice sounds sarcastic in my head, *"Duh."*

"You can do that?"

"Maybe. Or maybe I'm just a projection of your unconscious, and you're reading micro-expressions and other social cues to tell that people are bluffing. The only way that gets from your unconscious into your conscious thinking is through an intricate and borderline psychotic conversation with the disembodied voice of a mannequin you keep in your closet."

"I don't keep you in my closet."

"What else do you call that tiny room you sleep in?"

"Jerk. Well, can my unconscious projection do an intricate and borderline psychotic process where it tells me what to expect inside Devora's vault?"

"Indeed I can, my friend, just drive us on up, walk into the house, and...oh, we did that. No, I can't go into the house. It's protected from the likes of me, like an iron fortress."

"That's disappointing."

"That's what she said. And by 'she,' I mean Genevieve. And what she was referring to..."

"Nope," I say, turning the radio up loud enough that I can't hear my simulacrum insult me inside my head. The windows in my rented car rattle with each bit of percussive bass. It's pretty loud.

CHAPTER 9

I AM STANDING in the toy aisle of a large box store when my phone begins to vibrate. The caller ID is blocked, but I answer it anyway.

"Miles Ward, if there's a curse, call me first," I say cheerily into the phone.

Have I used that line before? I think I might have. Am I actually running out of material? The thought puts me into a brief panic.

"Hey, Miles," a familiar voice drawls, "Allen here. You know, The Wheel 'a Fortune."

"Hello, Mr. Fortune."

"It's Gilman, actually."

"What can I do for you, Allen?"

"Well, Miles. I was hoping we could have a little meet-up. A little tet-a-tet, something like that. How'd that be, us havin' a pow-wow?"

"Nope. I'll meet with you, but let's keep it culturally respectful."

"Well, aren't you, Mr. Politically Correct?"

"Allen, do you want to talk, or do you just want to be a jerk?"

“Yeah, yeah. Fine," he mutters, "Where’s good for you?”

“I’m at the South Napa Marketplace now...” I say.

“Heck yeah! Want to meet me over off Gasser, and we can walk up the river trail?”

I haven’t been to that part of the trail since the ill-fated night that Allen and his friends shot up the Lantern and Eric Walsh chased me.

“Sure. I’ll be down there in, say, fifteen minutes?”

“Heck yeah,” Allen says, and before I can respond in any way, he has hung up.

I sigh. I’m not sure where this is going, but I imagine I will be better off knowing anything he has to say now rather than waiting to find out on Saturday.

I manage to find the seasonal toy aisle and load up on modern, high-capacity squirt guns—a brief stop in the arts and crafts section for some little wooden craft disks and craft paint. Then I'm all set for shopping. I've spent far longer here than I ever want to, anyway.

Somehow, the checkout lines are all packed, and the self-checkout lines are closed. So I am about ten minutes late when I stroll down the paved path to the edge of the river trail where Allen is waiting for me.

“Well, if it isn’t my favorite Magician,” Allen says in a jovial tone.

“Wheel of Fortune doesn’t roll off the tongue quite as easily,” I say.

“Oh, a pun, I like it, I like it,” Allen says as he starts to walk. He motions me to join him with one arm.

“What’s up, Allen?”

“I like you, Miles. I think you are smart and funny. Quick, too.”

“Thanks,” I say, “But so you know, I’m in a committed relationship.”

“See, that’s what I mean, always quick with the quips,” Allen says, pulling his trucker cap up and scratching his hair. It is dirty blond with streaks of grey through it. "And so far as I can tell, you are scared of fuck all."

"Actually, I'm scared of literally everything."

Allen scratches his head again pensively, "I don't see how there's a difference."

"If you aren't scared of anything, you are deciding what to run toward. When you are scared of everything, you are deciding what to run away from."

He laughs a hearty belly laugh at that. I am not sure it was worth a chuckle, but he's amused.

“You probably don’t see it this way, I know, but we are on the same side, you and I,” Allen concludes.

“I’m not sure I believe in sides.”

“Oh, there's sides, al'right. There is a line, and everybody stands on one side or the other. Some people stand with a leg on each side, and so it’s hard to see the line without looking down. Even then, though, they are more on one side than the other.”

“I don’t follow your metaphor.”

“I mean, most people aren’t lookin' fer if they are doing good or doing bad. They are just trying to get through the day. Sometimes, that means doing good. Sometimes, it means doing some bad, but usually, it’s just doing, and it isn’t neither. But you and me, we are both over here on this side. I can see it. We both got a hankering to do good.”

“You know I was in the Lantern when you and your friends shot it up.”

Allen raises his eyebrows, crinkling the skin of his forehead up into rows of little furrows.

“That a fact?”

“Yeah. Kind of a miracle I survived.”

“Well, I am sorry about that. Honestly, I am. It probably doesn't help, but I wasn't there that night if that'll change your opinion of me. I was even against going in like that. We gotta be more subtle, I said. The scalpel, not the sword. But it wasn't me calling the shots.”

It does change my opinion of Allen a little.

“Your friends came in hot and hit heavy without sufficient information. The Lamia was dead by the time they got there. Or as dead as she was going to get.”

“I agree with you. Like I said, there is a time for the scalpel and a time for the sword. That's actually what I wanted to talk to you about.”

I cross my arms on my chest and raise my eyebrows. I am curious to see where Allen is going with this.

“See, there is a time for doing your research, looking at schematics, making a plan. All that stuff, that's what I call the scalpel. You know, a tiny little cut here, a tiny cut there. Precision.”

"Yes, I understood the metaphor. Then there is a time for the sword, when your plans are what they are, and you have to start hacking away. My father used to have a quote about that, 'On dying ground, fight,' he'd say."

"Sun Tsu's nine grounds, yeah, I'm familiar. Same idea, only I sorta condensed eight of Sun Tsu's grounds down to just one. There's a time for planning and subtlety and all that, but you gotta be ready for when the shit hits the fan, you know?" Allen says. His bearing, demeanor, and manner of speaking lead me to believe that Allen is an uneducated and unthoughtful man, but every time I talk to him, I am surprised at how well-versed and astute he can be.

"So, what, specifically, did you want to talk about, Allen?"

"Well, I didn't take this job because I want the money. I am not saying I can't use it. It's just not my reason. See Devora, he's a monster. A monster's monster. The worst, as bad as Redbrook, prolly worse."

I sigh and take a deep breath, "And you and the Knights of Saint George want to take him out."

"That's right. Strike while the iron is hot, and I think it's glowin' red now."

"But killing his body isn't going to work," I remind, "If the Hierophant is correct anyway."

"Soul Jar, like you said. Gotta destroy that."

"That isn't going to be an easy task. For one, he's not going to leave that laying out. It's going to be secured. It's going to have protections. Probably both magical and mundane."

"Secured, like in a vault. You got the magical. I got the mundane."

"You want us to work together to take down Devora."

"You got a track record there, brother."

"This isn't in the Hierophant's plans."

"Fuck the Hierophant's plans, man!" Allen exclaims.

"I suppose if I say no, you are going to do it anyway, but it's probably going to get messy without my help?"

"A familiar tale, ain't it?"

I shake my head.

"What are you proposing?" I ask.

We've come to a small bridge over a little creek that feeds down into the river. Allen stops. He leans on the rail and motions to a heron standing in the reeds.

"She's got chicks nearby. She's waiting to see if we're a threat."

We watch the heron for a minute in silence. It's calm, and probably the only peaceful moment I remember having all week. Finally, the heron seems satisfied with our peaceful intentions and goes back to fishing in the marsh with its beak.

"I am betting on the Soul Jar being in the vault. What I am getting at is that we work together to get it out of there. We grab it with the other loot and then figure out how to destroy it. Like you said, it's going to be the most protected thing he's got. I figure it's better to get it out and take our time destroying it. You know, the right way, rather than try to get rash and smash it. This is the scalpel method, right? It's precise and clean. If he ain't a lich? Well then, no big deal, right? Cause he won't have a jar to smash."

"So you want me to help find and grab the Soul Jar while we are in there? That's the ask."

"Yup."

"What's in it for me?"

"Mercenary all of a sudden. I guess I didn't know there had to be anything. We're still doing this heist. We're still getting paid. I am just suggesting that we add this little stretch goal while we are at it. "

I grimace and nod.

"Fine, if we see it, we will try to nab it. But like you said, it's a stretch goal, okay?"

"Scout's honor," Allen says solemnly.

"Were you a scout?" I ask. In my experience, most people in the modern world who say 'Scout's honor' never were scouts —making the expression a little disingenuous.

"Golden Eagle," he says, holding his hand up in a little salute.

I look back over at the heron, which takes to the sky. There is something squirming in its beak. It flies a few hundred feet before touching down in a particularly dense patch of reeds. I can suddenly hear a chorus of high-pitched chirping drifting in on the wind. I guess Allen was right about the heron having chicks nearby.

"Oh, I should probably mention: in case shit goes sideways on Saturday, I got the cavalry on standby. Go in prepared to use the scalpel, but bring the sword, just in case."

"The Knights of Saint George?" I ask.

"Yeah, if it gets all pear-shaped, it can't hurt to have a little backup."

"I'm not sure I agree with your logic."

He shrugs.

"Just out of curiosity, why are you telling me all of this? Why not try to loop in one of the others? It seemed like you and The World were chummy the other day," I say.

"Like I said, Miles, I like you. We're alike, you and I, even if you don't want to admit it. Besides, you're the only one in that bunch I trust."

"Oh?" I ask. I am curious what his assessment of the others is.

"The Hierophant, he ain't telling us everything. He's got inconsistencies that don't match up. He's real detailed in some places and not in others. I don't love his story. Suspicious."

"I agree, though that begs the question, why are you working with him?"

"Well, in part, to get my hands on that Soul Jar. But also, I reckon similar to you, because I think it'll go smoother if I am in. The money doesn't hurt, neither."

"What about The Hermit?" I ask.

"He's a weird one, and I don't get the impression he's too reliable. I feel like maybe he's got something else on his mind."

"Yeah, he's got a personal beef with Devora. I picked that up."

"The driver, The World? She's too happy. It's fake. She's frontin' something. I don't know your lady none, but I know having her there is pissing off The Hierophant. That leaves The Fool."

I nod but don't say anything. I am curious about his assessment of Magdalena, and I don't want to influence what he's going to say.

"I see that you two know each other, but she's a wild card. She's young, too young to be coming on an op like this, and she doesn't give me a real stable vibe, you know?"

Again, I simply nod.

"I met the type, you understand?" He says emphatically, "The kind that when shit gets crazy, they get crazier. The kind that you find dancin' naked in the enemy's guts, laughin' and frolicking like a kid in a candy store. I seen eyes like hers before."

He gets a distant, glassy look in his eye.

"It sounds like you are talking from personal experience," I say, horrified.

"Yeah, I served a couple tours in 'ghanistan when I was younger—met all the types there. She reminds me of one of em, crazier than a shit house rat." he says with a dark look in his eye.

"And that's your take on The Fool?" I ask. I agree that Magdalena has her moments. She's certainly packing enough trauma for the job, but I don't see her as that far gone.

"I'm not saying they don't have their time and place. In a mad world, it's the psychos that reign supreme. 'Nuff said," he concludes and then looks back at me.

"Anyway, I got a good read on you, Miles. You're a good guy. If I need someone to run into a burning building strapped with dynamite, I'll look to your Fool. You're the guy I want to watch my back."

"Well, thanks," I say. "You mentioned the military. Is that where you learned safe cracking?"

"Short answer is kinda. Long answer is I don't much want to talk about it if it's all the same to you."

"Sorry, not trying to be nosy."

"It's a'right. Well, you should better be getting back to readin'. I should do the same," Allen says.

I nod.

He motions down the trail away from where I parked my car, "I'm this way."

"See you tomorrow morning," I say as he walks away.

"See you."

I watch him walk down the trail. It's a good half mile to the nearest trailhead in that direction. That means he parked at least a good mile away from where we agreed to meet. Maybe he lives or works close to the trail. I keep watching him.

A hundred yards down the trail, he turns off the trail to the fence line. He pulls up a corner of the chainlink fence separating the trail from the neighboring railroad tracks. He crosses them, then vaults another chainlink fence on the other side and vanishes into the parking lot of an apartment building. Does he live there, or did he park in that lot and take a circuitous route to meet me? Something to ponder.

CHAPTER 10

In less than four hours, our little Tarot team will meet for the last time before we make our move on Devora's vault. I am still unsure how to deal with the wards on the vault. Sitting at my desk, phone at hand, I carefully copy the runes from the amulet I photographed onto the little wooden discs I bought.

Just copying the symbols, of course, isn't enough. I need to make something that is close enough to the real amulet to fool the spell. The symbols are a start. The wooden tokens are a start, but I will need something to bind them to the wards on the house. As with all magic, it will need blood. For this, however, each person is going to need to provide their own drop of blood freely for it to work correctly. To create a linkage from the person to the disc and the disc to the wards. The original pendants didn't need the personalization as they were part of the wards' creation. I would describe this as indirect, sympathetic magic. It isn't what I would call an entirely reliable approach, but it's the best I have on short notice.

I remove the tiny vial of shavings from the amulet I wore at Devoras and carefully glue bits of the original amulet onto the edges of these fakes I've manufactured. This should help confuse the spell about the origin of these amulets, each having a small piece of the real one incorporated into it.

I inspect each of the four false amulets I've created and compare them in detail with the pictures I took. They aren't perfect, but they should do. This isn't about duplication; it's about ambiguation. I set them aside to let them dry.

I am just pulling my laptop out when Genevieve walks in from the other room carrying her computer.

"So I've been looking through the Hierophant's files on Devora. The whole Devora-is-the-mad-hermit-writing-the-devils-bible thing is pretty speculative and wishy-washy, so I started doing my own digging. Check this out," Genevieve says, turning her computer around so that I can see it.

There is an illuminated manuscript page. It features a bearded, long-haired, and bedraggled figure holding a book. He is inside a box. Around the box is stylized scrollwork. Clearly woven into the scrollwork is an intricate series of sigils that have been highlighted so they can be identified. "Look familiar?"

"Yeah, these are the same sigils as the wards on the vault," I say. They aren't exactly the same, but the same series of sigils occur in both, and the pattern is what I would magically categorize as 'close enough.' "Where did you get this?"

"Libri Tauri Stercore."

"Book of Bull. I don't know the last word," I say.

"Shit," Genevieve clarifies.

"The Book of Bullshit? That hardly sounds like a credible source."

"It's a graduate dissertation from a decade ago. It's pretty erratic and has some questionable research, but they copied the illustration directly from The Codex Gigas itself. This page is originally from the Codex. The Libri Tauri Stercore highlights the sigils clearly, making it more useful to our purposes than the Codex. Here's a photo of the original."

She pulls up another image of the same page. I have to squint and puzzle a bit to see the sigils. They are there, but she's right; the highlighted image makes it much more obvious.

"Okay, so the wards on the vault are from the Codex Gigas," I say.

"And the person in the center of the illustration is Herman the Recluse."

"So you think that The Hierophant is right, that Devora is Herman the Recluse and an undead sorcerer?"

"I don't know about any of that. But it certainly means something, and Devora has done more than his share of evil shit," Genevieve says, shaking her head and leaning against the wall, "But again, there is a fair amount of that in the public record. The Hierophant has provided even more evidence of even worse stuff."

"Oh?"

"Yeah, you don't want to know. I don't want to know. It's bad."

"Bad?"

"Imagine the worst thing you can imagine. Now imagine buying a small private island off the coast of a nation with no extradition and very few laws so you can do that thing without interference."

I try not to imagine anything that Genevieve has suggested. I nod. Jim Devora is a pretty well-documented scumbag. I don't need more evidence of that.

I flip my phone to the pictures I took of the vault and do another comparison of them with the illuminated page from the Codex Gigas. The spell is complicated, the sigils diverse, and even though I don't recognize all of them, just looking at the flow sends shivers down my spine. This is evil magic, powerful magic. Something this big would take a lot of blood to activate, almost certainly numerous living sacrifices. If Devora isn't a dark sorcerer himself, he's at least got a very powerful one on the payroll. Whether he is the crafter of this magic or just a consumer doesn't really matter for our purposes.

"I don't need more convincing," I say, "But I do need more information. I think I am going to head down to Grape Reads to see if I can't use their books. Do you want to join me?"

"Eh," she says, "Not really. I mean, if you don't mind."

I shrug nonchalantly, "Okay, no pressure."

It's a lie. I am chalant as hell. Genevieve makes a slightly sour face at me and returns my shrug.

"Would you drop me off downtown? I thought it might be nice to go do a little window shopping before our big meeting this afternoon."

"Sure," I say flatly. I'm not sure why I am so annoyed.

It's a short drive downtown. Genevieve blows me a kiss as she jumps out of the car at a light on First Street.

"I'll meet you at Grape Reads," she says, flitting into a boutique.

"Okay," I say to the empty space where she was. I probably should have said something. The truth is, I do mind that she wanted to go shopping and left me to research alone.

I GET to Grape Reads a few minutes later. The new guy, Brady, is behind the counter. He's thirty-something and wears a porkpie hat, waxed mustache, and suspenders. It is a pretty noteworthy look, not one I could pull off myself.

"Hi, Brady."

"Hi," he says. I'm pretty sure he doesn't remember my name.

"Hi, Miles!" Emily says, flitting out from behind a bookshelf.

Emily is trying to look upbeat, but I can tell it is a facade. She hasn't been the same since the election. Lorelei Redbrook's gambit for mayor failed, ending in her assassination. Her death is not public knowledge. It's hard to prove someone has died when their body turns into black ooze upon their demise. On paper, this was a victory for our cause, but it doesn't feel like much of a win.

"Hi, Emily. How are things?"

"Well. Quiet, which is good."

I nod. We stand in awkward silence for a moment.

"Well, come on then," she says, walking toward the back room. "I know why you're here!"

I follow her. Using Sergei's special collection has felt even more awkward since I realized that Sergei is a non-profit organization, not a mystery man working behind the scenes. I am not sure why it is uncomfortable. I guess because every time I do, I am reminded of the mortification I got when I first discovered my misunderstanding.

We walk into the cramped little room that smells like old books.

"I'd love to help you out," Emily says, "But the annual Sergei board meeting is coming up next week, and I have a bunch of stuff to prepare to present."

"Oh," I say. I guess I didn't think of boardroom presentations as part of Emily's work here at Grape Reads.

"It's pretty stressful. Numbers keep dropping year after year. We might have to start shutting down stores and programs. We are all scrambling."

I nod. "I'm sorry," I say. There is an expression that a fool and their money are soon parted, and I am that fool. There is definitely nothing I can contribute to this conversation.

"Well, knock yourself out," she says politely but curtly as she turns to leave the back room.

"How are you doing, Emily?" I ask before she leaves.

"Hmm?"

"It's just, we haven't seen each other much since, you know, the election," I stammer awkwardly, "And I feel bad. I should probably have checked in with you. I don't feel like I've been a very good friend. Time gets away from me. You know?"

"You're spending time with Genevieve, I get it. It's all good. I am fine. There were some dark moments there, but it's over, and I am moving on."

I nod.

"I'm moving on from a lot of things..." She murmurs.

"Well, if you need anything..." I say.

"Yeah, yeah. Of course," she says, "And how are you doing? Gosh, it's not like I asked. And the election, her speech had to be hard on you. I mean, you saw her. You saw when Redbrook...you know."

Was murdered. Died. Exploded in a rain of putrescence. These are the things she isn't saying. She and Ren were knocked unconscious for that, but I saw it. What bothers me about it the most is that it doesn't bother me at all. It's like a dream I had that I can tell you the details of without actually remembering the dream. Like a story I told over and over again, but I don't remember myself. I guess repressing trauma is one of my secret skills.

"It's not that secret."

"Dammit, will you stop that?" I hiss.

Emily raises an eyebrow at me.

"Sorry, there was a fly or something," I lie.

"Well, thanks for asking. I mean it. I appreciate that you

took the time to check-in. You usually get so focused when you come by that it can seem like you only care about the books," she says.

I hang my head a little as I nod in shame.

"I didn't mean that to be mean. Believe me, I understand getting caught up in your work. I've just felt a little, I don't know, alone since all that. Ren took off on a road trip across the southwest; they needed to 'get away and reset,' and...Jeff...well, that didn't work out. My other friends, well, they wouldn't understand."

I nod again, "Yeah. Feel free to call. Always happy to be there. You, Genevieve, and I should get tacos and go bowling again."

"The taco place at the bowling alley closed. It's just not the same."

"What?!?" I ask incredulously.

"Yeah, their last day was like three days ago."

"Now I think I need a road trip across the southwest to reset!" I say melodramatically.

She laughs.

"Thanks," she says, "I should probably get back to that report."

"Yeah, I should probably figure out these wards," I say, motioning at the bookshelves.

"Good luck," she says.

"Good luck."

The door closes behind her, and I am alone in the small, book-encrusted room. I pull out my phone and laptop and get to work. I only have a little bit of time before I need to find Genevieve and make our way to our last meeting with The Hierophant. This is about finding references so I can actually figure out the wards tonight.

Most of my time is spent standing at a bookshelf, taking a

title down, shuffling through it, and looking for anything familiar. One in every ten or so books, I find something and then take quick pictures of pages that seem relevant. I hammer out some notes on my computer. An hour and a half passes in a frantic blur of rifling through books and recording data for later.

Ultimately, I am left with no concrete conclusions but a general impression. This spell is intentionally convoluted. It is constructed to make its ultimate function difficult to understand through a mire of secondary functions and failsafes. Each rune and sigil is carefully selected and arranged so that its removal will change the context of the spell in a functional way. That is, effacing any given sigil makes it a new and different spell. It's diabolically clever.

I am interrupted by a knock at the door, followed by it opening to reveal Genevieve standing there.

"Hey," she says, "Sorry to interrupt, but we should probably get going."

"Right," I say, putting the book I am looking at back on the shelf.

"How's it going? Got a plan for," she pauses and looks around surreptitiously, "you know, the thing?"

At first, I am confused as to why she's being covert. Then I realize that talking in a public bookstore about your plan to rob someone's personal vault is probably not the best idea.

"It looks complicated. I really wish I had more than a day to figure it out."

"Well, let's go get this last meet-up over with, and hopefully, you can get the time."

I finish putting books away and then grab my stuff.

"Thanks, Emily. See you later, Brady!" I say on my way out the door.

"Please come again!" Brady says with a rote little wave. Emily is nowhere to be seen or heard.

CHAPTER 11

Genevieve drives back Up Valley to Enchanté. I am not certain why, but she's quiet and clearly in a bad mood. In the passenger seat, I am chugging coffee, looking at my phone, and typing on my laptop simultaneously. I would really like to have a clear plan of action by the time we meet with Team Tarot, a name I just came up with.

I'd really like to keep the squirt gun filled with bacteria-infected water as a backup plan.

"You seem very quiet," I say after a gulp of coffee, "Everything okay?"

"Yes," she says curtly, "No. I don't know. This whole thing doesn't seem as good an idea as it did a couple of days ago."

"It didn't seem like a good idea a couple of days ago. What's changed?"

"I don't know; it just seems...it's just a feeling," she says, biting her lower lip. "You know?"

"I think I do. I call that feeling 'being awake.'"

"C'mon, Miles, this isn't a joke," she says scolding.

"I know, I know. I don't think it's a joke. I'm just saying I have that feeling a lot."

"Okay. There was this one time I was going to go skydiving. I'd never done it before, and I was excited. I got there, and the plane was just, like, a mess. It looked like it was held together with duct tape, and who knows, maybe it was. Anyway, the instructor had this smarmy attitude. Everything about the experience said that I shouldn't do it."

"Did you?"

"Yeah," she says, nodding slowly.

"And?"

"And, it was a little dicey, but it was fine. I jumped, we landed, you know, no problems."

"I'm confused."

"Well," she says, "The next week, I saw this post about a skydiver who died because of an equipment malfunction. It was the same company, same plane, same instructor. My gut wasn't wrong. I just got lucky."

"Okay," I say, "I can see how that could be upsetting, thinking 'that could have been me.'"

"So now I try to listen when some part of my brain says, this is a bad idea."

This is so far from my experiences with Genevieve that I am having difficulty accepting it.

"Really?" I ask, my voice sounding more incredulous and judgemental than I intended.

"Yes, really, Miles. I actually weigh risks before taking them, believe it or not. You approach everything like it's risky, so you don't have to burden yourself with making a judgment call. If everything is a bad idea, there is no reason not to do anything, right? You are always sniping at me for being a danger junky, but you are no better. You mitigate it by dressing it up with this whole burdened martyr act, but you're no different."

"Ouch," I say, sometimes the most cruel things are also the most honest.

"Sorry," she says. Her tone doesn't agree with her statement.

I grunt sullenly, and we sit in uncomfortable silence for a mile or so.

"I guess we should probably see this through," she finally says.

I nod and go back to trying to decipher the spell on the vault door.

"Can I confess something?" Genevieve pipes back up.

"Yeah, if that's what you need," I say.

"I think I'm also a little put out because I got stuck as the lookout," she says sheepishly.

"I know," I say as she pulls into the driveway to Enchanté.

I load my things back into my bag, and we leave my crappy rental car with the valet. A moment later, we are back in the Burlesque Room at a table surrounded by our coconspirators.

My nemesis is directly across the room from me, backdropped by a burgundy velvet curtain. Its baleful red eye stares at me, challenging me, daring me to say anything. The LavaJava 24K SXR, with its gold trim, looks like it is grinning at me, taunting me.

"You don't win today, coffeemaker," I mutter to myself.

"That's the spirit!"

"Hmm?" Genevieve murmurs quietly.

"I'm going in," I say, standing and rolling my sleeves up.

Genevieve gasps and hisses at me melodramatically, "No! Miles! It's not worth it. Last time, you complained about the coffee all day after we left."

"This is personal. You wouldn't understand," I say, stalking across the room to where the LavaJava sits on a little wooden table, surrounded by carafes of cream and little bowls of sugar and non-calorie sweeteners. I stare down at the machine, its lights like malevolent eyes, menacing me from the darkness. "This is something I have to do."

I stab at the buttons like a fencer with a sword. No, a sword sounds like I'm hacking it to bits. A rapier? No, I think that's just another sword. What do fencers use? A foil? Like a fencer with a foil, I jab its buttons repeatedly. I make the grind less fine and reduce the exposure time slightly.

"My name is Miles Ward. You killed my father. Prepare to die!" I declare as I go in for my final strike to the 'Errupt!' button. I step back and triumphantly watch my victory over the villainous machine.

It chugs and whirrs and dings. The little eruption animation begins on its display as the coffee pours out into my mug. When it is complete, I lift the mug and turn toward the tables, taking a huge, satisfied whiff of the steaming java.

Everyone is watching me intently. Again. Apparently, I was more dramatic about the whole thing than I thought. I take a big sip of the brown water. Sadly, hot brown water is the best description of this beverage I can give. If the last cup I got from the LavaJava was thick, dark, and bitter, this is thin, light, and tasteless.

"Touché LavaJava, touché," I whisper into my mug as I turn around and top it off with too much cream and too much sugar.

"Mmm! Delicious!" I follow up loudly. With insincere aplomb, I raise my mug in salute to everyone. Non-plussed, they all turn back to private conversations. I sit back down next to Genevieve and sip my brown water sullenly.

"Not good?" She whispers.

"Defeated once again."

"To be fair, that machine costs more than you make in a year."

I sneer over my shoulder where I imagine Hank to be.

"I'm trying to say that society values that machine more than it values you. It's too good for you."

"Shut up," I whisper.

Genevieve quirks an eyebrow. If she intends to say something, it is cut off by the Hierophant starting the meeting.

"It is my intention that we walk through the complete plan one last time, do equipment checks, and conclude by five so that we can all get a full night's rest before we reconvene tomorrow," The Hierophant says briskly.

There are nods and a general murmur of consent.

"Very well, we will meet at the rendevous point tomorrow. I will give you a time-encrypted file with the location. It will become unlocked tomorrow at noon exactly, giving you half an hour before our rendevous. If you are prepared, this should be ample time."

"I'm sorry, why all the cloak and dagger stuff?" Allen asks the exact question that I am thinking.

"We are coming into the most vulnerable portion of the operation. It is imperative that we confound any possible interference from here on out."

"Okay," Allen drawls dubiously.

"We will meet at the rendevous location tomorrow at half past noon. From there, we will don the World Wide Shipping uniforms provided by The World. I will be providing radios that are all tuned to the same encrypted channel at that time. The Tower, do you have a vehicle to take to your location?

Genevieve looks at me questioningly, and I nod.

"Yeah, I've got Mi...Magician's car."

"Good. I will provide you with all of the equipment you need for your part of the job. You will make your way there and signal us when you are in position."

"Okay," Genevieve says.

"The Wheel will sit in the delivery vehicle's cab. The magician, Hermit, and I will be in the back of the truck with the materials."

"Are there windows?" Howard asks.

"No," The Hierophant says.

"I get easily carsick," Howard says, "Can I ride in the front?"

"I apologize to The Hermit," The Hierophant says, "But you will need to ride in the rear. I will make sure that you have sanitary bags with you. It is a short drive."

"Why does The Wheel get to sit in the front? Why do I have to sit in the back? I don't like enclosed spaces. I don't want to sit in the back," Howard says. He seems on the verge of panic.

"The Wheel is far more convincing in a blue-collar layman's role than The Magician, you or I," The Hierophant says in his most condescending tone.

I glance over at Allen, who rolls his eyes and sneers a little.

"Once we are into the garage," The Hierophant continues to steamroll the conversation.

"Where is Mag...The Fool for all of this?" Genevieve asks.

"You do not need to worry about The Fool. She will meet us on site," The Hierophant says.

I glance over at Magdalena, who seems to be playing a game on her phone once more, disinterested and uninvolved in the conversation.

"Once we are into the garage," The Hierophant picks up as if there had been no interruption, "The Hermit will take this path to the security office to meet with The Fool."

The Hierophant hits a button on his remote, and a red line highlights the path on his projected map.

"The Fool will have already incapacitated the guards and

secured the security office. The Hermit will then disable the building's security," The Hierophant explains.

We all look over at Howard, who nods.

"Magician, you can get us past the wards on the house?" The Hierophant asks, drawing our attention back to him. His face is blank, emotionless, and unreadable.

"Yes, I have four amulets I've made that will bypass the wards on the house."

"Excellent," The Hierophant says.

"You sure they will work?" The World asks skeptically. I can't tell if she's skeptical that I can bypass the magical security measures or skeptical of why we are bothering to deal with magic at all.

"Are you sure you won't get a flat tire on the road coming in?" I ask.

"Well, I mean, no, but..." She begins.

"I'm as sure as I can be," I say, "But there is one little detail."

"I do not like 'little details' Magician," The Hierophant says.

"In order for them to work, each amulet will need a little dab of blood from the person using it. The blood needs to be fresh, meaning not dried. So if it starts to dry, you will need to put an additional dab of blood on."

"What happens if the blood dries up while we are inside?" Allen asks.

"Then the protective wards on the house may trigger," I say.

"May?" Allen follows up.

I shrug, and the Hierophant nods grimly.

"What effects are we talking about exactly?" Allen asks.

"A few things," I start.

"It will alert Devora that an unauthorized person has entered," The Hierophant says.

"It will also summon something, some kind of magical creature or construct," I add.

"Hellhounds," The Hierophant clarifies.

I turn and look at him through narrowed eyes. He suddenly seems to know a lot about the defenses for a guy who left me to figure everything out by himself.

"Hellhounds, are they really a thing?" Genevieve asks.

"I would not have said it if they were not," The Hierophant says flatly.

"What exactly do we do if these things get summoned?" Allen asks.

"We do not allow that to happen," the Hierophant says.

"I think that is the best option," I say. "So watch your amulets and make sure they stay wet."

Allen, Howard, and the World nod grimly.

"The good news is, if they do get summoned, I don't think they can leave the house, so get out quick?"

I glance at The Hierophant. He says nothing, but his grim and disinterested expression tells me he does not think that is much of a possibility.

"Once we are in, we make our way here," The Hierophant says, bringing up a blue line on his map that shows the way to the staircase down to the vault.

"What you don't see on the map," I say, "Is that the entrance to the vault is concealed."

"What do you mean it is concealed?" The Hierophant asks, his eyes narrowed in suspicion.

I look at him incredulous. How does he not know this?

"It's in a panel in the wall that is kind of hard to spot. Notable because it has a keypad on the wall to open it," I say.

"I do not have this in my notes on Devora's security," The

Hierophant says for the first time today. There is a whiff of emotion in his voice. He likes being in control, and this oversight is making him feel out of control.

"Did you get the code?" Allen asks.

"No," I say, then indicate The Hierophant, "I assumed he had it."

"Hermit, can you open this door from the control room?" The Hierophant asks.

"I'm. Um. I'm not sure. If it is on the same system, yes, but it wasn't included in any of the diagrams or schematics you sent me. If it was added later, maybe, but it could also be on its own circuit, in which case, cutting power to the house should do it unless it's on a backup battery. Then, of course, it would still operate, and cutting the power probably would make it fail closed, not open, so that wouldn't work and..." Howard babbles until The Hierophant's grumpiest voice cuts him off.

"Can you do it or not?"

"I don't know," Howard concludes.

"Fool," I say. Howard looks at me, hurt. "No, not you. I mean her."

I point at Magdalena. Howard looks slightly placated. I continue, "Do I have to call her that? I don't like it."

"Yes," The Hierophant says.

"It's fine," Magdalena says.

"Fool, could you bypass the keypad?"

She could look through the future, trying every possible combination until she finds one that works. Out of the corner of my eye, I see Allen, Howard, and The World looking at me curiously. The Hierophant doesn't seem the least bit surprised by my suggestion.

Magdalena shrugs without looking up from her phone, "Sure."

"I do not like alterations to the plan, but this doesn't seem drastic. Fool, after The Hermit has disabled the electronic security, you will join us in the garage," The Hierophant states.

"I don't have an amulet for her. This wasn't in the plan. The plan was that the four of us go in."

The Hierophant nods reluctantly, "The World will stay with the truck then, and the Fool will enter with us."

"Why do I gotta stay with the truck?" The World whines. "That wasn't the plan."

"A plan that is too rigid is sure to crumble when stressed. We adapt. Once the Fool has bypassed the keycode, we will make our way into the vault, where The Magician will take down the wards on the vault. Magician, you are prepared to do this?"

"We should be good. I am working on an elegant solution, but if I can't manage that, I have a little more inelegant one that will work," I say, trying to sound confident.

"How long will your inelegant solution take?" The Hierophant asks.

"As I estimated before, an hour tops."

"And your elegant solution, I assume, will be quicker than this?" He continues his interrogation.

"Yes, for sure."

"The Wheel of Fortune will then break into the physical vault itself. There are, I hope, no changes to your portion of this plan?" The Hierophant asks, looking at Allen.

"Nope. In fact, I think I can probably trim that down to forty minutes to get in. The drillin' is the hard part, but once we get through the casing, it should be a quick boom, boom, and it's open," Allen says. "It's a case of too high tech. They don't expect you to get your hands dirty."

"Then it is a matter of loading the goods into the truck. This should take no more than a half hour. Regardless, we must be through the gate on the way out by four o'clock exactly so that we are long gone by the time the next shift of guards comes. We will return to the initial rendevous location. There, I will give you information that will give you access to overseas accounts in your names with your respective payments in them. We will part ways. When I have successfully auctioned off the contents of the vault, I will deposit your shares in those accounts."

"Pardon me for being a mite skeptical," Allen says, "But that is asking a lot of faith on our parts."

"And I, in turn, am giving a great deal of faith. I assure you that I have little to gain by double-crossing any of you or making any more enemies than I have already. I find myself in a position to perform tasks such as this one with some regularity, and it does not behoove me to build a reputation for being anything but honorable."

"So there is honor among thieves," Genevieve snorts.

"We have all had ample opportunities to part ways if trust was an issue, and yet we are all still here. I assure you that I will pay you."

"Bullshit."

"Would you make a blood pact to that effect?" I ask. I've only engaged in one of those before, and both parties barely survived it. I have no desire to lock myself into a magically binding oath, but I am curious what his response will be.

The Hierophant raises an eyebrow. For a second, I think it might be alarm. He stops and seems to consider my suggestion.

"If that is the assurance you require. Yes, I would make an oath to pay you for this job upon its successful completion and your successful and complete participation in that completion. I vow that I fully intend to pay every participant and have the means to do it."

I note all of the caveats to his concession. He knows what he's agreeing to.

"Well, your willingness is all I need," I say because I know that whatever I ask of him, there will be something he asks in return as my part of the oath, and I don't want to be magically bound to whatever wording he tricks me into.

The Hierophant looks around the rest of the table. Everyone, in turn, nods. Apparently, my faith is enough for them.

That is upsetting.

"Are there any further questions?" The Hierophant asks.

He receives a sea of stares. Howard looks like a deer trapped in headlights. Allen looks slightly suspicious. The World looks excited and eager. Genevieve looks grumpy. Magdalena is still staring at her phone, disinterested.

"Oh yeah! Miles, this is going to be a barn burner!"

CHAPTER 12

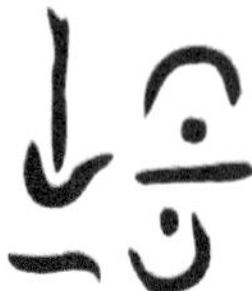

On the drive back to my apartment, Genevieve and I are quiet. I'm lost in my head, thinking over the challenges of tomorrow. The sigils that make up the spell on the vault door are an intricate puzzle, one I feel compelled to solve. I worry that it might be beyond my skills. How do we build skills, if not by trying to achieve things that are at the edge of our capacity?

I am certain that I cannot simply fill the carven sigils in with clay or epoxy. Eliminating any sigil will change the spell to do something dire. At least one of these potential outcomes is a huge pulse of energy. As I understand them, one recurring set of sigils translates to something like: Summon, River (of), Sun, Fire, and Spirits. I speculate that this means the room will be flooded with intense magical radiation. The only thing I am certain of is that I don't want to find out.

There must be an order in which the spell's sigils can be disabled. They are such a complex network of interconnected flows of magical energy. So far, I haven't found the order in which to disable them, at least not one that I would stake my life on. Since all our lives are on the line here, I'm not going to guess at this. Once more, Jeff's Acetobacter Magusficedula is looking like my best option. I am quietly irritated that Jeff's formula always feels like the only useful tool in my toolbox.

My reverie is interrupted by two blasts of a police siren.

"Shit," Genevieve says, "Getting pulled over."

I sit up straight and put my phone in my pocket. I glance over at the speedometer and see she is going basically the speed limit, maybe five over. She hasn't suddenly slowed down, so it isn't a speeding ticket. Genevieve slows down and pulls onto the shoulder. Normally, I wouldn't be worried about getting pulled over, but the circumstances have me on edge.

"Relax," Genevieve says, "Not a big deal, it's a rental car. They probably think we are tourists out wine tasting and driving."

She's right. I am far too tense. I hadn't even noticed how tense I was until she mentioned it, but I am barely breathing and white-knuckle gripping the door handle. I take a couple of deep breaths.

"You're right," I say, closing my eyes for a second. "No big deal."

I sit with my eyes closed. I can hear Genevieve's window roll down.

"Is there a problem, officer?" Genevieve asks in a calm, almost flirty tone.

"I need to talk to Miles," a familiar voice says.

I open my eyes and look over.

"Hi, Chris!" I say, surprised. At first, I am happy it is a familiar face. Chris Benson is a friend of sorts on the local police force. Then I see the look on his face, and the gears begin to click into place. The last time I talked to Chris, he considered going undercover in the Knights of Saint George, the same militant group of monster hunters that Allen belongs to. I realize now that Allen said he put out the call to be back up tomorrow. That means Chris probably knows something about tomorrow's job. Suddenly, I am less happy to see a familiar face.

"Miles, can we talk?" Chris asks, giving Genevieve a pointed glance.

"If it's about what I think it is about, she might as well be involved. This is Genevieve, my girlfriend. She's in the loop."

He looks perturbed, "The side of the road is probably not the place. There. Let's turn off there on Wine Country Ave. and talk in the parking lot."

He indicates the light about a quarter of a mile down the road.

"Okay," I nod to Genevieve.

Chris returns to his car, and we start driving.

"Chris is in the Napa PD. I've helped him with some magical problems, and he's helped me with legal problems. He joined the Knights of Saint George, so I am pretty sure he knows about tomorrow through Allen," I try to explain to Genevieve quickly while we drive.

"The Knights? Seriously?"

"It might have been my idea that he joined..." I say sheepishly.

Genevieve doesn't say anything. However, she does roll her eyes a little.

"I am going to play my cards close to my chest, though, see what he actually knows before saying anything."

"Probably wise."

We pull into the indicated parking lot. Chris is right behind us. Genevieve and I get out and stand between my rental car and Chris' patrol car.

"Good to see you, Chris! It's been a while."

"Damnit, Miles. Don't small-talk me. What the hell are you doing at Jim Devora's tomorrow?"

"Word gets around..." I mutter.

"Well, the KoSG guys are all talking about it, 'ready to move tomorrow afternoon.' I was about to do something about it when your name came up. So before I ran it up the flagpole, I wanted to see what you had to say."

I sit and think for a minute about how to reply. If I tell him everything, he will either try to stop me or want to help. I don't know him well enough to know which, but I do know him well enough to know that he will not lack an opinion.

"I want to honor our friendship and be completely honest with you. However, I am concerned that doing so will complicate what is already a very complicated situation. Do you know how, sometimes, in order to help someone, you have to break something? You know, kick in a locked door to get to a person having a heart attack in a house or something?"

"Sure, I deal with it all the time."

"It is like that. Jim Devora is a bad guy, a very bad guy, worse than anything you've heard. Some other people want to take something from him. If I help, maybe it won't get messy, and nobody gets hurt. Definitely, at least one bad guy loses. If I don't help, I think a lot of other people lose."

"More vague than I had hoped, but I understand you're trying to absolve yourself of responsibility for doing something bad with moral relativism," Chris says.

"No, it's not like that!" I exclaim. It isn't, is it?

"Why not come to the police? Why not come to me? Deal with this the right way," Chris asks, sounding tired and exasperated.

I nod and look him in the eye. It is hard to do.

"Because Chris and I don't mean anything personal by this; these people are going to do what they are going to do either way. Whatever philosophical pitfalls I may be trapped in, I am certain that if I bail, or you arrest me, or you have a full tactical squad show up tomorrow, they are going to try this anyway. Yeah, you might be able to stop them, but it's going to get messy. Very, very messy. I don't think Jim Devora's possessions are worth a single life, let alone a bunch."

"Miles, I respect you. You know I do. I know the world is a bigger, weirder place than I was raised to believe, and I know you are doing your best to manage that. But this isn't your job. No matter how you slice or justify it, none is your job."

"Whose job is it?" Genevieve asks.

"It's the job of law enforcement. It's the job of the courts. We have systems for a reason," Chris says, his face getting a little red.

"It's the job of the Knights of Saint George? They've done worse and not a single arrest. You want to talk about moral relativism? Is your job to protect and serve? Or is it just to protect and serve rich old white men?" Genevieve says flatly, staring Chris down as she does.

"Genevieve," I hiss at her.

"No, no, Miles. She's right. I am a hypocrite. I've been playing it fast and loose with the rules, too. I've been helping you when it was convenient, turning a blind eye when I had to—fudging there, nudging here. Shit, I only know about any of this because of the Knights of Saint George, a group that is so scared of what they don't know that they are always gearing up for a fight."

He looks down at his feet. His barrel chest is puffed up from holding his breath.

We sit there in silence.

"Okay," Chris says, "Miles, here's what we are going to do. I'm walking away this one last time. But then I'm done. I'm done with the Knights of Saint George, Miles Ward, magic, and boogeymen. Back to by-the-book, weird gets filed under W and mysterious under M."

I blink at him.

"I can't tell you what to think or do, Chris, but I tried that approach once upon a time. After Pandora's box is opened, it can never be shut again. There are so many things you can't unsee."

"I can try."

"Well," I say, feeling hurt and sad, "If you decide you aren't done with me, I'm not done with you. When I say it out loud, it sounds like a threat, like 'I'm not done with you yet, Mugsy' or something, but I mean, I'll still be here, and I understand and..."

"Yeah, I got it," Chris says, turning his back to climb into his patrol car.

"Okay, well then..." I start to say.

"Just leave me alone, Miles," Chris says as he slams his door slowly and methodically drives away.

"I..." I start to say something. I am not entirely sure what. Genevieve interrupts me.

"Just give him some space," Genevieve says.

"Are we doing the right thing?"

"I don't know, right and wrong are matters for historians. In the present, we can only do our best."

"Are we doing our best?"

"Was there a better option? As you told him, The Hierophant has made it clear, he's doing this one way or the other."

"That's what he said, but I am really starting to wonder what 'the other way' is. He can't shoot his way into that vault," I say.

"Do you want to find out? I'm asking as an honest question. I'll back your play either way."

"For me, I guess, it boils down to Magdalena. If I knew where her loyalties lay, it might change my perspective. But if she will stick it out even if I bail, then I don't want to find out."

"Why not?"

"There are two reasons. First, I think she's trying to improve, to be better than she was raised. It's a trial I am familiar with. I think she's right on the cusp, the tipping point. I think we, you and I, are, don't laugh, the best influences in her life right now. I think if she does this job without us, she's going farther down a slippery slope."

I pause to take a breath. Genevieve nods for me to go on.

"And the second?" Genevieve asks.

"The second is that Magdalena is terrifying. Genevieve, you've never really seen what she's capable of. Actually, I don't think I've seen all that she's capable of. I think she could do this whole job herself if nobody cared about the crater she left behind her. I don't think Chris or the Knights of Saint George are prepared for someone like Magdalena. And we don't know anything about the Hierophant."

"If you have all these questions, then ask her," Genevieve says. "Ask her if she's going to do this without you."

I sigh. It's that simple, isn't it?

CHAPTER 13

Back at our apartment building, I knock on Magdalena's door. The lights are out, and there is no answer. She must not be back yet. Genevieve and I retire to my apartment.

"I am going to try to figure out this knotwork puzzle of sigils. I think I've almost got it," I say.

"I am going to keep digging on Devora. He's a piece of shit, but a lot of the other stuff that The Hierophant said seems speculative. He said there was hard evidence in these files, but it's really only circumstantial. Mostly, it just proves that Devora was born to some privilege and has had some stunning good luck," Genevieve says, pulling out her laptop.

We sit on opposite sides of my desk, facing each other with laptops back to back.

"You sunk my battleship!" I say because the laptops remind me of that childhood board game. Genevieve smirks at me but doesn't say anything.

"Do you want coffee?" I ask, "I need coffee."

"No, I'm good. You've been drinking it like water all day. Maybe you should take it easy."

"I do my best work with java in hand. And mouth. And stomach."

"When you can't sleep, don't go waking me up."

So I go to the kitchen and brew a pot of coffee, which I bring back with cream and sweetener, and pour myself a mug at my desk.

Hours pass, with Genevieve and I sitting at my desk. The only sounds is the clack, clack, clacking of computer keys and the occasional tinkling as I stir more sweetener and cream into another mug of coffee.

I feel like I haven't made any progress. Whenever I think I have figured out every possible permutation of this spell and an order in which the sigils can be removed benignly, I see something I missed. It is frustrating. I also can't tell exactly what its intended function is. It creates a potent exclusive boundary, shunting magical energy out. But that is all it seems to do, a task easily done with a far less complicated spell. Most of the effort has gone into building a series of fail-safes. The fail-safes all have to do with either summoning things or emitting a pulse of energy. I am certain I don't want to trigger any of them. However, so far as I can tell, if I were to walk into the vault, I would be fine. Any person who just walked into the vault would be fine. I believe that if the wards aren't tampered with, the spell is just an intricate exclusive boundary.

This revelation makes me worry more. The way this is constructed doesn't make any sense to me. I must be missing something. I am wallowing in frustration and the beginnings of a mire of self-pity when I hear Magdalena's apartment door open and close.

"I should go talk to her, right?" I ask Genevieve.

"Yeah, probably. But first, I've been piecing together Jim Devora's life. He came from an upper-middle-class suburban family. He went to college. He wasn't really anyone of note, right? He went to film school, where he made his first film, Sintrix 8, a low-budget sci-fi film that borders on softcore porn," Genevieve explains.

"No, it was clearly on the other side of that border," I add.

"That was, like, fifty years ago. It was played at a local film festival and was forgotten until he got big. He dropped out of film school after that and traveled. His biography claims that he went looking for inspiration. He basically vanished for five years. Then he reappeared with 'The Lost Sceptre'. It became an instant blockbuster, and he went from a no-name film school dropout to an international star literally overnight."

"The Lost Sceptre, I saw that when I was a kid. That's the one about the guy who joins an archeological dig and finds a magic staff and all the weird, surreal adventures it takes him on?"

"Yeah, I've never seen it, but it has a reputation for being very hokey by today's standards. Anyway, until a few years ago, everything he did was gold. No matter what, if his name was on it, it was a blockbuster," Genevieve says.

"Then the allegations started coming out, and now he's basically in hiding," I conclude, "That pretty much lines up with what the Hierophant said. Maybe in those five years, he got possessed by the Mad Hermit and came back unstoppable."

"It lines up, sure, but there is no reason to believe that magic has anything to do with it. There are a dozen more plausible explanations."

"Well, he certainly does not look his age. He's got to be, what, in his seventies? He doesn't look a day past fifty,"

"Sure, but there are plenty of explanations there, too. Makeup, collagen treatments, botox, magic. I mean, how old will Magdalena look when she's seventy?" Genevieve says.

I nod and bite my lip in thought.

"You go talk to her. I will try to watch The Lost Sceptre. I think it might be allegorical, and there are entire online threads that agree, though most of them equate the allegorical scepter to the inspiration he discovered in his five years of travel. Or, you know, whatever," Genevieve says, "You want to watch?"

"Yeah, maybe I'll throw some popcorn in the microwave when I get back, but go ahead and start without me," I say as I walk to the door.

"You betcha," Genevieve says.

I walk out into the walkway and knock on Magdalena's door. She opens it a minute later. There is a weird, oily, chemical smell that wafts out of her apartment door.

"What's up?" She says curtly.

"I wanted to ask you a couple of questions," I say.

"Sure, come on in. I hope you don't mind if I work while you ask."

I shrug, "Fine by me."

I follow her into her kitchen, where an array of knives and firearms are laid out on the table, all in various states of repair. Gun oil is the weird smell I noticed. She sits down and begins quickly and methodically stripping, cleaning, and reassembling each item. She hones and oils knives. It is all done with a meditative focus.

"How well do you know this Hierophant guy?" I ask.

"We have a professional relationship; I trust him because he's always held to the letter of his deals. I've never known him to double-cross anyone. He's a professional fixer, and he keeps it professional. I don't know him beyond that, and I don't want to."

"Is he always this hands-on?" I ask.

"No, actually, he usually sets it up, and then I don't see him till the job is done. He doesn't usually get his hands dirty. That is new," she says with a quirked eyebrow before returning her attention to a rifle she is cleaning.

"I think this job is a mistake," I say, "I want out, but I don't want to leave you."

She nods, "I figured."

We sit in silence. She seems quieter and more contemplative than usual. I get that strange sense of déjà vu once more. I wonder what she's trying.

"I am going to do the job either way. If you want out, I won't stop you. However, I don't think the Hierophant will like it."

"You did the time thing just there. What did you do?"

"I tried a few dozen ways of answering the question to see which got the best response from you. I keep forgetting you can tell when I loop."

I had never thought of her using her power like that. I feel a little betrayed, as if some bit of my free will has been stolen from me.

"Oh," I say.

"I don't know what he's going to do if you bail. But I know he's going to be pissed."

"I am not going to bail. I'm not going to leave you behind. I just wanted to see if you'd leave with me."

"I can't. I have a professional reputation to consider. I start bailing the last second on jobs, and the word is going to get around."

"If jobs start going down in flames every time, word is also going to get around," I point out.

"Going up in flames is my specialty. You should know that by now," she says with a smile like she's trying to be funny, but the smile doesn't leave her mouth.

"Well, after this, you should be able to retire," I say.

"I could retire now."

"Why don't you?"

"What does a carrot peeler do when there are no carrots left to peel?"

"You're not a single-use kitchen tool, Magdalena. You've got lots of other things you could do."

She nods but continues cleaning her guns.

"How did my name come up for this job?" I ask. It's something I've been wondering and now seems like a good moment to get a straight answer.

"He asked if I knew a good spellbreaker. I told him I knew a guy who had fended off the best the Hizarin and the Lamia had to offer without breaking a sweat, but that he had a conscience, so it had to be a 'good' job," she puts down her tools to air quote the word good.

"What did he say to that?"

"He said that he could work with that," she shrugs.

"So he didn't ask for me by name?"

"Full of yourself much? No, he didn't ask for you by name. In fact, I'm not sure he'd heard of you until I mentioned you."

"Do you know why this job is so important to him? It seems personal, which is part of what concerns me."

"Nope," she says, "Like I said, we have a good professional relationship; I get a job, I do a job, I get paid."

"So all that stuff about Devora being a Lich, that's all info you got from him?"

"Yeah, but he had some data. Also, have you seen Devora's aura? It's...Whew, it's a train wreck."

"No, I've never met the man. What do you mean?"

"I don't know how to describe it. It's all tied up like a knot, with...I don't know, shit folded up inside. It's not normal, not at all."

"I see."

She nods and looks down at her work. I can't think of anything else to say.

"Okay, well, I have work to do. Have a good night," I say and start toward the door. As an afterthought, I add, "Let's carpool tomorrow. I'm driving. Your car stands out too much."

"No can do. I have some errands. I'll be meeting you at Devora's," she nods pensively, "Remember, that's the plan."

"Oh, right. Yeah. Okay. Um, g'night," I say.

"Night." She responds as I close the door behind me.

CHAPTER 14

"What did I miss?" I whisper as I plop down on the bed next to Genevieve and put a bowl of microwave popcorn between us.

"You really need to get a couch. I don't want to sleep with popcorn crumbs," she whispers back.

"Bah," I grunt, "Pause it. I'll go get a sheet or something to throw down."

I rummage through my linen closet for something that will work, but I can only find a couple of old, faded beach towels. I don't recall ever owning or using a beach towel in my life, and conclude that they must have been in the apartment when I moved in. I don't mention that to Genevieve as I lay down my improvised popcorn barrier.

"Okay, catch me up."

"That guy," she says, indicating a man in khaki shorts and a white short-sleeved shirt, his face frozen into a nightmarish mid-sentence expression. "is Bennett Welles, an archeology student. He is smart, cunning, and has a rakish way with the ladies that might have been considered endearing fifty years ago but is creepy now. And frankly, rapey. How did anybody watch this and then get surprised when all the allegations came out about Devora?"

"Yay," I say sarcastically.

"That guy you see behind him, he's pretty blurry. The guy with the white beard that is Dr. Arnett Cockswallow."

"Cockswallow?"

"Oh, yeah, there is a lot of overt homophobia, too. This movie is pretty awful. The opening credits ended like six minutes before this, and we've already lost sixty years of cultural progress. So, Dr. Arnett is an array of blatant and demeaning homosexual stereotypes. He's also a blundering fool. He pretty obviously represents Devora's perceptions of academia."

"All right, I saw this as a kid, but the only thing I remember is a scene where the protagonist, I assume that is Welles, wrestles a giant snake. I remember thinking the snake was just a big rubber hose with scales painted on it. I was eight, so if I wasn't impressed, then..."

"Yeah, Welles is portrayed as a man of action, so snake wrestling is definitely in his future. Anyway, Welles has just been informed that he is to join the Doctor's expedition to find the lost city of Mu. Welles has made at least six homophobic jokes at the Doctor's expense, kissed three unconsenting women, and defeated the football team's captain in a fistfight."

"I thought you said you were only six minutes in?" I say in confusion.

"We are. There was absolutely no context or storyline. It shows him walking down a hallway, grabbing three unsuspecting women, and kissing them. They swoon. He proceeds to punch a guy in a football uniform. Someone makes a point to declare that it was the football team's captain. Then he walks into a classroom slinging reprehensible insults," Genevieve says.

"And this was an award-winning film?"

"For cinematography and a best supporting actor for Sir Edward McKinnery's portrayal of the villain."

"They got McKinnery to be in this steamer?" I ask in disbelief.

"Yeah, it was his first nominated role. Long before the knighthood, it opened the door for him to get the like twenty-nine best actor awards."

"He got an Emmy for his two-episode role in Craven's Gate."

"Nooo! Was he in Craven's Gate? And they got an Emmy?" Genevieve says, taking her phone out for an internet search. A moment later, "He did the full EGOT. Craven's Gate got a daytime Emmy? And a Tony? There's a Craven's Gate Musical? My world is crumbling."

"There is a Craven's Gate Musical?" I ask. I had no idea.

"You want to watch it, don't you?"

"No," I lie in outrage.

"Yes, you do."

"Yes, you do," Genevieve grins as she echoes Hank.

"Can we get back to the movie?" I say, crossing my arms and sulking melodramatically.

"Right, The Lost Sceptre," she says, scrunching her nose like she smells bad.

"What is the difference between sceptre with a re and scepter with an er, by the way?"

"Oh," I say, "It's the same word. One is more popular in the US, and one is more popular in the UK."

"Mansplain much?" Genevieve says, glowering at me.

"Oh, no, Hank asked," I say.

"It's getting a little old, the whole 'I was talking to Hank thing.' Anyway, the re spelling is actually more popular in the US, with just over fifty percent of the population preferring it, where it's a much larger majority in the UK at around ninety percent," Genevieve says.

"Mansplain much?" I ask, grinning.

"Oh, no, Hank asked."

"Did Genevieve just summon a fire demon? Cause ya got burned!"

"Stop ganging up on me, and let's watch this tasteless excuse for a movie that is older than anyone in the room."

So Genevieve unpauses the movie, and we resume The Sceptre.

The Sceptre is a movie that invites heckling, which all three of us do—a lot.

"There is probably a fan game where you drink whenever the protagonist kisses a stranger or winks at a thug before he knocks them out with one punch. Where you drink whenever an enemy shoots at him point blank and somehow misses," I say.

"Nope, you drink after every time he says, 'You're going to feel that one in the morning!'" Genevieve says.

"Those are both the same thing!"

"This is so bad. This thing won an Oscar?"

The plot is pretty basic. Bennet Welles is an impulsive man of action who, for some reason, is also an archeology student on an expedition with Dr. Arnet Cockswallow. They travel to a remote jungle location in an unspecified country on an unspecified continent. It is filled with horrifyingly racist portrayals of the local culture—the imagery and symbolism are a blind mashup of non-European cultural stereotypes. They plod off into the jungle following a map, the origin of which is unspecified, but our group consensus was that they got it in the gift shop at the airport.

They run afoul of cannibals, most of whom are played by white people, in the most horrifyingly racist and culturally insensitive garb; wrestle a giant snake; free a blond-haired, blue-eyed 'princess' from a band of pirates, also played by race-painted extras; Welles has a protracted and shockingly graphic, for the era, sex scene with the 'princess.' Finally, the remnants of the expedition find their dig site.

Now, things start to get strange with the movie at its halfway point. When the expedition arrives, Edward McKinnery's villain, Otto Von Crupe, already occupies the dig site. He is a bald, one-handed German with glasses and a stutter. Otto Von Crupe and his gang of knock-off Nazis are searching for The Sceptre of Ranmook.

A protracted fight between Von Crupe and Welles ends when they crash through some weak stones and fall down into the dark catacombs below. Once locked in the dark, the film becomes more like a horror movie, as it is revealed that Von Crupe is, in fact, a vampire. Suddenly, Welles is crawling alone in the dark, being stalked by a creature of the night. Welles is all but blind, while Von Crupe can see perfectly. This is demonstrated by a series of cuts back and forth, from Welles crawling in near blackness to first-person shots from Von Crupe's perspective. At the climax, Welles falls and hurts his ankle, and Von Crupe closes in on him rapidly.

In a flashback scene, Welles is told an old folk tale by his Romanian grandfather. The grandfather explains all of the weaknesses of vampires. The flashback ends with the grandfather explaining, "And if legumes are spilled upon the ground..."

Welles throws a handful of beans onto the ground before Von Crupe. It's never really clarified where the beans came from, but I guess everyone who goes adventuring in an unnamed jungle carries a handful of dry beans, just in case. Von Crupe is compelled to count the beans before he does anything else, and Welles uses the opportunity to escape.

Using a lighter and some very questionable logic, Welles

follows the direction of airflow to a chamber. As Welles enters the chamber, Genevieve interrupts.

"Hey, wait, pause it," she says.

I pause the movie, "What's up?"

"Go back like, I don't know, ten frames."

I roll the movie back a few frames to a point where Welles is ducking through the entry to the chamber.

"You see? There?" Genevieve says, pointing at the arch around the chamber entrance.

I squint. It is hard to see clearly in the grainy old film. But sure enough, the arch around the entrance has sigils adorning it. The sigils are, while not undeniably, almost certainly the same sigils used on the vault.

"Huh, I think you are right. He used the same sigils in the movie as he put on the vault. The same pattern as the Codex Gigas."

"That's interesting."

"Interesting, but I'm not sure what it means."

Genevieve shrugs, "Something to think about."

I grunt an affirmation and unpause the movie. Welles ducks through the arch and into the final chamber. There, he finds the unquestionably phallic Sceptre of Ranmook. Von Crupe makes a surprise attack at that moment, and Welles uses the Sceptre to absorb Von Crupe's power. After informing Von Crupe's ashes that he will feel that one in the morning, Welles returns to the surface, where he uses his newfound power to save the Doctor and return everyone to civilization.

The final scene ends with a reporter asking Welles where the Sceptre is now. Welles says that it is in the National Museum, then turns to the camera and winks.

As the credits roll, Hank chimes in, *"Well, that's two hours, four minutes, and thirteen seconds of my life I won't get back."*

"It was two hours and eleven minutes long," I point out. I think we were all tracking the minutes.

"The sex scene was six minutes and thirty-eight seconds I'd watch again."

"Ugh," I groan at Hank.

"Yeah, why did it have to be so long?"

"The movie? The sex scene? The snake? The scepter? There are many subjects about which questions could be asked."

"Well, yes. But I meant the movie. I mean, half the movie had nothing to do with the plot!" Genevieve says.

"Did we learn anything from watching this?"

"Yeah, that I really want to make Devora suffer. The writing was offensive. The acting was weak. The dialogue was tepid. The sex scene, which you'd think that pervert would have at least done right, was meh."

"Hey, now!"

"But I mean, do we think that he actually found this Sceptre? That he used it to gain power?"

"I don't know, but after watching that, I need to take a shower and wash the stink of it off me. And I will need you to never wink at me or say 'you're gonna feel that in the morning' to me again," Genevieve says.

"I've never said that to anyone."

"Well, let's keep it that way," She replies.

"Not true, bro. I've heard you say that to yourself in the mirror at least a dozen times."

"Shut up. And don't call me bro."

Genevieve looks like she's about to say something, but her face scrunches up.

"Talking to Hank again? It was cute at first, but it's getting...confusing."

I shrug helplessly as she goes off to shower.

CHAPTER 15

Sleep evades me all night, so the alarm has barely squawked before I am out of bed and getting dressed. I want to say the alarm woke me up, but that's not true. After watching The Lost Sceptre with Genevieve, I spent another hour drinking coffee and staring at a series of runes that continue to confound me. Genevieve was quietly snoring long before I climbed into bed. I've been staring at the ceiling for hours.

"Good morning, sunshine!" Hank says.

"Shh, I don't want to wake Genevieve."

"Then stop talking genius. It's not me making all the noise. She can't hear me!" Hank yells at me in his loudest voice.

"Dick."

"I know you are, but what am I?"

"I don't know. What do they call a rubber copy of a..."

"Hey!" He howls at me again. I smile. This is my first time getting one up on Hank in a long time.

I slip out into my kitchen, quietly closing the door behind me. I skulk to the kitchen and make myself a cup of coffee. I have that weird, gummy-eyed, slightly nauseous feeling you get when you haven't slept but get out of bed anyway. My body is lamenting the lack of rest but acknowledging that the window for sleep has passed.

I sip my coffee and stare out the window at the grey light of the morning. The marine layer has rolled in, and the air is thick and misty. I hold my coffee mug between both hands and run through the day in my head.

We have about six hours before meeting the crew and starting this whole caper. I start to feel jittery and anxious thinking about it. I pace back and forth in my tiny little kitchen and sip coffee.

"What's the problem?"

"There is no problem."

"Come on, Miles, I know you better than that. Give me a little credit."

I roll my eyes and groan, talking into my coffee mug.

"Then you know the problem," I mutter.

"You want to see yourself as a good person, but you are going to break into Jim Devora's vault and steal a bunch of stuff from him. Which, by most social norms, is not considered good."

"That, but also: Dangerous. Risky. Stupid? Anyway, this whole emotionally insightful Hank is freaking me out. I prefer when you insult me and throw witty quips my way," I snort.

"You aren't giving me a lot to work with here."

I take a big chug of my coffee.

"I'm just anxious. This is kind of crazy. My mind keeps spiraling about all the things that could go wrong."

"Don't worry about it, Miles. If there is one thing I am certain about, it's that everything you could fuck up, you will fuck up."

"Gee, thanks, that is very comforting."

"It should be very freeing. The bar is very low, bro."

"Don't call me bro," I say, my jaw clenching.

"Talking to your mannequin again?" Genevieve asks from

behind me. I must have been so lost in my conversation with Hank that I didn't notice her come in.

"Yeah," I say because while it's awkward, there is no sense in avoiding it.

"Do you think you do that more when you are stressed out?" She asks. Her brow is knitted, and her mouth pursed. She's concerned.

"Yeah," I say, but I don't actually feel that way. I think it just sounds more healthy than saying I talk to him all the time and that his voice has started following me even when he's not around.

"I'm curious about the story behind Hank. I know, simulacrum, magic, protection, but it seems like...I don't know. It seems like there is a story there."

I sit quietly for a minute. I don't really want to talk about this. It is uncomfortable. But I feel like I owe Genevieve something. She's been awfully understanding about this. She's been awfully understanding about a lot of my quirks.

"I named him after my brother," I say quietly.

She nods and doesn't say anything.

"He died a long time ago. I don't really like to talk about it. I don't even like to think about it, if I am honest."

I have a weird, panicky sensation in my body. I can feel my heart racing in my chest. I take a big sip of coffee to cover my discomfort.

She nods, lips still pursed.

"So, today is the big day," she says after a long silence.

"Yeah."

"We should do something to take our minds off of it. Sitting around mulling it over is not going to help. Let's go for a hike or something, get some morning air, stretch our legs."

"It's probably a good idea. Clear our heads," I say as I grab some toaster pastries for breakfast, "Oh, and I will need to swing by Jeff's on the way back. I can't figure out how to deal with these runes, so I'm going to need a lot of his Acetobacter."

"I get to meet the infamous Jeff," Genevieve says with a lack of enthusiasm. Although she's never met Jeff, she doesn't seem to like him for some reason.

Well, this will be fun.

CHAPTER 16

We are back on the trails of Skyline Park. A narrow dirt path winds its way through a maze of manzanita. It all burned back a few years ago and has just started to re-establish. The red and green boughs are interspersed with charred black sticks.

Genevieve is walking maybe ten feet ahead of me on the trail. We haven't really spoken in about fifteen minutes. My mind keeps jumping back and forth between the impenetrable mystery of the vault and the mire of my moral ambivalence.

"What are you thinking about?" I ask, breaking the long silence.

"Hmm?" she asks, clearly lost in thought. "Oh, mostly about the conference I have to be at next week. It's a writer's thing. I was supposed just to be attending, but they had someone drop out at the last minute, and they'd like me to fill in on this panel."

"Well, that has to be flattering," I say, "Do you think you will do it?"

"Yeah, I already agreed. Now I am just trying to get my head in that frame of mind."

"Really?" I ask. With the afternoon we have planned, I can't even think about making Jeff's party this evening, let alone what will happen on Tuesday.

"Yeah. I know this afternoon is a lot for you, but I am just sitting on a hilltop with binoculars and a radio. It's not exactly going to be a thrill ride for me."

"Well, it's all I can think about. I am pretty anxious," I say.

"I know."

"What's the topic of the conference?"

"It's like publishers, writers, editors, marketers, getting together to talk about the future of the industry, new tech. At least that's what they say they are getting together to talk about, but really, it's just an excuse for everybody to get drunk and get strange."

"So, what do you think you will talk about?"

"Eh. I'll figure it out."

Genevieve picks up the pace until we are going fast enough that I am too busy focusing on my footing and breathing to talk much. Our hike concludes in silence. We are back on the road before I speak again.

"I need to swing by Jeff's before we head Up Valley."

"We should stop by your place, shower, and grab our stuff first," Genevieve says.

After a quick stop at my place, we are back on our way. I pull off the highway at Wine Country Avenue, and we wind our way through the suburban maze to Jeff's house.

"This is nice," Genevieve says as I pull up in front of Jeff's. "A lot of house for one guy."

"Yeah, I think in his mind he was always going to start a family."

"Does a family want to start him? That's the question," Genevieve quips.

"You haven't even met him. I know he and Emily went through some stuff there. But that's a very one-sided view you've got. Jeff's my best friend, so can we try to save the judgment until after you've met him?"

"How did you two become friends?" Genevieve asks. She hasn't opened her door yet.

"We worked together at the same winery for a while. He was a cellar rat, and I was working in IT. We hit it off and stayed in touch after we both moved on to different jobs."

She nods in silent judgment.

I climb out of the car, and Genevieve follows suit. We walk to the front door without talking. The energy between us feels somber, as if we are going to a funeral.

Jeff answers the door quickly after I ring the bell.

"Hi, Miles!" Jeff says,

"Hey Jeff, this is Genevieve. Genevieve, Jeff."

"Hello, Jeff." Genevieve holds out her hand for a brief handshake. "I've heard a lot about you."

Genevieve's energy has changed. She is suddenly bubbly and enthusiastic. I'm surprised by her change of demeanor.

"Hello Genevieve," Jeff says, "I have heard basically nothing about you!"

He seems mirthful and gives me a skeptical look, which gets a smirk from Genevieve.

"He doesn't talk about me at poker night?"

"No, he usually regales us with stories of his derring-do," Jeff replies.

And immediately, the tone changes from one in which Jeff is on trial to one in which I am on trial for not talking about my girlfriend. I don't know how he does that.

"Does he give intricate explanations of what different sigils mean and how he figured out how to take spells apart?" Genevieve asks.

"Only when he isn't giving us the definition of a word we will never use again."

"Well, I am glad it's not just me!" Genevieve says.

"Okay, okay, we can plan a Miles Roast for another time. We are here on business," I interrupt before they touch any really sore spots.

"Right, right, you were here for the Acetobacter?" Jeff asks.

"That's right. Also, do you have any more of that catalyst?" I ask, "That could be useful."

"Yeah, though, did you use the bottle I gave you?"

"No,"

"It's stable. It doesn't seem to go bad, so that should still be fine."

I nod, and he walks us to his cellar.

"Here she is," Jeff says, pointing at the large plastic carboy on the floor.

I try to lift it, but it's too heavy to carry more than a few feet.

"I've got a dolly in the garage," Jeff says, "One sec."

Jeff vanishes, leaving Genevieve and me standing over a large plastic carboy of magic-eating bacteria.

"He's more charismatic than I was expecting," Genevieve says, "The bad ones always are."

I scowl, "Look, he's doing me a big favor here, so can we be polite?"

"I've been perfectly polite. I know his type, though. I've met a thousand like him."

I glower at her, but the conversation ends when Jeff returns with a little wheeled platform. It's little more than a two-foot square frame of wooden boards with four caster wheels and carpet tacked on the top. He helps me lift the carboy on top of it. Then we wheel it out to the sidewalk, where he helps me load it into the car.

"You going to unload this yourself?"

"No, I will use it to fill squirt guns."

Jeff laughs for a moment but then sees my facial expression.

"Oh, you're serious?" Jeff asks.

"Yeah, I think it will be easiest to deliver via squirt gun. I've got some industrial-grade soakers for this job."

"You are going to knock over a vault with a squirt gun," Jeff laughs.

Genevieve gives me a sudden, wide-eyed look of alarm.

"Yes, I told him," I say to her.

"I won't say a word, Scout's honor," Jeff says, holding one hand over his heart and the other up in a three-fingered salute. I know Jeff was never a Scout.

Genevieve doesn't look impressed.

"Well," I say, trying to change the topic before this gets potentially uncomfortable, "Thank you for the magic eating juice. We should be getting on the road. We have timetables to keep."

"Okay," Jeff says, nodding, "See you this evening?"

"Yes, for sure," I say.

"This evening?" Genevieve asks.

"Oh, yeah, Jeff is having a little soiree. I told him we'd come by."

"Oh, did you now?" Genevieve says, "Great to meet you, Jeff. I guess I will see you this evening!"

"Perfect!" Jeff says, "Good luck, break a leg, or whatever means good luck, you know, doing what you are doing."

Genevieve and I get into the car while Jeff returns to his house.

As soon as the door closes, Genevieve turns on me, "Why would you tell him about the heist?"

"He wanted to know. He has helped me out a lot. He is helping me out a lot. I didn't feel comfortable asking my best friend for help and then lying to him about what that help was for. I trust him."

She grunts, and then we fall silent for a moment. The sound of the engine purring its way along the highway is the only sound I can hear.

"Ugh, you and your ethics. Fine, I think you are right. You would be a crappy friend to ask for help without giving him any reason."

"Thank you," I say.

"Why didn't you tell me about the party tonight?" She says, suddenly changing topics.

"Honestly, I had forgotten about it until he asked."

"That sounds on brand," Genevieve quips as I turn onto Silverado trail.

CHAPTER 17

I'm doing fifty northbound on Silverado Trail. I turn east up a road that winds past Lake Hennessy and into the hills. We come to a long, straight stretch. The GPS tells me that I have to turn off in a quarter mile, but I don't see where I am supposed to turn. I begin to slow down.

There is a red sportscar behind me. It's already borderline tailgating me when it lays on the horn and gets so close I can't see its headlights in the rearview mirror. I turn my turn signal on, and they cut hard into the oncoming lane to pass. There is a pickup heading westbound, and the sportscar swerves back in behind me. An angry chorus of car horns ensues.

Finally, I see a small gravel road dipping into a gap between two large stands of Himalayan blackberry. This must be the turn, as there are no other possible turns. I turn, and the red sportscar roars around me. I can see the driver flipping me off over the sleek roof of the car.

"What's their problem?" I grumble.

"Impatient to find the bottom of a ravine. This isn't a road I'd be driving like that on," Genevieve says. She's right. This stretch is steep and windy. It's not a wise place to be driving like it's a speedway.

The little gravel road opens into a wide circle of dirt, with old rotted logs laid out as a perimeter. A small brown metal sign notes this as a trailhead, with no indication of what trail it is the head of. There is a pickup truck parked there. It is older and has clearly seen some use. There is also an immense box truck with the World Wide Shipping logo on the side. Allen, Howard, and Elizabeth, aka The World, are talking in the clearing. They are all wearing coveralls with the World Wide Shipping logo on them.

I park, and we get out.

"Hey, Miles," Allen starts to say, then seeing a glower from The World, he corrects himself, "Magician, Tower, much obliged."

"Hi," Howard says shyly.

"Welcome to the party," The World says, "Let's get crackin'."

"Where's The Hierophant?" Genevieve asks, looking around.

"He's waiting in the back of the truck," Allen says.

"Magician, Tower, and Hermit, you're riding in the back with him. The Wheel is going to ride up front with me."

"And I get to drive myself up to be lookout," Genevieve says grumpily as I toss her my keys. The World hands Genevieve a radio.

"Tower, this is yours. It's all programmed. Keep it turned on, and don't touch the dial," The World says. Genevieve nods in acknowledgment.

"Good luck," I say quietly to Genevieve.

"You too," she says with a touch of concern. I give her a wink, and she returns a lopsided smile. I'm trying to appear calm, but as I watch the car vanish between the blackberry bushes, I get a sinking feeling I might never see Genevieve again.

The World opens the back door of the shipping truck. It rolls up to a stop with a loud clang. I glance inside. There are a couple of large crates on pallets. Behind them, the space is inky black. I can't see The Hierophant in the gloam.

I give Howard a hand up and follow him in. Once inside, I can see that the blackness is hanging there like a curtain, but it isn't fabric or any other physical material. A literal wall of darkness hangs midway through the truck. I press through it, and there is a slight cold feeling like I've just walked through a rivulet of water, but I am not wet.

On the other side, it is still dark, but not to the point of being completely blinded. I can see the others in front of me through the twilight. The Hierophant is there, sitting on a crate.

"Welcome. I've thrown up a little shadow charm so that if anyone looks in here, they won't notice us," The Hierophant provides.

I glance around and see sigils drawn about the inside of the truck. I don't get much chance to examine them before The World slams the rolling door shut behind us, plunging us into complete darkness. I can hear the latch chunk into place. I feel a little panic begin to swell in my chest. I'm not terribly claustrophobic, but being latched in the back of a dark, moving truck would trigger panic in almost anyone. The Hierophant flicks on an electric lantern that casts a dim light through the back of the truck. The darkness spell reduces the lantern's brightness to that of a birthday candle.

Howard isn't doing so well. He immediately looks sweaty, nauseous, and terrified.

"I can't do this," Howard mewls as the truck's motor rumbles to life.

"I fear that we are beyond the point of no return," The Hierophant says.

The Hierophant hands Howard a stack of plastic bags and napkins. "In case you feel ill."

The Hierophant motions me to a jumpsuit with the World Wide Shipping logo. I start trying to put it on over my clothes. Putting on a jumpsuit in the dark in the back of a moving truck is a lot harder than it sounds. Eventually, I managed to wrangle myself into it. Backwards. So I have to wrestle my way out of it and put it back on the right way.

"It's like a three stooges bit, but there is only one stooge."

"Not now." I hiss as I finally zip the front of the coverall up.

"I'm sorry, what not now?" The Hierophant asks.

"Nothing, I just talk to myself when I am stressed. I can't imagine why I'd be stressed trying to get dressed in the back of a moving truck. In the dark! Why couldn't you wait till I got dressed to leave?"

"We have a timetable."

"I got there exactly on time."

"You were two and a half minutes late. That was your time to dress."

I throw my hands up in exasperation, but The Hierophant ignores me. We all sit down on crates and grab onto the rails on the side of the truck. The ride is bumpy and sickening. We are bounced, jounced, and flopped around for what seems like forever. The clock on my phone insists it is only twenty-five minutes, but it has to be at least a day and a half of terrified bouncing in the near blackness before the door is once more thrown open.

To his credit, and much to my great surprise, Howard hasn't vomited once during the trip.

We all stagger out of the back of the truck and into a large loading bay. During our briefing, it was called a garage, but it's immense and has plenty of space for the shipping truck. A half-dozen very expensive sports cars are parked here. One is bright red and looks familiar.

"One second," I motion for everyone to stay put as I walk over to the car and put my hand on the hood. It's cool. If it were the same car, the engine would definitely still be warm. I let out a sigh of relief.

"Is there a problem, Magician?" The Hierophant asks.

"No, this just looks a lot like a car that passed me on the road. I wanted to make sure we weren't in for an unexpected surprise. The engine is cool, though. This isn't the same car."

The Hierophant gives me a curt, businesslike nod, "Good."

The World begins handing out radios with earbuds to each of us. I hand out the amulets I constructed to everyone who will be going into the main house with renewed instructions to keep a fresh drop of blood on them.

I put blood on my amulet and hang it around my neck. How many times have I done this? How many times have I sat in this garage and put this little wooden amulet around my neck? Deja vu. With that, Magdalena arrives. I'm not sure where she's come from. She suddenly comes sauntering around the corner of the shipping truck.

"What'd I miss?" Magdalena says.

I toss her an amulet as The World tosses her a radio. Magdalena casually catches both, one with each hand. I notice that Magdalena is wearing her tactical harness with three pistols. Two are clearly air guns, but the third isn't.

Magdalena sees me eyeing her firearm, "No killing, I promise! I like to be prepared."

My head feels light, my stomach feels tight, and my vision is swimming a little. It's just nerves. Once we get into things, I'm sure this will all go away.

"Okay, Fool, Hermit, you're up," The Hierophant barks impatiently.

Magdalena nods and puts a firm hand on Howard's shoulder. With Magdalena moving gracefully in the lead and Howard awkwardly following, they leave through a side door.

Allen, The Hierophant, The World, and I sit silently, staring at each other. Occasionally, there is a faint creak or groan. Maybe trees blowing in the wind outside or the foundation of the house settling. The fire damage all seemed cosmetic when I was here a few nights ago, so hopefully, it's not creaking because it's going to fall down. We all strain our ears, waiting for a report over the radio.

The Hierophant stands erect and still. His face is an impassive mask, and he barely blinks. It almost looks like he's in a trance.

The World keeps moving around the shipping truck, checking the tires, looking underneath. She opens the engine compartment and looks the engine over for a minute before closing the hood again. This seems like due diligence the first time through, but by the time she's halfway through her second time, it's fairly obvious this is how she is dealing with nerves.

Allen unloads a couple of large bags from the back of the truck and starts poking through them. They are filled with tools. Drills and saws, I recognize, but a number of devices I don't.

I find myself checking my phone to see the time. I look at my amulet to see how dry the blood has gotten. I look back at my phone. I check through my bag of tricks to make sure that everything is there. I turn to watch the others for a moment. Then, I check the time on my phone again. It's only been a minute and thirty seconds.

No one talks. It is a protracted and nerve-wracking silence.

Eventually, the silence is broken by a crackle of static followed by a tinny voice.

"Phase one is complete; the drawbridge is down," Magdalena says over the radio.

"That is go time," The Hierophant indicates to Allen and me. "Fool, we need the portcullis lifted. Move into phase two."

"When did we come up with all the code phrases?" I say, "Why was I left out of that."

"They are all in the overview documents he gave us," Allen mutters.

"Oh, I guess I missed that part," I say. I skimmed through them. I really don't remember seeing that part.

"'Skimmed' doesn't mean you just opened the file."

Allen snorts at me. Out of the corner of my eye, I can see The Hierophant giving me a dirty look.

There is a set of stairs leading up to the first floor of the house, and this garage is on the ground floor. Based on the locations and length of the stairs, I surmise that this means the vault is actually under the hill that the house abuts, not the house itself.

I lead Allen up the stairs to the main floor of the house. As the only person who has been in this building before, I have a better sense of where we are going. We turn a corner at the top of the stairs and move briskly and quietly across the foyer to where the hidden door leads back down to the vault.

We've only just arrived when Magdalena joins us. I indicate the keypad to her.

"There," I say.

She walks over to it and types the passcode in. Deja vu washes over me. Combined with the lack of sleep and anxiety, the déjà vu almost knocks me over. I have to put a hand on the wall to brace myself. I feel seasick.

"You okay?" Allen asks me, sounding concerned.

"Fine, it's just when Mag...The Fool does that magic. It kinda messes with me."

"Oh," Allen says, sounding confused. From his perspective, there isn't any obvious magic going on.

"I am going to watch the front. The Tower isn't in position yet." Magdalena says as if she didn't just enter a hundred thousand passcodes into a keypad in an instant. She saunters to the front of the house, where we can see her take up position by a large bay window.

I pull the door open, and Allen and I descend into the vault.

The vault looks exactly the same as it did before. We are in a large room made of concrete with an immense metal door. It has a keypad on one side, and the concrete encircling the door has sigils cast into it. Deep in the recesses of the sigils, I can see a patina of dried blood.

"Wat..tower...go." Genevieve's voice comes in over my radio. It's crackly and almost impossible to make out. Like before, with my cellphone, the ferro-concrete walls of the vault are interfering with the radio.

"Come again, Tower," Allen says into his radio.

"Watchtower...a go," Genevieve's voice comes in a little clearer, but it's still hard to determine exactly what she's saying. It takes a second for me to process what I am hearing.

"Understood Tower. Hierophant, where you at?" Allen says.

I am staring at the vault door and its complicated, intricate runes.

"Keeping eyes topside," I can hear the Hierophant's muffled voice come down the stairs with a tinny broken echo through the radio.

"That wasn't the plan," Allen mutters to me.

Shortly after that, Magdalena comes down the stairs. "What's the delay, Magician?"

"Fooldelena, look at this," I say, pointing at the runes, "Is it me, or in this state, is this just a very intricate exclusive circle?"

She glowers at me, blending her name with the handle, but then turns to examine the runes. We sit there for a quiet minute while she does so.

"Yeah, I guess that's right," she concludes.

"Blow the lock," I say to Allen.

"What do you mean 'blow the lock'? I thought if we didn't do this in the right order, the whole thing will blow up in our face!" Allen says incredulously.

"I've spent days staring at these sigils, trying to figure them out. By themselves, they will have no impact on us. They only affect us if we take them apart. So our best bet is to blow the lock."

Allen looks at me, then looks at Magdalena. Magdalena shrugs.

"Fuck it," Allen says, "I trust you."

Allen opens up his bag and starts unloading a bunch of equipment. Drills and fancy-looking bits. He's got a little box with stickers all over it, cautioning the handler that the contents are highly volatile. He still has even more tools in the bag. He really came prepared.

Magdalena slips back upstairs as Allen begins to measure the vault door and make a number of marks with permanent markers. I stand by and watch, scratching my chin and thinking.

"Hmm," I say.

"What's up?" Allen says as he begins assembling a drill.

"Nothing, just thinking."

"Wheel! Do not blow the lock," we hear the Hierophant's voice echoing down the stairs, "Magician, destroy those wards now. That is what you are being paid to do: do your job."

His usually calm, bordering on annoyed tone has changed.

Now, he has a strong, resounding emotional tone. He sounds angry.

Allen turns and looks at me quizzically, stopping what he is doing.

"It's safer to leave it alone and open the lock. The wards in their current state do nothing," I call back up the stairs.

"Get back on track, Magician. I'm warning you."

I stare at the radio. I stare at Allen, I'm puzzled. Then, the last bits click into place.

"Oh," I say.

"Oh?" Allen says quizzically.

I reach down and grab a hammer out of Allen's bag.

"Do you trust me?" I ask.

Allen gets a pensive look on his face, his mouth scrunched to one side.

"Yeah, I trust you."

"Okay, blow the lock."

He shrugs and begins drilling into the vault door. I move to stand on the far side of the door, near the hinges. I heft the large hammer in my hand.

Allen's drill is whining and sparking as it starts to bite into the hardened steel door.

"This'll take a while. First, we get a hole here and here," he says, motioning with his head at the spot he is drilling and another spot he's marked. "That's the hard part. Then we put in the explosives and pop, and it should come right open."

I nod and wait. A minute later, The Hierophant comes barrelling down the stairs with Magdalena at his heels.

"What in the nine holy hells are you doing, Magician?"

Magdalena is standing at his right heel, looking confused.

I don't give him a second to act. I bring the hammer down hard on one of the runes carved into the concrete. It doesn't budge, so I swing again. Out of the corner of my eye, I can see the Hierophant's face contort in a rage-filled sneer. He pulls his sleeve up, revealing rows and rows of sigils tattooed there. I strike the concrete again; it is harder than I thought, and nothing breaks.

I glance back to see what the Hierophant's response to my vandalism is. A knife appears out of nowhere in The Hierophant's hand, and he casually stabs Magdalena in the thigh. She doesn't expect it and has no defense. Magdalena staggers back with a scream. With a practiced movement, he brings the bloody knife up to rub into the runes on his left arm.

Magdalena starts to draw a pistol, but The Hierophant casually swings his arm back.

We all have those days when we go looking for something in our house. Maybe it was our keys or our sunglasses. Not long into looking, we forget what we were looking for but keep searching. Soon, we forget why we are searching at all; the search becomes the point, and the idea of finding something is long gone. Soon, a day is spent opening a drawer, looking through it, closing it, opening a cabinet, searching it, then going back to the first drawer and searching it again, over and over, frustration building but never any closer to our now long lost goal.

In this way, I find myself mired in déjà vu. I've been sitting in this moment for so long that I've lost what the moment is. I've lost where I am, who I am, or why I am here. I gaze drunkenly as a distinguished-looking, middle-aged man backhands a young, dark-skinned woman. Her face contorted in shock and horror as his arm catches her in the stomach. Moving with the speed of a striking snake, he flings her eight feet back and into the wall like a ragdoll. She slumps to the floor unconscious as he begins incanting a spell.

I am stunned and dazed. It takes a few seconds for my brain to adjust to the present—a few seconds I really cannot afford to lose. Magdalena must have attempted to dodge his arm by bending time, but it didn't work. I cannot imagine how many countless iterations she spent trying to do so. Apparently, there are some things that are just inevitable.

The Hierophant finishes his incantation. I lock eyes with him. His eyes have a cold, dead, dark look to them. His skin suddenly seems pallid, dry, and drawn. He sneers, and his teeth are yellowy stubs. Whatever mask of magic and deception he was hiding behind has been lifted away. The creature before me isn't human, at least not anymore.

"I just want to be free," he hisses. "I've been trapped for decades, fulfilling the whims of a hedonistic imbecile. It is no way to exist."

I can feel the hairs rise on the back of my neck and go taut. The follicles hurt from the pressure. There is a weird tingling sense that rushes throughout my body. This is magic. I don't know what the spell is doing to me, but I know it isn't good. It is rare that magic has an overt visible or identifiable effect. The production of light, sound, and heat all require energy. Energy that could be directed somewhere more useful, like killing me.

I try to raise my hammer up for another blow at the concrete, but I can't move. My muscles begin to cramp and shake. I quickly glance at Allen and see that he, too, seems paralyzed, holding his drill. His whole body is shaking. Allen begins to emit a high-pitched whine of agony.

"You'd have figured out my secret, so you were all going to die anyway, but I would have made it quick and painless. We are beyond that now," the Hierophant howls, a tone of excitement, almost glee in his voice.

I close my eyes, and will my warding tattoos activated, I freely give a little bit of the blood from the vessels in my skin to the tattoos and open my connection to Hank. My arms begin to darken and bruise in response. I hate doing things this way, but it's really my only option. As the spell redirects to my simulacrum, the rigor in my muscles releases.

I grimace and shake off the last of the spell, raising the hammer above my head. I hear The Hierophant approaching me fast, howling with frustration and rage. I really hope I translated the runes correctly, and this does what I think it does.

"Summon River of Sun Fire Spirits!" In my best anime-signature-move voice, I announce. I bring the hammer down again. I see a bit of the concrete crumble away, defacing the rune.

There is a brilliant flash of light.

CHAPTER 18

White. Brilliant white light. That's all I can see. Even with my eyelids closed, it is like staring into the sun. I scrunch my face against the searing glow. It quickly fades from blinding white light to absolute blackness. I feel dizzy. I feel sick. My stomach is churning. I am lying on the floor now, curled in a fetal position. I must have blacked out there. How long have I been here on the ground?

"What the fuck!" Allen is yelling. I think he's been doing it for a while.

I try to talk, but a gurgling moan is the only sound I manage to make.

"Goddamit, Miles, what did you do?" Magdalena says.

"I'm fucking blind!" Allen responds.

I push myself up and sit with my back against the wall, hands raised over my face and head in a defensive posture, and listen carefully.

"Fuck!" Magdalena screams.

"Quiet," I say.

"Why would we be fucking quiet? I'm blind, and everything hurts!" Allen says.

Come to think of it. My skin is hot and itchy, like I have a bad sunburn.

"Just shh for a second, trust me."

"Not sure how much trust I got left," Allen says.

"Shhhh!"

We sit in silence for a minute. It's very, very quiet. I can only hear Magdalena's ragged, pained gasps and Allen's more subdued breathing.

"Okay," I say, "I think we are good."

"What the fuck was that Miles?"

"The spell on the door wasn't for us. It was for the Hierophant. Specifically, to keep him out."

"Come again?"

"Okay, so hear me out. He wanted to get into that vault. It was personal for him. That was obvious from our first meeting. He knew all about this place. He knew how the wards on the building worked. He even knew how the wards on the vault worked, though he pretended not to. He had a full, detailed map of the building and its security. He has been here before, probably a lot."

"Okay," Allen says.

"Yeah, get to the point, Miles."

"The wards on the vault kept confusing me because they didn't seem like they would be a problem. The wards weren't to keep just anyone out. They were intended to keep one specific person or thing out. The wards, as they were designed, would prevent magic from entering the vault, but a person could walk in. A magical creature, on the other hand, couldn't. The only way that changed was if you removed a sigil. Any permutation of removing sigils changed the spell, causing it to, well, basically explode in energy. But it wasn't fire or anything. In fact, the sigils made it sound like solar radiation."

"Is that why I feel like I got the worst sunburn of my life?" Allen asks.

"And I can't see a goddamn thing?" Magdalena asks. She sounds very grumpy.

"Yeah. Whatever they were trying to keep out was harmed, or I am thinking, destroyed by sunlight. Then it occurred to me: The Hierophant was upset that I hadn't disabled the runes. Every time I've met him, it's been in a darkened room. He had a magical shroud of darkness in the back of the delivery truck, and he didn't come out until we got into the sealed garage. Have you ever seen him in daylight, Magdalena?"

"Sure," Magdalena begins, but her voice tapers off, and she falls silent for a few heartbeats. "Actually, no. I had never really thought about it, but he always meets at night or in places with no windows."

"Which isn't really suspicious for someone planning crimes; not really a red flag under the circumstances," I say.

My vision is beginning to return, just a blurry little spec of light at first.

"My vision is coming back," Magdalena says. Soon, her hand is on my elbow, and she's helping me to my feet.

"I can just see a blur," Allen says.

"Me too," I add.

"Your old eyes just can't keep up. My vision is back. He stabbed me good, though. I am losing some blood," Magdalena says.

"There's a first aid kit in my bag," Allen says.

There is some rustling and grunting. I can now see Magdalena and Allen's blurry shapes across the room.

"Shit," Allen says.

"What?" I ask.

"Radio's out," he replies, "There must have been a big EM pulse with the flash of light that shorted everything out."

I try my radio, but it's dead too.

"So, why didn't he have us go in the vault and bring him whatever he wanted? Why all the theatrics?" Magdalena asks.

"Because, like in the movie, whoever has it controls his power. Welles absorbs Von Crupe's vampire powers with it. I think it's metaphorical."

"What movie?" Allen grunts.

"The Lost Sceptre, but never mind that. The point is, he didn't want any of us handling it. He didn't trust us," I say.

My vision is blurry and dark at the edges. Opening my eyes all the way hurts, but if I squint, I can at least move without running into anything.

I looked to where The Hierophant had been standing. His clothing, his radio, and other possessions all lay on the floor, covered in a silt of ash or dust. The dust seems to stir slightly like a breeze is blowing across it, though the air is completely still.

"We need to get into that vault."

"Why?" Allen says.

"He's going to come back. Devora isn't the Lich. The Hierophant is. His Soul Jar, or bottle, or whatever it is...Oh! I bet it is a scepter! It's in the vault, and Devora has been using it to coerce The Hierophant into aiding him. That's why Devora has had such good luck. That's where all the magic is coming from."

"What?" Magdalena says, "That's ridiculous."

"No, the more I say it, the more it makes sense. That's why he called himself The Hierophant but used the reversed card. That card is about freedom. This was about him finding his freedom."

"But if he's been forced to help Devora all this time, why is he trying to break free now?"

"He said it himself. There was a brief window of opportunity provided by the fires. This is the first time he thought he had a chance."

"So why did you break the rune? Why not just let him free?" Magdalena says.

"Cause," Allen drawls, "He wasn't gonna let us leave alive."

"Magdalena, you saw how fast he turned to stabbing you. We were just tools to him. You are lucky he didn't hit your femoral artery. I saw him. He didn't even care. He couldn't use his own blood, probably because he had none. We need to get into that vault, find whatever he was after, and destroy it. If we don't get that soul jar soon, he will come back, and he will be pissed."

"But you don't know that, Miles," Magdalena says, "You have no evidence."

I point to the pile of ashes that seems to be swirling slightly higher in the non-existent breeze.

"Well, shit. I got some bad news," Allen interrupts.

"What?" Magdalena and I ask simultaneously in the same exasperated tone.

"Remember how you said to keep the medallions wet?" Allen asks.

I look down at my amulet. My eyesight has improved tremendously, and I only have a little black circle missing in the middle of my vision. The drop of blood on the amulet is completely dry. Probably, the intense flash of energy dried it out. Dried them all out.

I look over at Magdalena just as we hear a howl reverberate through the house. It's a loud, intense, and absolutely horrifying howl. It creates a sort of sensation you feel in your bowels first as it slowly crawls through your central nervous system to your brain, the sound itself only registering as an afterthought.

"Allen, get that vault open. Magdalena, you and I hold the stairs while he does."

"How long is that going to take?" Magdalena asks.

"Best case, twenty minutes," Allen says, picking up his drill again, "More likely closer to forty."

"Shitake," I say.

"Crimini, you old guys have porcini taste in puns. No morel of those!" Magdalena says flatly.

"Did you just pun-up me?"

"Is this really the time?" Allen shouts testily.

Magdalena grimaces and pulls the handgun out of her holster. I get two super soakers out of my bag, both loaded with Acetobacter Magusficedula.

"We are going to have to make this work," I say, and use the copious amounts of Magdalena's blood on the floor to start inscribing an inclusive circle around the base of the stairs. No sooner have I completed it, than I hear a deafening report from Magdalena's gun as she discharges it toward the top of the stairs.

CHAPTER 19

THE 'HOUND' portion of 'Hell Hound' is probably a misnomer. The nightmare thing at the top of the stairs far more closely resembles a shaved aardvark whose body is covered with rheumy white eyes and tiny human-like mouths. Minuscule, half-formed, misshapen hands and feet bristle out of it like quills on a porcupine wrought from sheer madness. Its long proboscis and each of the horrifying little mouths on its body emit what I can only describe as screaming shadow fire.

I've seen some horrors in my life, but this creature is probably the most weird and terrifying thing I have ever seen. To make matters worse, I can see at least four more crowded in the doorway behind it at the top of the stairs.

The first one leaps forward. It seems unaware and unimpacted by the huge gaping hole that Magdalena put in its torso. It lands heavily at the bottom of the stairs, right in the middle of my inclusive circle. It howls so loudly that the whole room seems to shake. As hoped, it is more magic than matter and becomes trapped in the circle. I scoop a squirt gun off the floor and begin dousing it with Acetobacter Magusficedula. It emits a sound that I can only describe as a growl, but even that doesn't do it justice, as each little mouth on its body emits a sound in unison. However, due to the variations in size and shape, they each have a different pitch and timbre. The result is a cacophonous chorus of nightmare chuffing.

There are more at the top of the stairs. I can't count the total number. Two are crouched in the doorway, ready to pounce. They don't advance, almost as if they are watching, assessing what happens to the trapped one.

Magdalena mutters something I can't quite make out and exchanges clips in her pistol. She sees me looking at her.

"Magic bullets," she says curtly.

"Like the one that took out Lamia?"

"No, I only have one of those left. I am saving it for a special occasion."

She raises her pistol and aims it at a Hell Hound. For a long minute, the only sound is the whining of Allen's drill punctuated by an occasional low rumble from one of the Hellhounds.

I glance back at Allen. He is drilling away, staying completely focused on his work. Most people would break rank at this point, panic, and try to flee. But Allen stays on task. His face is now locked into a grimace of focus, his usual, more jovial expression forgotten. This is not Allen's first time in a tight situation.

Suddenly, I get a familiar sense of déjà vu as Magdalena takes a shot.

I shouldn't be surprised by Magdalena's preternatural accuracy at this point. I know her trick. It is still shocking to see the heads of three Hellhounds implode as Magdalena has improbably taken the shot at an instant they are all lined up. Just her time bending alone couldn't make this shot. An incredible amount of skill and focus must also be required. The three Hellhounds collapse to the ground in a spray of ichor.

"Holy shit," Allen says from behind us. I glance back at him. He's turned now to look. The drilling is momentarily forgotten.

"Time," I remind him. He nods and returns to drilling.

I look back. The remaining Hellhounds at the top of the stairs have retreated out of line of sight. I can still hear their chuffing and growling. The smell of acetone draws my eyes back to the one trapped in the circle. It appears to be slowly melting, like a candle with bits of bone and hamburger suspended in it. While much of the Hell Hound is just phantasm, there are bits of real material in the center, the flesh sacrifices used to summon it. Soon, what's left is a chunky pile stewing in an acetone puddle. I notice with some discomfort that the pool is slowly washing away the magic circle.

"I can't take a shot through the walls," Magdalena says, "It won't penetrate the concrete. They seem to be cowed now, but we are going to be attacked as soon as we clear the stairs. Anybody that comes in to help will get chewed to pieces."

"Didn't you say the same thing that summons them sets off some kinda magical alarm?" Allen yells over his shoulder, almost drowned out by the screeching of his drill.

"Yes, that's right. This is bad. I'm going to see if I can get a radio working again. Magdalena, make sure that none of those things comes down the stairs. Allen, get that vault open."

I take my radio out and fiddle with it. I'm not sure what the magical energy pulse did to it. I disconnect and reconnect the radio's battery and flick it on and off again. Finally, it comes to life, and I hear Genevieve's voice.

"Mi...ddamit, c...you hear...? Come...n. Worl..Anybody?"

"I'm here. Our radios got knocked out."

"Miles...trucks park......house, ar...guards. Evac..ate," Genevieve voice stutters as the encrypted signal breaks up.

"We are pinned down, repeat, pinned down. No exit," I transmit over the radio.

There is a loud clunking behind me, followed by the ceasing of the drills whining.

"I'm through," Allen says, "But I don't know why we are spending time on getting into this vault. We should be spending time on getting out."

"At this point, I think we can use the vault as a more defensible location. Hoping that there is a way out."

"Tell yer gal to text 911 to this number," Allen says, and then he gives me the number.

"Why?"

"Calling in the cavalry might buy us some time to get outta here. Any other intel she can provide on our situation would be good."

"Shit," I say. I remember that Allen had the Knights of Saint George on standby in case things went sideways. I consider it for a long minute. Is that really what we need right now? More feet on the ground? Or is that bodies in the ground? I'm not sure it could get any worse. So, I decide to pass the information along to Genevieve.

"Tell them do not, repeat, do not enter the house. Hellhounds," I complete my message to Genevieve.

"Can you blow the vault and get us in there now? Please?" Magdalena says.

"I'm working on it," Allen drawls back. I'm unsure what he's doing as my eyes are glued tightly on the stairwell.

"Miles, that concoction of yours, will it work if it isn't in a circle?" Magdalena asks.

"Yes, on these Hellhounds, maybe, they are mostly magic. It's faster and more effective in a circle, though. It needs lots of magic to work."

"Cool," she says, grabbing the second squirt gun off the floor. It has a large two-liter tank full of Acetobacter Magusficedula. She throws it up to the top of the stairs and, with a brief whiff of déjà vu, shoots it. It splits and hits the wall, showering liquid down the stairwell and around the corners where the remaining Hellhounds hide.

"That might slow them down, but I don't think it's going to destroy them."

"How long before optimal effect?" She asks.

"I don't know, a minute or two. Or ten? I don't know," I say, frustrated.

"That's about how much time I need to finish this vault door," Allen chimes in.

"Movi...front doo...r..." Genevieve's voice comes in over my radio.

We sit in silence. I can hear the distant sound of people shouting directions, followed by the sounds of Hell Hound claws scrabbling on the floors. Interesting. Could it be that the guards coming in don't have protections against the Hellhounds?

"Cover your ears," Allen says. Magdalena and I cover our ears and duck down, hunching our heads by our knees.

There is a sudden change in air pressure. The sound is not as intense as the palpable physical sensation, like suddenly being shoved to the bottom of a swimming pool. Then it passes. I don't feel well, and my vision is swimming. My heart is racing. I feel sick and dizzy. By the time I stand up, Allen and Magdalena are pulling the vault door open.

CHAPTER 20

I DON'T KNOW what I expected the inside of Devora's vault to look like.

This isn't it.

It isn't a vault at all. The floor is carpeted with a thick, plush pile. Two couches and a handful of seats are arranged around a coffee table in a simple but elegant Norweigan style. Blue, black, and white are the clear color motif. The walls are hung with trophies. Many of them wouldn't be identifiable as trophies except for their mounting. An old corncob pipe, a wooden mask, a broken sword, an antique mason jar filled with some unidentifiable chunky blackish-yellow substance. I can't tell if the contents are solid, liquid, or gas. A small refrigerator stands in the corner.

This is less a vault than a trophy room, a panic room, or both.

Allen tosses all our bags into the vault and steps inside, with Magdalena and I both close on his heels. Allen swings the vault door shut behind us.

"The lock is blown. Can we seal it?" I ask.

Allen glances around the door, "Yeah, it's designed to be barred from the inside."

"So it's not a vault. It's a panic room," I say.

"Weird panic room," Magdalena says.

Allen bars the door behind us and says, "What's the plan now, boss?"

"I'm thinking."

I check the radio, but it doesn't work in here at all.

"We need to find a way out," I say. "Past the guards and the Hellhounds."

"Yeah, I don't know how that's going to happen," Allen says, "We are locked up pretty tight in here."

I hold up a finger for silence and think. It is quiet in here. The vault's thick concrete walls and hardened metal door make this space soundproof.

"There is no way Devora is locking himself in here blind. He's got to have access to the closed-circuit video feed," I say.

Allen nods, and he, Magdalena, and I start poking around. Magdalena opens a set of low cabinets on one wall, revealing a number of flatscreen monitors on pneumatic arms that swing up. She pulls them out and flicks them on. Video feeds come up on some of the monitors, though a surprising number are black.

"There's the parking lot. Goddamit, if that's not a lot of cars," Allen says, indicating many black SUVs on one monitor. Milling about is a group of men in black BDUs with assault rifles ready.

I point to a monitor with a blur of action on it. It is the main foyer, where a number of the hired security are engaged with Hellhounds. The Hellhounds are more horrifying than ever as their flesh slowly peels away and crumbles from the Acetobacter. One security guard is thrust to the ground by two Hellhounds. They begin feeding upon him like starving dogs, only to be torn to ribbons by automatic weapon fire a moment later.

"Your squirt guns worked. I don't think those guards would stand a chance if the Hellhounds weren't already falling apart," Magdalena says with a tone of appreciation in her voice.

"Yeah," I nod, my stomach churning and my head swimming.

I glance at a screen showing the driveway leading up to the front gate. A number of pickup trucks are pulling up. The license plates have been removed, and they are filled with men carrying rifles and wearing balaclavas.

"That was fast. It looks like your cavalry is here," I say with a resigned sigh.

"Shee-it," Allen says, his voice subdued. I think he just realized how bad this situation is.

"There is no way we are getting out of here the way we came in," Magdalena says.

"A guy who has invested this much, gone through this much trouble, isn't going to lock himself in a vault without an exit strategy," I say.

"I wouldn't," Allen says. Magdalena gives a confirming nod.

"There is something we are missing. Keep looking around. Something weird, anything weird."

We all keep looking around. I search the walls with all the various bric-a-brac displayed there. There are no labels or plaques. These are clearly trophies kept as personal memorabilia, each a memory not intended to be shared.

After a few minutes, I hear Allen say, "This is all weird. But I might have found the weirdest."

Magdalena and I head over to where Allen is looking at a piece of art hung on the wall. A sheet of leather has been stretched over a wooden frame. It is about four feet in circumference. Sigils have been drawn all about the perimeter. Looking closer, I see that they aren't drawn. They are tattooed. The ink is inside the skin.

"Human skin," Magdalena says.

I feel ill. I believe that she is correct.

"How do you know?" Allen asks.

"You can tell by the grain and the less pronounced hair follicles."

"It's a spell of some sort, that's for sure. I've seen these sigils before," I say.

"Me too," Magdalena says, "Circe has something like this."

That is where I recognize the sigils from. The Phantasmigoricon.

"It's a portal into the Dreamtime. It just needs blood to activate," I say.

"What the hell are you talking about?" Allen asks, sounding mildly alarmed.

"If we activate this spell and walk through the portal, it will dump us outside reality," I say.

"No," Magdalena says, "Circe used something almost exactly like this. There is another identical one somewhere. They are linked. Once this is activated, you walk through and come out of the identical copy, passing through the outside to get there."

"So it leads into another vault somewhere else, is what you are saying?" Allen inquires.

"Or he might not know what he has here, and the other side might be hung on a wall in a museum. It might be in a sunken ship at the bottom of the ocean. Who knows."

"We have to ask ourselves," I say, "Is staying here less risky?"

"I think we're dead if we stay here," Allen chimes in.

"I agree," Magdalena says.

"So we take our chances with the weird human skin portal spell?" I ask.

The other two nod grimly.

"How much blood are you going to need?" Allen asks.

"A pretty good amount," Magdalena says, looking down at the crudely dressed wound on her leg. Her skin is ashen, and despite her stoicism, she is obviously weak. She's already lost a lot of blood, and clearly, she isn't available as a donor.

I bite my lip, but then something occurs to me.

"You know what? I might have something better than that."

Allen looks relieved, but Magdalena looks very suspicious and confused. I reach into my cooler bag and grab the flask that Jeff gave to me, his blood-free magical catalyst.

"Grab your stuff, get ready to go."

I splatter the catalyst onto the stretched leather wall hanging. At first, it seems like nothing is happening, but then slowly, I see a tiny black pin-prick in the center of the leather. It slowly spreads and grows outward. I have a strange sense of vertigo and a feeling like something inside of me is being tugged at, as if this black whorl before me has a sort of gravity pulling at my very soul. Some atavistic part of my brain knows that I am seeing reality itself tearing apart and responds with barely suppressed panic.

I glance at Allen and can tell he is having the same sensation. His face is contorted with animal terror. On the other hand, Magdalena seems completely unperturbed, but I reflect that this is not her first time doing this.

Soon, a black pool is in the wall before us. It looks just like the gate that the Demoglorbin came through. It is just large enough for a person to climb into. Magdalena hops in without hesitation, vanishing suddenly into the darkness. I usher Allen in. He is more cautious in his approach. He tosses his bags through and then timidly slips a hand in.

"It's cold, and...my hand feels like it's dying," Allen says in all but a whisper.

"The known or the unknown," I say back. He nods, biting his lower lip in a pensive expression.

"Fuck it; you only live once, right?" Allen says, grinning back at me with a forced rictus of a smile. He plunges into the black pool and vanishes.

"If you're lucky," I say, thinking of the shifting pile of dust that was The Hierophant.

I am left standing in the room by myself.

"Hey buddy, are you forgetting something?" Hank's voice comes whispering out of the black portal on the wall.

I start and jump.

"Where did you come from suddenly?" I ask.

"I've been here all along. It's you that left. But again, aren't you forgetting something?"

"Shit," I say. In all of the chaos, I forgot about The Hierophant and his Soul Jar that he was looking for in here. I need to destroy it to make sure that he doesn't come looking for revenge or that Devora can't use his power anymore.

I quickly sweep the room with all of its trophies and content. It could be literally anything, though, and I don't have time to make careful examinations of each object and its aura. I take up the remaining squirt gun full of Acetobacter Magusficedula. Once I am done, I will need to make a hasty exit, so I toss my bags into the inky black portal on the wall.

"That is a solution," Hank's voice whispers at me, with a hard and skeptical emphasis on the 'a'. *"Spray and pray, spray and pray."*

I begin to hose down the room, spraying the trophies and couches. As I spray the monitors, I notice that even more cars have arrived outside the compound, including a line of police cars and black sedans. People are being arrested in the parking lot, and chaos has erupted throughout the compound.

"I'm glad I am not going to be here to see how this plays out," I say as I spray the last drops from the squirt gun. "Hank? What, no witty retort? Hank?"

I turn to face the portal, the origin of Hank's voice. My stomach lurches as I see that it is gone. Just a blank piece of stretched hide hangs on the wall.

The smell of vinegar and acetone has become incredibly strong. My head feels light, my vision swims, and my heart pounds in my chest. I try to walk to the hide to reactivate the portal, but my feet feel leaden. I run into a couch and fall. How did I miss the couch? Probably because it's so dark in here. Why is it so dark in here?

"Oh crap," I murmur as I start to feel myself fall over. I never hit the ground, though, because oblivion comes to envelop me like a merciful blanket.

CHAPTER 21

I'M WARM. All the pains of life are gone. I can hear kind, angelic voices calling to me. I can't see them, but I know they are there, holding me up, embracing me, and taking away my pain. Am I dead? Am I alive? Where am I?

My eyes drift open. I'm sitting in a hospital bed. I've got a catheter in my arm, little electrodes attached to my chest, and a blood oxygen monitor on my finger. I've been awake for a while, but time is hazy, fleeting. I'm not sure how long I have been here. An hour? Two? Five? I can't tell.

My head hurts, especially on the right side. I raise my hand and gingerly feel the bandage there. I must have fallen and hit my head.

A nurse comes in. He wordlessly takes my temperature and jots down some notes on a clipboard.

"When will I see a doctor?"

"The doctor will be with you shortly," he says curtly.

I feel like we have had this conversation a dozen times already, but this is the first time I can remember. I can see the shoulder and arm of someone in a Deputy Sherrif's uniform sitting on a chair outside the door to my room. Some chairs are meant to be sat *in*, I reflect. Big, plush, soft, and pillowy chairs you sit in them. Other chairs, though, are to be sat *on*, like the metal framed, plastic shelf the hospital has for visitors. The Deputy, rigid-backed and square-kneed, is definitely sitting on their chair.

The Deputy seems to be looking intently at their phone and doesn't even glance in my direction. I suspect that is putting a damper on the nurse's conversational spirit. It has certainly deterred me from asking if I can leave.

"Can I get you anything?" The nurse asks me.

"Some coffee would be nice."

"I'm sorry. No coffee, doctor's orders. I can get you some jello or some water. I might be able to dig up an apple juice if you like."

"Water then," I say grumpily.

There is nothing to do in the cramped little room. There is no TV. I am wearing a hospital gown I don't remember getting into. I have no phone. I have nothing.

A few minutes later, the nurse returns with a plastic cup of water. Now, I have one thing: I have a small plastic cup of water. The nurse leaves. A few seconds after that, I have just a small plastic cup. I was a lot thirstier than I realized.

I sigh, set it down, and go back to staring at the ceiling, counting the number of holes in the tiles. I don't feel well. I can't describe exactly how or why I don't feel well. I just don't feel like myself. I'm exhausted but awake, agitated but lethargic, anxious but calm.

At some point, a man in a white lab coat comes in. He has a stethoscope around his neck and an insincere smile on his face.

"Mr. Ward, I'm Doctor Samik," he says, "Do you mind if I ask you a few questions?"

"No, I guess not," I say.

"Do you remember being brought into the Emergency Room today?"

"No, I blacked out and woke up here."

"You have a concussion, and we are going to be keeping you here overnight for observation. Do you remember how you hit your head?"

"No, I don't. I assume it happened when I blacked out and fell."

"Have you ever blacked out like this before?"

"No."

"Do you have any preexisting medical conditions? Epilepsy, diabetes, anything like that?"

"No."

"How often do you consume alcohol?"

"Occasionally," I say, then add, "I know everyone says that. I mean, I'll have a glass of wine if I am out at a fancy dinner on a date or something and a beer on poker night, but that is about it."

He nods and jots something down on his clipboard.

"Do you use drugs recreationally?"

"No."

"Are you on any prescription medications?"

"No."

He furrows his brow.

"I am asking because you seem to be severely hypertensive. Your heart rate and blood pressure are concerningly high. Can you tell me about the events leading up to your blackout?"

"No," I say flatly, looking at the Deputy sitting by the door.

The doctor looks over at the Deputy, nods, and turns back to me.

"I am not interested in legal events. I am simply trying to assess your current state of health so that I can suggest a course of treatment. How has your sleep been?"

I nod and think.

"Not great. I didn't sleep last night. At least, I think it was last night. What day is it?"

"The fourteenth."

I do the math in my head, "Yeah, I didn't sleep last night. Not much the night before, either. I guess I don't get a ton of sleep."

"Do you use caffeine to help stay alert?"

I laugh, "Yeah, I've been known to drink a cup of coffee or two."

"How much coffee do you drink?"

"Um," I say, suddenly feeling very uncomfortable with where this is going, "A lot."

"What is a lot?"

I shrug as I think. "On a regular day, I drink, I dunno. Ten. Fifteen cups."

He raises an eyebrow.

"How much did you drink last night and today if you didn't sleep well?"

"Um..." I stammer, trying to see if I can estimate a number, "More than that. A lot more than that."

"So if a lot is ten or fifteen cups, you drank twenty-five or thirty?"

"Um, yeah, that sounds about right."

"A cup is eight ounces," the doctor begins.

I feel my ears burning, "Okay, so maybe double that."

"Ah." The doctor nods.

"I'd like to have some blood drawn for some tests. I would like to rule out a heart attack. Would you mind that Mr. Ward?"

In my profession, giving blood is something you don't do lightly. It might be one of the reasons I find myself avoiding the doctor so often. Blood has power. The power not only to catalyze magic, but it is also a link to the individual. When someone asks you to give blood freely, you always want to consider it. So, it takes me a moment to agree.

"Sure."

"I can't help but notice you have a pronounced erythema. Why is that?"

"You're erythema looks a little petite and flaccid there, doc!"

I suppress my smirk and look puzzled at the doctor. I have no idea what he is talking about.

"It is a reddening of the skin associated with irritation or injury," he clarifies.

"It's a sunburn."

"Do you regularly spend a lot of time in the sun?"

"No."

"Well, in the future, I would recommend sunscreen if you are going to spend any time outside. That's a pretty bad burn. I will prescribe a topical ointment for you."

"Thanks, doc."

"Lack of sleep, excessive caffeine consumption, sunburn, seems like you just stressed your body out and had a vasovagal syncope. Basically, your vagus nerve, it runs here," he begins to explain, running one hand up his chest.

"I know what a vasovagal syncope is," I interrupt him, "It's a fainting spell."

"Have you had one before?"

"No, but my father used to have them anytime he'd get hurt. Like bumping his knee on a bench or something. Lights out."

"I see," the Doctor says, jotting down more notes on his clipboard. "Is there anything else worth mentioning?"

My first inclination is to say no. Part of me is screaming not to share information with the doctor. On the other hand, if I don't tell him everything, he's not going to be able to help me as much.

"Yeah, there is one more thing. When I passed out, I inhaled a good quantity of acetone fumes."

"Acetone? That alone could cause you to pass out. I'm going to add a few more panels to the blood test to make sure," the doctor says, jotting down notes.

"Can I get my phone?" I ask.

"I'm sorry, I don't have your phone. You will have to ask the officer outside."

I nod.

"Mr. Ward," the doctor says, "I am going to recommend you cut back on the coffee. At your age, the quantity you are drinking can have a lot of bad side effects. In addition to hypertension, it's hard on your stomach and liver. Some studies are indicating a possible linkage with high cholesterol. If you can't eliminate it from your diet, at least consider reducing it."

I stare blankly at him and don't respond. I've stared down ancient Greek monsters, demons made of burning cows, Hell-hounds, vampire assassins, and an ancient undead sorcerer, but this is the most horrifying experience of my life. Stop drinking coffee? I feel like my world is ending.

"All your lab work and my recommendations will be available after you are discharged. I recommend you follow up with your doctor," he pauses and glances at the Deputy outside the door, "Or a doctor within the week."

The doctor turns to leave, and I interrupt him.

"Am I free to leave now?"

The doctor looks at the Deputy sitting outside.

"I don't think so," the Doctor says with a shrug, then slips out the door, pulling the curtain shut behind him.

Time blurs. A nurse comes to draw my blood and take my

temperature again. I count holes in the ceiling tiles. At some point, I fall asleep. I wake up to being poked and prodded for my temperature again. No one really talks to me any longer than they have to. I ask the time here and there. I get some water. I have a little jello and instantly regret it. Even hungry, I don't like jello.

CHAPTER 22

It is late the next morning when, through the curtain in front of my gurney, I can see a silhouette of a man approaching and talking to the Deputy. I make out the phrase "attorney-client privilege" in the hushed conversation. The Deputy moves away from the door, and a figure comes in, closing the door behind them. I can only see their silhouette through the curtain.

"Miles!" An unpleasantly familiar voice says as the curtain slides back.

The smiling, obsequious face of John Hale appears. No matter how fancy his suit is or how expensive his red power tie might be, he will always look like a scumbag to me. He has a briefcase in one hand and in the other a paper cup of coffee from that chain whose name I dare not speak.

"Hale," I grunt, "What the hell are you doing here?"

"I'm your attorney!" He says jovially, "You haven't talked to anyone about yesterday's events, have you?"

"How the hell are you, my attorney?" I ask incredulously.

"Business first. We can get to small talk afterward. This is time-sensitive."

"I didn't hire you. I don't want to work with you."

"Listen, Miles," he says.

"Mr. Ward," I say, more to be ornery than anything.

"Listen, Miles," he continues, "You have two choices. You can work with me and leave here this afternoon a free man. Or you can refuse my services, and you'll be in prison by the end of the week. Not jail; prison, a federal prison to be more specific. In addition to burglary, breaking and entering, and assault, there are at least seven murder charges. There is plenty of evidence and witnesses that will testify against you."

He sits silently to let that sink in. Somehow, if I don't work with him, I get pinned with everything that happened. I could say I wasn't behind it all, that a mysterious man calling himself The Hierophant was. When they ask where to find him, I can only point them to a pile of dust. In order to get witnesses to confirm my testimony, I'd have to find Genevieve, Magdalena, and Allen and drag them into this. All of whom, so far as I know, are in the clear. I have no idea what happened to Howard or Elizabeth Barnes, but neither have any reason to support me and lacking another scapegoat, I make the perfect one.

I don't know how I got out of the vault, but I assume the authorities found me there. That's a pretty damning bit of evidence. There is a lot I don't know, but it's difficult to imagine that filling in the blanks will make it look any better for me.

"You haven't talked to anyone about the details of yesterday's events," Hale repeats. I cannot tell if it is a question or a statement.

"No, the Deputy has stayed outside the whole time."

"Good, that's very good. I advised them that you wouldn't speak to anyone without your attorney present."

"How can you get me to walk free?" I ask.

"I have this affidavit signed by Jim Devora, certifying that he hired you as an independent security consultant to prevent theft and incursion into his Napa property and that you were incapacitated there while performing that function."

"And if I don't comply..."

"Then I have a very hungry paper shredder."

"I see. But then, you pretty much own me."

"Well, not me, personally, but my boss does," Hale says with a mysterious smile.

"And who is your boss?"

"I can't tell you that, of course. But let's say that the world is a giant chessboard, and you and I are just pawns."

"You're just a pawn?" I ask. It seems out of character for him to put himself at that level.

"At least we are on the board," he says, "I am a pawn placed to get to the other side and become a queen."

"And I'm a sacrificial one," I observe.

"Possibly," he says with a shrug.

"So, your boss is, what, the King?"

He laughs. It's a deep, hearty laugh, authentically amused.

"No! The boss is one of the chess players, the one that is winning."

"So, who was Redbrook?" I ask. As oblique as this metaphor is, I am actually getting some answers out of it.

He shrugs, "I don't know, maybe a rook."

"How do the Hizarin work into this metaphor?"

"I don't know, Miles, it's not a perfect metaphor. My point is that there are bigger things at play here. The game goes on with or without you. Your choice here is to be on the board or get taken off. I prefer you stay on. But ultimately, that's your choice."

I sigh and lay back on my gurney.

"Can I think about it?"

"Take as much time as you need. So long as," he pulls his sleeve up and looks at his Rolex, "the time you need is less than thirty-seven minutes. I have to get some things filed, or they are going to transfer you to a 'more secure location' once the doctor gives you a clean bill of health."

"How do you know that will take thirty-seven minutes?"

"Everyone has their price, Miles," he says with a suddenly serious look, "You should probably figure out what yours is while there is still someone willing to pay it."

Right and wrong are two ideas that we have firmly fixed in our heads. Few people, maybe no one, choose wrong for the sake of doing wrong. There are always mitigating circumstances.

For example, letting Hale bail me out of this one is wrong because I will forever be under his and his mysterious overlord's thumbs. I'd spend my entire life knowing that at any moment, they could get me whisked away to jail. He's suggesting keeping me out of court, meaning I'd never be tried; therefore, if new evidence came to light, I could still be tried. The double jeopardy principle wouldn't protect me.

On the other hand, knowing that Hale is representing Devora and has specifically prepared this as a binary choice for me, I know that any evidence that comes up, should I be tried, would be damning. Hell, he's probably got evidence of every misstep I've taken in my life. Spun the wrong way, the last few months could be made to look very, very bad for me. I would certainly go to prison for that list of crimes, and it's unlikely that I'd ever see the light of day again.

These are mitigating circumstances; It doesn't even seem like a choice. Once I go to prison, I think that's it for me. I have no opportunities to correct the situation. But under Hale's thumb, at least I have opportunities to find a way out.

"Okay, fine, you win."

"It was never a game, Miles. I know you have doubts, but you are making the right decision," Hale says with a sudden note of tender sincerity. I'd think it was genuine concern if it were anyone else but Hale.

He pulls out a bunch of paperwork and a pen and lays them on the little rolling table next to my gurney. He rolls it over my lap and hands me the pen.

"You are going to need to sign a little paperwork."

It's not 'a little' paperwork. It's not some paperwork. It's a lot of paperwork. There are non-disclosure clauses, contracts, and other legal documents, and I do not know what I am signing. I thoroughly read what I am signing in the beginning, but by the end, I don't care if they get my firstborn child. I want to finish with the signing and get out of here.

Once I am all done, Hale packs everything into his briefcase and vanishes.

"I'll be in touch," is the last thing he says before bustling out past the curtain.

True to his word, thirty-seven minutes later, I am walking out of the hospital without a law enforcement official to be seen.

This magic of Hale's might be the most terrifying magic of all.

CHAPTER 23

I'M STANDING in the parking lot of the emergency room at the Queen of the Valley, our local hospital. I have no phone or wallet; I don't know if I lost those at Devoras; maybe I left those in my rental car with Genevieve; the last few days are so hazy. I am exhausted, shaken, and miles away from home with no money or way to contact anyone. I don't even have keys to get into my apartment if I did make it all the way there.

I have no idea if anyone knows where I am or how much Genevieve stuck around for. Did Howard and Elizabeth get away before everything went wrong? Where the hell did Magdalena and Allen end up? I walk a hundred feet across the parking lot to Trancas and sit on the curb to think.

I slept a little in the Emergency Room, but it wasn't restful sleep. I'm exhausted, and the world seems surreal and crystal clear, but I can only focus on one thing at a time. The drone of cars driving by is hypnotic, and I zone out, staring at the aged sign of the steak house across the street.

"Miles?" I am broken out of my reverie by a familiar voice, and I snap to attention. A minivan has double-parked in front of me. One of my poker night buddies, Mike, is in the driver's seat. I can see his wife, Barbara, in the passenger seat, and his two kids are in the back.

"Mike!" I say, "I am so happy to see a familiar face."

I look down at my clothes. They are stained with dirt, blood, and god knows what else. They have a weird, funky smell and fit stiffly. My hand drifts to the side of my head where a bandage still covers the stitched-up cut I got when I passed out.

"What happened to you?" Mike says. Though, it seems more like a formality than an actual question.

"I just got out of the ER. I hit my head pretty badly. I lost my phone, my wallet, and my keys. I feel lost."

Mike sighs. "Hop in."

The back door to the minivan opens of its own accord, and I push myself to my feet. Standing hurts more than I think it should.

"Thanks," I say as I climb in. I have to clamber over one kid's booster seat and squeeze between it and the bulky car seat on the other side. I am comedically squished between the two. I see a mountain of groceries in the back that would prevent the third row from being raised.

"Hi," I say, looking at each of the kids. I can't remember either of their names. I've only interacted with them maybe once ever.

"Where to?"

"I don't know," I say. "Could I borrow your phone? I don't have mine or my keys, and I can't get into my apartment."

Barbara murmurs something to him. It's one of those couple speak things that aren't words, but he understands what she's getting at. He grunts in reply and then says over his shoulder, "You can come back to our place. We'll get you a cup of coffee and something to eat, and you can use the phone. How does that sound?"

"It sounds great, thank you," I say, but after a moment's thought, I add, "Though I am going to have to pass on the coffee... doctor's orders."

Mike looks at me incredulously, as if he's trying to determine whether I am some alien doppelganger imitating Miles.

"Yeah, I know. It's been a bad day," I say miserably.

The two kids, whose names I loosely interpret based on contextual cues are Anthony and Sydney, stare at me for the whole ride to Mike's place.

At one point, Anthony, the older of the two, complains, "Daddy, he smells like a dead cat."

"Honey, that's very rude. We don't talk about people like that," Barbara lightly scolds.

"Even if it's true," Mike pipes in.

"Mr. Miles is having a rough day," Barbara says, glowering at Mike.

We get to Mike's house, and he guides me to a phone on the wall in the kitchen. I didn't know people still had landlines. I sit with the phone and try to think of who to call. The problem isn't that I don't know whom to call. I should call Genevieve, but I don't know her number off the top of my head. It's programmed into my phone, and I've only dialed it once. The only number I can think of off the top of my head is my childhood phone number, but nobody I know would answer that anymore.

I'm still staring blankly at the phone when Barbara brings me an egg salad sandwich and a glass of orange juice. I can hear in the next room that Mike is settling the kids down to a cartoon about talking dogs with Australian accents.

"Are you okay?" Barbara asks.

"Yeah, I just don't know any phone numbers anymore. My phone remembers them all for me. Without it, I'm lost."

She nods knowingly.

"Do you want a shower? Can I get you some clean clothes? I'm sure Mike has something that will fit."

Mike comes in from the other room. He's quite a bit shorter than me but pretty stocky, so anything that does fit probably won't fit well.

"My brother left some clothes here last time he visited. They are in the guest room, and they will probably fit."

Barbara slips off to find those clothes.

"Miles, I can tell you've been through hell. Does this have anything to do with why you missed Jeff's party and all that stuff that happened Up Valley?"

I forgot about Jeff's party. I don't want to say yes, and I don't want to lie, so I stay quiet and avoid eye contact.

"Let me rephrase," he says, "I mean, I know this has to do with what happened Up Valley and why you missed Jeff's. What I really mean is: is having you here a danger to my family, Miles?"

I shake my head no.

We sit there silently for a moment.

"I know you say that if I am going to be a friend, I can't just call about the weird stuff. I'm sorry that I ended up falling in your lap like this. Thank you. I know you could have driven on by."

He grunts, "Thank Barb."

Barbara returns with some clothes and a towel as if summoned by her name. A few minutes later, bathed and wearing a clean pair of cut-off jean shorts and a t-shirt for a music festival that I've never heard of, I return to their kitchen and finish my orange juice.

"I'm pretty sure your brother is just using your house to dump unwanted clothes," I say as I come out.

"Yeah, probably," Mike says.

"Can you get me the number for Grape Reads? I am going to call Emily there. She should have Genevieve's number."

Mike obliges, and I call Grape Reads. Emily isn't there, but Ren gives me her number, and within a couple of minutes, I am calling her.

"Um, hello?" Emily asks.

"Hi, Emily, it's Miles."

"Miles, Oh, thank goodness, Genevieve is here. We've been worried sick! Where have you been."

I am about to answer but am interrupted when I hear her clarifying away from the phone, "It's Miles!"

"I've been in the hospital."

"May I talk to him?" I can hear Genevieve ask in the background.

"Yeah, he's in the hospital," Emily says, and then more loudly, "Miles, Genevieve wants to talk to you."

"Hi, Miles," Genevieve says into the phone before I can get a word in, "Are you okay? You are in the hospital? What happened? No, don't tell me over the phone. I'll come pick you up. When do you get discharged?"

"Calm down, I am not in the hospital anymore. I'm at Mike's house. I got discharged this morning."

"Are you safe? Are you hurt? Were you arrested?"

"I'm safe. I had a little concussion, but I've been released. No, I'm not arrested. Well, not anymore, but that's a story for later. I just want to get home and get some rest."

Mike is trying to pretend he isn't listening, but I can see him give me a sharp look when I say the part about getting arrested.

"Okay, we will come right over and pick you up," Genevieve

says, then I can hear her say away from the phone, "We can go pick Miles up, right? He's at Mike's house. Mike's house, right? Who the hell is Mike?"

"Relax. Everything is fine for now. Put Emily on. I think she should drive. She sounds a little calmer than you."

"Of course, she's calmer than me!" Genevieve raises her voice a little, "She wasn't sitting on that goddamn hill watching a fucking war movie!"

Soon, I am talking to Emily and giving her Mike's address. We get off the phone quickly. Mike and I sit in his dining room in silence.

I've never really been in Mike's house before. It's a pretty non-descript ranch, probably built in the seventies. It's boxy and utilitarian. Clean but cluttered with toys and bottles and the other paraphernalia and bric-a-brac that seem to come with having young children. The kitchen has a faded yellow wallpaper, an old-fashioned button phone on the wall, and a small electric stove. The only thing that has been updated is the very modern refrigerator, an imposing glass and chrome deal with six kinds of hot and cold water in the door.

"Thank you, Mike," I say blearily.

"Yeah. You're welcome."

"About all the arrest stuff..." I begin.

"I don't want to know Miles."

We sit for another minute in silence. I want to make small talk, but I can't think of anything to say that doesn't have to do with the insanity of the last few days.

"See you for poker Thursday?" I ask.

"Will I?" Mike says skeptically. He makes a good point. I have no idea what's going on.

"Actually, I don't know. I'll try," I say weakly.

He only nods.

Barbara comes quietly in from the other room, holding a plastic bag in her hand.

"I couldn't help but overhear. You have someone coming to pick you up?" She says.

"Yeah."

"I put your clothes into a prewash. Maybe the stains won't set," she says in a hushed tone.

"Not much of it is my blood," I say. As soon as I say it, I regret it. It was a weird thing to say. In my mind, it was a reassuring thought, but when I said it aloud, it sounded wrong.

"Oh," Barbara says, "Well, I am glad to hear that then."

"I mean, I didn't hurt anybody, but a friend of mine got stabbed. Nobody died," but then I realize that isn't true, "Well, I mean, the blood isn't from anyone that died."

"You can stop now, Miles," Mike says. I can tell he's trying to be gentle and understanding about it, but his voice has an edge. Barbara is having a difficult time hiding her shocked expression.

"Sorry," I mewl, "Thank you for helping with my clothes, and thank your brother for the loaners. I will get them back to you."

"No need," Mike says.

"Oh. Okay. I will just go wait outside."

Mike walks outside with me, and we stand in silence on the curb. It's only a few minutes before Emily and Genevieve arrive. They jump out of Emily's car and run over to me. Genevieve gives me a big hug and a kiss on the cheek. When she's done, Emily gives me a smaller, more reserved hug. No kiss on the cheek, though. That would be awkward.

I introduce Mike and Barbara to Genevieve. It is quick, and curt, and immensely awkward.

I thank Mike and Barbara once again and get into the back seat of Emily's car.

No sooner have we turned the corner than Genevieve turns over the seat and demands, "What the hell happened? Where is everyone else? Magdalena, The Wheel, The Hermit? The Hierophant?"

"It got...complicated," I say. I give a meaningful look at Emily.

"Oh," Genevieve says, "Don't worry, I already freaked out and told her everything."

"Ah," I say.

I am tired, and my body hurts all over. I want to eat something and sleep. I do my bleary, foggy-brained best to explain everything that has happened since I saw her last.

"So the Hierophant is a djinni?" She asks.

"I don't know if he's a djinni, exactly. I think he was more a Lich, a sorcerer who made himself immortal by binding his soul to an object, than a spirit from Arabic mythology. Though, I'm pretty sure Devora was treating him like a Djinni in a fairy tale, forcing The Hierophant to do things with the Soul Jar. Was the Hierophant a person? An undead? I don't know, but getting a sunburn turned him to dust."

Genevieve nods and then tells me her side of the tale.

"From where I was standing, everything was going according to plan. I talked to you for a bit, then lost contact. Then, the shipping van drove off. I hadn't heard anything on the radio, so I thought maybe you got the job done ahead of schedule."

"The World left before things started going sideways?"

"Yeah, and she left in a hurry. Then, immediately afterward, these black SUVs pulled up, and guys in riot gear got out. They charged into the house."

Did Elizabeth Barnes sell us out to Devora?

She pauses for a breath, "Then pickups arrived, and there was shooting. That was when all hell broke loose: police arrived and black sedans. It was like a warzone for a few minutes. I got you back on the radio for a minute, then nothing. I decided it was time to get out of there, so I went back to your place. I sat up all night. When you hadn't returned this morning, I freaked out and went to Emily's. She's the only person I could think of who I could talk to about this."

We pull up into the parking lot in front of my apartment building.

"I'd love to talk about this more," I say, "but I just want to sleep. I can barely remember my own name."

Genevieve nods, and we get out. She thanks Emily profusely and promises to call her tomorrow.

"I'm glad you are alive, Miles," Emily says before driving away.

Genevieve walks me upstairs to my apartment. I stagger straight to my bed and fall asleep face down, still wearing Mike's brother's cutoff shorts and festival t-shirt.

CHAPTER 24

It is late in the morning when I get up. By my standards, very late. I'm still sore, and my skin is beginning to peel from the burn I got from whatever radiation we were bathed in. I get up and shower, and when I come out of the bathroom, Genevieve has a cup of coffee waiting for me. I am bleary-eyed and tired, and I've taken a big chug before I remember the doctor's recommendation.

"The doctor said I should cut back on the coffee," I say, putting the coffee back down on the counter.

"Cut back or cut out?" She asks quizzically.

"Cut out, but if I couldn't manage that, cut back. I was thinking I'd at least talk to my doctor before I started drinking coffee again."

"Do you have a doctor?" She asks skeptically.

"Okay, I need to get a doctor and talk to them before I start drinking coffee again."

"That is going to be hard."

I nod, sit on the corner of my bed, and stare, lost in thought.

"Do you want me to cook you some eggs or something?"

"Um, yeah, that would be great. Thank you," I mutter. Do I have eggs? She must have gone shopping while I was in the hospital.

She leaves. I find my mind wandering, thinking about everything that has happened over the past few days and wondering how everything went so very, very wrong. Genevieve returns in what seems like seconds later, but it must be at least five or ten minutes. She has a plate of eggs with a couple of slices of toast. I take it gratefully and start wolfing it down.

"How are you doing?" She says softly.

"My head hurts. Well, everything kind of hurts, but it's better than yesterday," I say between mouthfuls.

"No, I mean, you know, after Saturday, how are you doing? That was...I was watching from the hilltop, which was traumatic for me. You were right in the middle of it, and it sounds, well, insanity-inducing."

I shrug and think while I chew my last mouthful of egg.

"Honestly, and this is probably not a healthy thing to admit, but honestly, it's getting routine."

She nods. She seems more shaken than me. Apparently, even Genevieve 'Adrenaline' Gale has her limits.

Our conversation is cut off by the doorbell ringing.

"I'll get it," she says, jumping up before I can move.

She comes back a moment later with a cardboard box. It has the World Wide Shipping logo on the side.

"It's a package for you. I had to sign for it," she says.

"Why did you rush to the door like that?" I ask. She seemed jumpy and frantic.

"I didn't want to tell you," she says, "but there's been people loitering outside looking to get a photo. What happened made national news. Devora is a public figure. I guess this was always going to make national news, but your name is now part of it."

I stiffen.

"What?"

"Devora's house was the location of a massacre: private security, an armed mob, wild animals, police, federal agents, and a gang of armed kidnappers. What did you think was going to happen? And you, you're like the hero, maybe that's the wrong word, you're the guy they are saying single-handedly saved Devora's life and thwarted his kidnapping."

"Is that what they are saying happened?" I ask incredulously.

She nods and pushes the package into my hands.

I stare down at it. It is addressed to me. It has my address as the return, but the name on the return address is just "HP." I carefully examine the whole box and notice the stamp says it was picked up last Thursday in Napa. I look at Genevieve, and she shrugs.

"This was mailed before we went to Devora's."

I consider putting the box down and saving it till later. After a moment, I decide I want to get everything associated with this last week behind me as quickly as possible. I carefully open the box. It is filled with shredded paper, and a smaller cardboard box is in the middle of the paper. It is about four inches wide, six inches tall, and maybe an inch and a half thick. "For The Magician" is written on the box with ballpoint pen in a neat, practiced script.

I take the small box and open the top. Before I see its contents, I have a good idea of what it will contain. It is a deck of large cards. Each card is hand-drawn and colored. The artist is very talented. It is a tarot deck. All the cards are customized.

The minor arcana cards are all the usual, but each major arcana is clearly inspired by the events of the last week.

They are not in an immediately recognizable order, so I surmise that the order is intended to tell me a story. I preserve the order of the stack of cards and move it to my desk.

"Genevieve, if you wouldn't mind, I want to photograph the order of these cards," I say, "I think these are supposed to tell us something."

She nods and has already produced her phone to do so. It makes me wonder where my phone is, but I decide to ask later.

We sit down at the desk and go through the cards. Many of the cards have repeats, so I conclude it is intended to be done in multiple readings. I start with a standard cross and rod spread of ten cards. There are fifty cards in the box. This would make for five ten-card readings.

"One for each day of the caper," I say as I place them in ten card sets in order.

"How do you know how to do this?" Genevieve asks.

"My dad was into all this crap. He used to do readings as a side hustle."

The whole process is about interpreting symbols and commonly accepted archetypes of the tarot. But even with the potential vagueness there, it is easy to identify each day's events. When it is all done, I sit staring at the last ten cards. My eyes are focused on one in particular, my head pounds, and my heart races.

It is the tower, but it's not so much the reading that has my attention but the art itself. The tower in this card is a familiar, tall, black structure. It looks much like the Syzmek building but is all black—The Donjon. Lightning is striking it, and there is a figure falling from it. The figure is clearly intended to be me. Down below at the base is another figure, arms outstretched to catch the plummetting man. The figure at the bottom is also intended to be me.

"What's this message supposed to mean?" Genevieve asks over my shoulder.

"It's one reading for each day since we met The Hierophant. At first, I thought that was Tuesday through Saturday, but I think it's actually Wednesday through Saturday and then a reading afterward."

"So this one," she points at the penultimate cross of cards, "Is Saturday. I don't really know this stuff, but is he predicting his own death here?"

She points at the Hierophant and Death cards in the mix.

"The cards' meanings are intentionally myriad and vague. They are really a vehicle for storytelling. The reader gets a reaction from the cards. They customize their story based on what the reader wants the audience to hear or thinks the audience wants to hear. So, there are a lot of potential interpretations of the cards. However, my interpretation is that, yes, it's saying he dies."

"How could he know that?"

"Oh," I say, "That's not magic."

She looks baffled at me.

"It's more like one of those 'if you are reading this, then I am already dead' letters. Because I think he intended to kill me, kill us all, at the end of the job. So, I think this was sort of like a plan B. The only way I was getting to see this was if he didn't make it."

"Oh," she says, "Then can you trust it?"

"I don't know."

We look over the cards in silence.

"I notice that," Genevieve says, pointing at the Fool card, which does not have Magdalena on it, but instead, there is one version of me standing at one end of a bridge while another me falls off the bridge, "there is someone that looks a lot like you depicted twice on most of the cards."

I point to a couple of tiny figures in the corners of other cards, "All the cards, I think. Yeah, he clearly knew something that I don't know."

"How do you figure?"

"Because some of the drawings are referring to things that either few other people know or no one else knows about my life."

"No one else?"

I shake my head no, "Nobody living. It's a message that only I can understand."

"That's weird. What does it say?"

"I think it's saying that if I want answers to the questions I haven't asked, I have to return to where it all started. I have to go home."

"Cryptic," she murmurs.

I feel ill looking at the cards. I feel lost and out of control. It's weird to say, but this message from a dead man has shaken me. I'm not even sure if the Hierophant is dead. Or a human.

"Well," Genevieve observes, "It couldn't hurt to get out of town for a bit."

"Yeah."

I carefully pack the weird custom tarot deck into its bland, brown cardboard box and put it on my desk. We sit silently for a moment. My head is pounding. My skin burns and itches. I feel sick and miserable.

"Where is my phone?" I ask.

"Oh!" She says insanely loud, and I wince with her exclamation, "I left it in the rental car. I'll go get it."

She slips out the door, and I sit at my desk, staring at the wall. She comes back a minute later with my phone. I stare at its blank black screen. The battery is dead, so I plug it back in.

Once it's charging, I turn it back on, and after waiting an eternity for the load screen, it comes back to life.

I have a lot of missed calls and messages. There are too many to go through, so I look at the names and numbers. Many are from Genevieve, some from the last day are from unknown numbers, and a few are from other friends.

"Sorry," Genevieve says, "I was kind of panicked and forgot I had your phone with me."

A number with an international dialing code, my phone says it's from France, is mixed in among my missed calls, so I check the voicemail from that number. It's Magdalena.

"Hi, Miles. I'm in France, which is less fun because Allen is with me. I am working on getting us home, but it might be a few days. Or weeks. It's been difficult trying to get papers for Allen," she groans after she says this, and I can see her eye-roll in my mind. Did you know that Jim Devora has a lovely villa in Rhone? Quite a collection of antiquities there, too, might I add."

"Howdy, Miles!" I can hear Allen drawl in the background.

"Anyway, if you could pick my car up, that would be great. The code is 33839547186. A spare key is in a magnetic box under the passenger's side dash."

I can hear Allen having an argument in the background with a third voice. It sounds like he is speaking Spanish, which confuses me. Magdalena stops, barks at the pair in French, and then says, "For the like, hundredth time, Allen, he doesn't speak Spanish!"

Magdalena groans loudly in frustration.

"What a dick," Magdalena continues into the phone, "As I was saying, get my car so it doesn't get towed. But you can keep it. I owe you a car anyway. Strangle you soon! Byeee!"

I put my phone down. "Well, apparently, Magdalena and

Allen got out okay but are stuck in France, I guess. We should go get Magdalena's car."

"What about Allen's truck? I could hot-wire it."

I look at her askance. I'm always surprised by the criminal skills this woman has.

"How would we get there and get three cars back?"

"We could ask Emily to drive us."

I shrug, "Why the hell not."

CHAPTER 25

I AM surprised at how willing Emily is to drive us to the rendevous point where Magdalena and Allen's vehicles are parked. Once we get going, however, some of her interest becomes clear. She absolutely grills me about Devora's magical security details: Hellhounds, The Hierophant, the magic portal; she interrogates me like a cheeky detective on a cop show. I do my best to tell her, but my brain is foggy, and it's hard to concentrate as my head pounds worse with every passing minute. I feel shaky and sweaty, like I've got the flu.

By the time we arrive at the cars, I have an epiphany.

"Can you get withdrawal symptoms from quitting caffeine?"

"Absolutely," Emily says.

"Yeah," Genevieve agrees, "If you consume enough, which you do."

"Like sweats, body aches, headache kind of withdrawal?"

"Yeah, if your body is used to enough of it, it can be like withdrawal from hard drugs," Emily says.

"How did I not know this?"

Emily shrugs, "Wait, did you stop drinking coffee?"

"Doctor's orders," Genevieve says.

"Oh, you poor thing," Emily says. She mostly seems sincere, but there is a hint of irony to it.

"I feel like I am dying," I say. I do. I can't remember when I felt so sick.

"Are you sure you aren't just getting sick?" Genevieve asks.

"Yes."

"How?"

"Because this little voice in my brain says that all I have to do is drink a cup of coffee, and it will all be better, and somehow I know it is right. I just want a cup of coffee."

"Just one cup, Miles, and everything gets better."

"I don't need to be ganged up on by voices," I quietly growl.

"Okay...are you going to be okay to drive?" Emily asks.

"Yeah, I think so. Maybe. Yeah."

"Encouraging," Genevieve mutters.

When we arrive at the turnout where we met before the heist, Magdalena's little sports car is next to Allen's truck. Both have tickets stuck to the front windows. There is an SUV parked on the other side of the turnout from them with no ticket. Hikers, probably.

I enter the code that Magdalena left me in the voicemail, and the car opens. I find the hidden key that Magdalena mentioned in her message. I quickly put it in the ignition and turn, and the car purrs to life. I look around the interior. I reflect on every terrifying hour I spent in this car on the way to Portland. I look at the passenger side safety handle and wonder how my hand didn't squeeze a permanent imprint into it.

"Oh, what horrible times we've had together," I say.

I turn the car off and get out. Genevieve has already made her way into Allen's truck and is in the process of hot-wiring it.

"It's a good thing it's a little older," she says, "I wouldn't know how to do this on a new truck."

"How'd you learn to do that?" Emily asks.

"What can I say? I like the bad boys," Genevieve says with a grin at me.

"So, how'd you end up with him?"

I grunt at the disembodied voice in my ear but don't say anything. Allen's truck engine suddenly roars into operation.

"Let's go. Meet back at Miles's apartment?"

Emily gives the thumbs up and jumps back into her little hybrid. I climb back into the sports car. A few minutes later, we are driving in a caravan back on the road.

Magdalena's sports car wants to go fast. It's almost as if it has its own spirit that possesses me once we get out on the highway. Before I know it, I can't see Genevieve or Emily in the rearview mirror. I get back into town and notice I am parking in front of Soothsayers. I didn't intend to drive here. Again, it's almost like the car was possessing me.

"I'll just get a hot chocolate and a scone," I tell myself. It really is my intention, but once I smell that roasted, nutty goodness, I can't help myself, and I order a latte. Just one won't hurt. I don't want to get crumbs all over Magdalena's car, so I sit at a table in Soothsayer, drink my latte, and eat my scone. I'm definitely not avoiding letting Genevieve scold me for drinking coffee against the doctor's orders.

"Liar."

My phone rings, and I see that it is Genevieve. I ignore it and drink my coffee.

"You are acting like a junkie, you know that?"

"What do you know?" I mutter into my coffee.

It is uncanny; my head still hurts, and my skin is still sensitive, but it's already better. I haven't even finished my first cup yet, but I can tell I'll feel all right soon. I take a nibble of the scone, and it no longer hurts to swallow. I sigh and lean back in my chair, feeling more at ease than I have in days.

"You were right!" Genevieve's voice says from the front door. I glance over. Genevieve has come in, with Emily at her heels.

"Where else would he be?"

They stand beside me and tower over me, arms crossed in disapproval.

"You don't know what it was like," I mewl, holding my hand out. "See, I've stopped shaking already."

Genevieve shakes her head.

"Maybe cold turkey was a bad idea," Emily says from behind my other shoulder.

"Bring the coffee, and let's go," Genevieve says, looking around the room. There are a couple of people staring at us.

She takes my elbow and guides me gently outside.

"Your face has been all over the news, Miles. You should probably lay low for a while," Genevieve murmurs to me once we are on the sidewalk.

"Maybe get out of town," Emily adds.

"I am heading to Atlanta tomorrow. You should come with me," Genevieve offers.

"What would I do while you are at a conference in Atlanta?"

"Well, I have a nice room. You could sit by the pool, have a mint julep, or whatever. Go see a movie, you know, take it easy."

She looks me up and down.

"A break and some rest would do you good, Miles," Emily chimes in.

"Hotlanta! Here we come!"

"Can I leave Hank at home?" I ask.

"Would you normally take your mannequin with us?" Genevieve asks skeptically.

Emily quirks an eyebrow but doesn't say anything.

"No, no. Nevermind."

"Well, let's get home and pack and see if we can't get you a plane ticket," Genevieve says.

We thank Emily profusely for her help and then head back to the apartment. I park Magdalena's car in her spot, and Genevieve parks Allen's truck on the street nearby.

I didn't really agree to go, but regardless, it seems I am going to Atlanta.

CHAPTER 26

"I HAVE a mixer to go to in an hour. I was hoping to get up to the room and take a quick shower beforehand," Genevieve says.

"Sounds like a plan. I might take a nap," I say. The flight from San Francisco to Atlanta was a harrowing ride of turbulence and squalling children. I can't remember being more tense.

"Oh," Genevieve says, sounding disappointed, "I was hoping you'd come to the mixer and be my arm candy. You are too handsome to leave in a hotel room."

Ambivalence takes me. On the one hand, I don't want to disappoint her, but on the other hand, I don't really want to come. The entire pretense that brought me along was that I would take it easy, rest, and keep my head low.

"Oh," I concede, "Okay, flattery will get you everywhere."

I smile, but it feels forced and fake.

We get to the front of the hotel check-in line. While Genevieve gives her name and details to the clerk at the front desk, I take the opportunity to scan the lobby. This is a huge hotel and conference center in downtown. Like all such hotels, it could be in any city in almost any country and the only tip-off as to which one would be the language the signs were in.

The lobby is crowded with people bustling about, some with huge carts of bags, others with a single carry-on bag. They are arriving, departing, and loitering everywhere. Some are sober, but most are not. I like people but not crowds, and this lobby gives me some anxiety.

I notice two men about twenty feet away who keep looking at me. They are both wearing slacks and collared shirts, one blue and the other dark pink. They are having a conversation and referring back and forth to one of the men's phones. They glance at me, look down at the phone, glance at me, and exchange words before looking back at the phone. They look up from the phone to find me staring back at them, and they both quickly drop their gazes and mill about awkwardly.

I guess that is the price for having my face plastered all over the national news. Somehow, my participation in trying to steal from Jim Devora has turned into me being the 'savior' who stopped an 'armed kidnapping attempt.' This might not be so bad if Devora weren't a known rapist with the most despicable and villainous of reputations. But he is, and so I am a hero to the sleaziest category of incel-bros, and everyone else who recognizes me thinks I'm also a sleaze. I want to run up to everyone who looks at me and scream, "I was trying to steal from him!" But I don't know that this would actually help my cause.

Soon, Genevieve has room keys, and we start toward the elevators.

"Can we maybe do that thing where we go a couple of floors above our floor, then take the stairs back down?" I ask. I am feeling paranoid that someone will follow us to our room and harass us.

"Um," Genevieve says, "Sure, I guess. Are you okay?"

"I just feel like everyone is staring at me."

"You are being paranoid. That's yesterday's news. The world moves fast."

"Maybe."

"Fine, we will take the 'duck-the-paparazzi' route."

"Thank you."

We take the elevator to the eleventh floor, then wind our way down the staircase to the ninth. I am fascinated that the staircases almost always look the same, whether you are in a moderate, no-frills hotel or a fancy upscale one like this. The stairwells are always basically the same. A big, clanky steel frame in a giant, echoing concrete shaft. No carpet, just slip-proof tiling on steel stairs. There is something about it. It makes me feel like I've just walked off the set and behind the scenes. Like I am getting the back-lot tour of the hotel. It's always quiet, lonely, and empty; you could get murdered in one of these stairwells, and there would be no one to hear you scream.

My nobody-in-the-stairwell theory is blown apart when we turn the corner onto the ninth floor and interrupt a man and a woman in the middle of something. Both of their clothes are disheveled, and the woman's lipstick is smeared. However, when we turn the corner, they seem to be vaping.

"Good evenin'," the man slurs at us. He's clearly pretty intoxicated. The woman lets out a drunken giggle.

"Hi," I say curtly.

"Evening," Genevieve replies, "How's the wife, Will?"

"Genny! Is that you?" He says drunkenly.

"You know this guy?" I whisper to her.

"Works in the industry. He's at all these things," Genevieve whispers back.

"How's things, Will?" Genevieve turns back to the man.

I take a closer look at him. He's probably in his early thirties, with a dark, bushy beard and glasses. He's wearing a nondescript shirt and slacks, with wingtip shoes. His companion is a young Asian woman in a blue dress and heels. Her black hair hangs down to her lower back. I'd guess she is in her twenties.

"Things are great, things are always great. I signed on with the SyzmekZinnergy team," Will says.

"Going to the dark side, are we?" Genevieve says, her voice is mirthful, but I can tell she isn't amused.

Will laughs too loud and too long; finally, he stops and stares at me. He sways drunkenly, and when he starts to speak, he stabs a finger in my direction to emphasize his sentences.

"Who's your friend? He looks familiar." Will says a little too aggressively for my tastes.

"Who's your friend? She looks familiar," Genevieve retorts, eyebrows both raised in a suggestive fashion.

Will laughs too loud and too long again, "Fair enough."

"Well, we need to get ready. I assume you won't be attending the mixer?" Genevieve asks.

Will makes a dismissive hand gesture and turns back to his companion. Genevieve takes my hand and leads me through the door into the hallway. We walk down a hallway, around a corner, and up another hallway. I am thoroughly lost by the time we find our room.

"So, who is Will?" I ask as I flop down on the king-sized bed. The suite that Genevieve got is huge. I think the television is larger than my bedroom.

"An absolute piece of shit, who I run into at every one of these conferences," Genevieve says flatly as she sets her luggage down. "He's an agent. He always seems to find some desperate young woman willing to do anything to get published."

"I see."

"I am going to get cleaned up. At least we know he won't be joining us for happy hour," Genevieve says as she starts to disrobe.

"Yeah, I think he's already a couple of hours into happy."

"Want to join me?" She asks over a bare shoulder as she sashays into the bathroom.

"Yes," I say, "But if I am going to do this elbow-rubbing, hand-shaking thing, I will need some rest. That flight was stressful."

She pouts at me, then shrugs. "Suit yourself. You don't know what you are missing."

"There will be plenty of time later! We have all week, right?"

She closes the door behind her.

CHAPTER 27

My eyes snap open. I am lying on a large bed in a room unfamiliar to me. It takes a moment of blinking, bleary-eyed, to remember that I am in a hotel room in Atlanta. My mouth is dry, my eyes gritty, and my muscles sore. I've only been drinking a single cup of black tea in the mornings, just enough caffeine to stave off the full DTs; it's better than cold turkey, but it's still been pretty rough.

I notice a little yellow post-it note stuck to my chest. I pull it off and read it.

"Went to mixer. See you there?"

I take a cool shower and then get dressed. On the way down to the ballroom, I tug and pull at my collar. I'm not used to wearing collared shirts, and it feels like a noose around my neck. The elevator opens on the ballroom level, and I hear the music reverberating through the hallway. A handful of people are standing in groups of two or three, sipping wine and chatting in the hallway, getting away from the din of music in the ballroom.

The ballroom is a huge space. The lights are dim, and music

plays entirely too loudly through the PA. It is dark and feels more like a high school prom than a happy hour for people in the publishing industry. I stand near the door and lean against the wall, one foot pressed against the wall behind me, knee sticking straight out, ready to kick off and run at a moment's notice.

I never went to prom in high school. My senior year was the only year I might have been interested in going, but my father had to skip town two weeks before prom, and I never got to go. My eyes scan the crowd. The room is packed with people of every possible description. They are all wearing light business casual and, based entirely on facial expressions and hand gestures, all are mired in the most phony conversations possible.

This is exactly how I imagine my senior prom would have gone.

A server comes by and offers me a glass of wine from a tray of half a dozen identical glasses. I shrug and take one. I don't really intend to drink it, but it feels like the prop of the moment.

I take a sip of the wine. It is an over-oaked chardonnay. I swallow it resentfully and vow not to repeat this mistake.

After a few minutes of people-watching and posing with my wine, a woman comes to stand beside me. She's about my age, maybe a little younger, and heavy-set with broad shoulders. Her hair is darker, but it is hard to tell the exact color in the shadowy ballroom. She wears glasses and a button-up sweater over her floor-length dress.

"I hate these things," the woman says. She is all but yelling to be heard over the music.

"Makes me think of a high school prom."

She laughs too loudly. "Yeah, I hated those things too."

We sit in awkward silence for a moment.

"So, SyzmekZinnergy huh?" She says speculatively, trying to reinvigorate the conversation.

I remember Will mentioning this.

"You going to the dark side?" I ask, emulating Genevieve's comment.

The woman laughs too loudly again, "No! No! I can't believe they are announcing the release here, of all places. Can you imagine?"

I have absolutely no idea what SysmekZinnergy is. I can intuit that it is a new program by the Syzmek corporation related to the publishing industry, but that's it.

"No, I can't imagine," I say. It's not a lie. I really can't.

"I'm Gretchen. I work mostly in editing. I mean, I write, but the money is in editing."

"I'm Miles. I don't work in the industry. I am a plus-one."

"Oh," Gretchen says, her attitude seems to cool.

"Sorry," I say, shrugging. I'm not sure what I am sorry for. I can't tell if she was talking to me because she thought I might be a good industry contact or if she was flirting with me, but either way, I seem to have shut her down with one sentence. I don't like shutting people out, but on the other hand, I don't really feel like chatting.

"Well, it's good to meet you, Miles. I think I see Barry Moore over there, so I'm going to go," she says, making a vague gesture toward a group of people before bustling off.

I'm alone once more. My eyes keep straining to find Genevieve in the crowd, but I have had no success so far. I've been told that if you are lost, the best thing to do is stay in one place and wait to be found. Since my only reason to be here is for Genevieve to see me, I decide to follow that advice.

A group of three women break away and stand by the wall near me. They huddle together in conversation, wine glasses held out to the sides of their little triangle. It almost looks prearranged, like part of a choreographed dance. Under normal circumstances, I would try to eavesdrop out of bored curiosity. However, it is far too loud in this room to do so.

After a few minutes, one of them taps me on the shoulder. I look over with a start.

"Excuse me," she says. Her trio breaks up and shifts to include me in their circle. She and her friends must all be on their third or fourth glass of wine, based on their demeanor and slight slurring.

"Hi," I say.

"I'm sorry, but you look really familiar. We were all just wondering where we know you from," the first woman says. She's short and cherubic with blond hair. She's wearing a summery dress with a short open sweater on top.

"You are the cover model for the new Craven's Gate series, aren't you?" Another woman chimes in. She has dark, curly hair and mocha skin.

"Um, no," I say, blushing, "I'm not a model. But what was that about a new Craven's Gate series?"

"Are you a fan?"

"The show was sort of a guilty pleasure," I say. The curly-haired woman gets a wicked grin on her face.

"Oh, well, you know the show was based on a series of novels. It's at thirty-six volumes now," she says.

"You don't read that trash, do you, Marsha?" The third woman asks. She's tall and thin, in slacks and a polo, her hair cropped in a short pixie cut.

"It's better than that weird historical-fiction-smut you read, Sandy," the curly-haired woman I can now identify as Marsha says.

Sandy, the tall, short-haired woman, opens her mouth wide in mock shock.

"You want to hook up with this guy because he kind of

looks like the model from your favorite wizard porn!" Sandy says.

Marsha looks scandalized.

"Yeah," Sandy says, leaning in very close. Her breath smells bad, like stale wine and inebriation, "That's right, she wants to take you back to her room and..."

She is thankfully cut off by the blond-haired cherubic woman, who puts a hand on her shoulder and gently pulls her away.

"Sandy, you're drunk."

"Mind you're own business, Anne! I am as sober as a...a...what's something that is sober?" Sandy drunkenly argues, "Okay, maybe I'm a little bit drunk."

Sandy breaks into peels of laughter, bending double at the waist and spilling some wine on the floor. Anne rolls her eyes. Marsha is standing with her arms crossed, staring angrily at Sandy.

"So," I say, feeling immensely uncomfortable, "How about that SyzmekZinnergy thing, huh? Welcome to the dark side, am I right?"

"Yes!" Anne says, "Seriously, what is the world coming to?"

Marsha gives a little smirk, "I heard that Walt Carmichael is speaking tomorrow. The gall, right?"

"Really? You'd think a guy like that would have better things to do," I say.

"It's just a rumor," Anne says, "It will probably end up being some VP of marketing or someone with some other random, made-up title whose real job is to sell Syzmek snake oil."

Sandy recovers from her fit of laughter. She stands up and looks me square in the eye. She has that look of someone who is very drunk and trying to pretend to be sober. She leans in toward me conspiratorially.

"Seriously," she says at full volume, trying not to laugh again, "Marsha will take you to her room right now and do things that are illegal in three states. She's not wearing her wedding ring, but she is married."

"Jesus, Sandy," Anne scolds, grabbing Sandy by the arm and dragging her away.

"Sorry about that," Marsha says miserably.

"It's okay. Just to be clear, I'm spoken for," I say.

"Oh," Marsha says. She sounds disappointed, which is flattering. This is my first time being mistaken for a male model, so that is a highlight.

A hand wraps around my waist from the side where I can't see. I start before I realize it is Genevieve. She has slightly exaggerated body motions and a glint in her eye, which I have come to identify as 'drunk Genny.' I'm less fond of this persona each time I encounter her.

"Miles!" Genevieve says enthusiastically, then curtly nods to Marsha, "Marsha."

Marsha's facial expression speaks volumes. She smiles, and it might even be a reasonable facsimile of a sincere smile if she were sober. However, what comes out is more of a sneer. Contempt and jealousy radiate from her suddenly.

"Genevieve," Marsha says in a tone that nonverbally adds an 'I should have known' to the end.

"Do you two know each other?" I asked. I didn't think the situation could get any more uncomfortable, but my rock-bottom expectations were too high, as usual.

"We are old conference pals," Genevieve says, venom dripping from every word.

"Is that what we are calling it now?" Marsha retorts. She crosses her arms and gets a confrontational look in her eye.

"You know what? I really don't like this wine," I say,

starting to move away, "I am going to get a beer. Can I get either of you anything?"

Genevieve clamps her arm tighter around my waist.

"It's okay," Genevieve says, "I'm sure Marsha was just leaving."

Genevieve and Marsha have a long staring contest. Genevieve is a few inches taller and has a generally more aggressive posture. From the outside, Genevieve has the advantage. The venom in their glares seems to suck the sound out of the room like a vacuum. Is my girlfriend about to get into a fistfight in the middle of a conference?

Genevieve still has a death grip on my waist. I sit in awkward silence, waiting for the tiniest slack in her arm to indicate that I can run. However, freedom is not forthcoming.

Finally, after what seems like an eternity, Marsha heaves a big drunken sigh while breaking eye contact with Genevieve. No sooner does Marsha break eye contact than Genevieve grabs me and kisses me hard and sloppy on the mouth. It isn't pleasant, and knowing this is some territorial thing with Marsha doesn't make it any better.

Marsha turns and stalks away. I am sure I hear her mutter "Bitch," as she goes.

"What the hell was that all about?" I ask, pushing back from Genevieve.

"She's always trying to fuck with me at these things," Genevieve says.

"I don't think that is what was happening here," I say. I can't imagine that Marsha knew Genevieve and I were together.

"Yeah, you don't know Marsha like I do. She's been stabbing me in the back for years now."

"I admit, it's kind of a weird coincidence that you happen

to know one of the like, three people who have talked to me here."

"Oh, that's no coincidence. I know everybody here," she waves her hand around the crowded room. It's more people than I have met in my life.

"So, why does Marsha hate you so much?"

"Oh, this whole thing. Like three years ago, we were at a convention. Albany, I think? Anyway, some of us had a few drinks, and we thought playing a prank on one of the keynote speakers would be funny. Sean Jacobs was speaking."

"The actor?"

"Yeah, this was right after that movie about the flowers came out. You know the one where he's the florist whose ex-wife dies and leaves him with three kids that aren't his?"

"I have no idea what you are talking about," I say. It sounds like one of those intense dramas I am not interested in.

"Whatever, anyway, it was a thing. I can't remember the name right now, but it was nominated for an Academy Award or something that year. Anyway, we decided to fill his room with flowers. We got into the cooler room, where they stored all the flowers for the tables and stuff. We bribed staff, we got a cart, and I picked the lock on his room. It was like a whole thing."

"Okay," I say, curious where this is going.

"We filled his room with flowers, I mean all over the bed, in the bathtub, on the counters, in the sink. It was pretty hilarious."

"Yeah, not sure I get the humor, but okay."

"It would be funny if you'd seen the movie. Flowers! It was called Something-Flowers! Tending Flowers? Raising Daisies? I don't remember!" she says, laughing so hard she almost falls.

"If you say so. Anyway, how does that relate to your friend Marsha there?"

"Right, right. Anyway, like I said, we were all pretty drunk, and Marsha passed out in Jacob's room. When we left, we missed her, well because there were flowers everywhere, you know, couldn't even see the carpet."

"So she got in trouble for it?"

"Oh yeah, I am pretty sure she had to go to court. Sean Jacobs has a restraining order on her. She's banned from that convention for life. It was, like, a whole thing."

"And she blames you for that?"

Genevieve averts her eyes from mine and wrings her hands together.

"Well..." She draws out guiltily, "I probably could have done more to help her out than I did."

I quirk an eyebrow at her curiously. She bites her lip. We sit there for a moment, the pulsing music and background din of chatter filling the space.

"I ghostwrote Jacobs's biography for him. I had an in and could probably have convinced him not to make as big a scene as he did. But it would have meant confessing that I was involved and maybe sacrificing some of my credibility. I'm not proud; it probably wasn't the right decision, but it's the one I made. She's hated me ever since."

I glower at Genevieve, "I'm not sure I can blame her."

Genevieve glowers back at me, "Don't judge me."

I'm just batting a thousand tonight.

"What about that SyzmekZinnergy thing, huh? That's crazy, right?" I say.

Genevieve crosses her arms and glowers at me.

"I don't know, it's worked to change the topic with everyone else here," I say defensively.

"Do you even know what SyzmekZinnergy is?"

"I haven't got a clue. People keep mentioning it, though."

"The whole theme of this conference is the role of AI in

publishing. Syzmek is about to release this new product, Zinnergy. It's basically a system that replaces the entire publishing industry from writing to delivery. It strips the human contribution out of the whole thing. If it takes off, almost everyone in this room is unemployed."

"I can see why a product like that might ruffle some feathers."

"And they've somehow arranged for this symposium to be the venue for their launch announcement. That's why there are so many people here. This is probably three times larger than most years."

"Huh," I say.

My face is suddenly cold, and my eyes sting. The smell of oaky chardonnay fills my nostrils.

"Creep!" I hear Marsha's voice as I blink the wine out of my eyes.

"Fuck off, Marsha!" I hear Genevieve yell as I wipe my face clean with the back of my sleeve.

"Genevieve Gale is boinking Jim Devora's bodyguard. That sounds about right!" Marsha screams, "That's why he looked so familiar."

I glance around. A few dozen people have stopped to turn and stare at the spectacle unfolding. Phones are already out and recording. Genevieve throws her glass of red wine in Marsha's face. Marsha lunges at her, but Genevieve is prepared for this. She grabs Marsha's wrist and twists her arm behind her back before tripping her to the floor.

I am tired, my head feels fuzzy, and I really don't want to be here. Genevieve is kneeling on Marsha's lower back, holding Marsha's arm up by her scapula. Marsha screams an incoherent cry of rage and frustration.

"Settle down, Marsha!" Genevieve is yelling.

"Come on, let's go," I mutter and put my hand gently on Genevieve's shoulder. She swats me away.

After an instant of hesitation, I decide to take that as a cue. I run out of the ballroom like a Disney Princess at midnight, run back to the stairwell, and dash in. Once in the stairwell, I stop and take a moment.

I want a cup of coffee.

I don't feel well. I haven't felt well since I cut coffee out of my life. My brain is fuzzy. My head feels tense and tight. It's not a real headache, but it's not well. My stomach is queasy and roiling. Coffee would fix all of this.

Why can I only think about coffee at this moment, with all the craziness that just occurred? Addiction is a double-edged sword. If I drink coffee, even a single cup, my heart starts racing until it feels like it's about to explode. Then I start sweating, and I have the constant sensation that I need to do something, but I can never remember what it is. But if I don't have it, I feel sick and incomplete, like there is a part of me missing, maybe the best parts of me.

So far, I have opted to follow the doctor's orders. Now, between the stress of the trip and the whole detox process, I feel like I am losing it. I didn't want to come to Atlanta. I didn't want wine thrown in my face. I didn't want Genevieve to get into a fight in the middle of the conference.

"I don't want to be here!" I scream; I can hear it echoing through the steel-sheathed stairwell.

"So go away!" a drunken male voice replies. The way it echoes, I cannot tell how far away it is or if it is above or below me in the stairwell.

I have to get out of here. I have to get some space.

Instead of heading upstairs to our room, I go downstairs and exit to an alleyway behind the Hotel.

CHAPTER 28

I WANDER the streets of downtown Atlanta. It's dusk, and I am not really looking where I am going. I stick to streets with more foot traffic. I might be in a funk, but I am not looking to get mugged. Eventually, I come to a street with a couple of nightclubs and food trucks parked outside. It isn't late yet, and the food trucks are just getting set up. I sidle up to one and order a cheese steak. It smells like salt and fat. It's not necessarily my favorite flavor profile, but it fits the bill under the circumstances.

Armed with a huge, greasy sandwich, I sit at a small plastic folding table and begin to wolf it down. The task I have set before myself is greater than I anticipated, and I have to stop halfway through.

I'm upset. I keep wishing that I had stayed home. I don't want to be in Atlanta. I don't want to be at a conference. Genevieve has been weird since we arrived, and I want to go home. The fact that the only enjoyable moment I have had all day is eating half of a cheesesteak should speak volumes.

I feel up to my neck in a cauldron of steaming, dark

emotions. This foul mood has seeped through my skin and is festering inside me. Part of me wants to stand up, scream, and throw my half-eaten sandwich at some random passersby. Another part of me wants to run home, hide in my bed, and sob. Unfortunately, the less useful impulse is the more convenient one.

I look up from my half-eaten sandwich and see someone looking at me. They look at their phone, then look back at me. Am I being paranoid? Probably. But as the old adage goes, just because you're paranoid doesn't mean they aren't spying on you.

My phone vibrates, and I glance at it. A message from Genevieve is waiting there.

"Where R U?"

"Taking a walk," I respond.

"Going 2 bed. B Safe"

"See you soon," I reply.

It's still not late, but the nightlife is just getting going. People are lining up at the nightclubs, and groups of young people wander the sidewalks. I get up and meander my way back toward the hotel. I am overreacting. I am freaking out because I have been through a lot of things in the past week, and I've got a lot of pent-up emotions. Empirically, I know this. However, it doesn't mean I don't feel overwhelmed.

"It's okay to be upset, it's okay to be scared and confused, and it's okay to want to go home," I remind myself out loud. I am glad I can't hear Hank right now. I don't think he'd be too kind to me on this one.

My phone vibrates again, and I glance at it. This time, it is Jeff.

"Hey," he writes.

"Hey, what's up?"

"Hang out? Saw the news. Talked to Mike."

"I can chat, but I am in Atlanta right now."

"Atlanta? How did that happen?"

"Genevieve had conference. I thought I should get out of town for a bit."

This isn't true. Genevieve thought I should get out of town for a bit. I accepted the narrative, but I am noting with increasing intensity that I'm feeling slightly bitter toward Genevieve.

"Oh that makes sense. I guess," Jeff replies.

"I am sorry we missed your party. Things did not go according to plan."

"Yes"

"I will let you know when I am back in town."

"Ok"

"We can grab lunch or something."

"Ok"

I feel like I should reply. It has always been my problem with text conversations. I feel like I should try to get the last word in. But I don't know what else to say, so I leave it as is. I'll reply again if Jeff says anything, but after a moment, it's clear he isn't going to.

There is a little a-frame sandwich board sitting on the side-walk. Big chalk letters read 'Magic Shop' with a cartoony-looking arrow pointing into an alleyway. I stop and look at the sign. I look down the alleyway. I am a little interested to see what an Atlanta Magic Shop looks like. But I also want to go to bed. I start to walk past the sign, then stop. I turn and take a few steps down the alleyway, then stop. After a minute of internal turmoil, I walk down the alley.

The alleyway seems to go all the way through to a parallel street. It is littered with trash and overflowing trash bins, and the smell of urine is pervasive. I squint in the darkness to see if there is anyone sleeping or lurking here, but it seems empty.

Halfway down the alley is a short set of brick steps leading up to a steel door. The door is brown and has a window set into it. The window is clad in a heavy iron grating to prevent it from being broken. I can see through the grate that, despite that, it has a large crack running through it. A wooden sign hangs on a steel rod above the door. The sign reads "Dweomercraft" and has a series of pentacles and Enochian characters. I roll my eyes to myself.

There is an 'Open' sign in the door's window, and I can see the light inside of Dweomercraft, so I walk up the brick stairs and open the door. A speaker somewhere emits a reverb-filled tinkling of bells that sounds like a cartoon pixie is casting a spell.

The interior of the shop is exactly what I expected—displays of wands and crystals, herbs, and tinctures—two low bookshelves full of books and a glass display case filled with gaudy jewels and baubles. There is a counter with a modern point-of-sale system and a tablet computer on a revolving arm. Behind the counter sits a bored young woman in a lacy black dress that is only a touch darker than her skin tone. She's got black lipstick and purple eye shadow and press on nails as long as daggers. Her curly hair has been meticulously braided back into cornrows with beads and adornments on the ends.

"Good evening," she says in a dramatically melancholy tone.

"How's it going?" I ask in response.

She shrugs a long, languid shrug. She's fully committed to the job, apparently. It probably makes the time go faster. Then, in a long, low, and spooky voice, she says, "It is well this fine Mabon eve."

"Mabon was like two weeks ago."

She laughs, "Busted. I don't even know what Mabon is. Just trying to set the mood."

I nod, "I like the laughing better than the Dracula bit."

"Fair, me too. So what can I do for you? Palm reading? A spell to speak to the dead? Or are you more of a love potion kind of guy?"

She says the last part with her face twisted up in concern.

"Just browsing," I say, picking up some crystals and looking them over.

You find magic shops in cities all over the place. They usually sell the same crystals and bric-a-brac everywhere, but very little of it is useful, at least in my line of work. I still like to stop in, every now and again, to see what it is people are buying under the guise of 'spellcraft.'

"Out of curiosity, how does that work? Spells to speak to the dead, that is." I ask. Many people claim to be able to do this, but I've never seen any evidence of actual success. Usually, this sort of necromancy is the work of con artists and grifters.

"Well, I don't really do that stuff myself; my boss does all the rites and rituals. Basically, you'd make an appointment and bring something in of the deceased, something they owned, or a lock of hair or, you know, something like that."

"Pay up front?"

"Not the whole thing, just a fifty-dollar deposit."

"And you take credit cards?" I say, indicating the point of sale system.

"We only take credit cards."

That's what I expected. You pay upfront with a credit card and schedule it. Then, they have your name, address, and enough time to do some research. The internet has made these sorts of scams a little too easy.

"Are you interested in making an appointment for a contact?" She asks.

"No, just curious. Is your boss in?" I ask. I don't know why I am asking. It is sort of like an annoying scab I want to pick at.

"Nope," she answers, but her brow knits in concern. Maybe my tone sounds confrontational, "Why, is there a problem?"

I shake my head no, "I'm kind of in the business, and I am always curious about what that looks like in other places."

"You run a magic shop?"

"No, I am an apotropaist," I reply. She nods comprehension, though I am unsure if that is just to placate me or if she knows the word.

"Look, the readings are crap, but you need someone hexed; we can do that for real. Good luck. Bad luck. Warts. Erectile dysfunction. We can do that," she says, looking around conspiratorially, "Not cheap, though, not for the real stuff."

"I'm not looking, but I am curious. What's not cheap?"

"Depends on the outcome, but an entropy curse for a year and a day'll run you seventy-five hundred starters. You want their 'johnson' out of commission, double it."

"You sell a lot of those?"

"A lot more than you'd think, especially that last one."

"Where do you get your blood?" I ask, making eye contact with her.

"We got a butcher around the corner," she says without hesitating.

I nod.

I take a small crystal amulet off a necklace tree and put it on the counter. When she rings it up, I almost bite my tongue at the price, but I pay for it anyway.

"This all?" She asks, holding the amulet up.

"Yup. Thanks for the talk."

"You know this is just a pewter necklace, right?"

"Yeah, I know. I thought I might give it to my girlfriend."

"Okay," she says, putting a receipt and the necklace into a bag. "Enjoy, and come back if you need one of those hexes."

"You can count on it," I say, knowing I will never return here again.

It is happening slowly but surely, and magic is becoming commercialized. There was a time when if you wanted to buy a hex, you'd have to find some weird hermit in the wood and bring them a live goat to sacrifice. Now you can just put it on the credit card. The world is changing.

I walk back out the door and to the street. I slide the little paper bag with the pendant in it into my pocket. I'm not sure why I bought it, really. I think I mostly bought it because it felt awkward to take up her time and then not pay for something. I consider giving it to Genevieve as a peace offering, but I am not sure I feel like I am the one who needs to be bartering for peace right now. I'm still feeling pretty upset about being dragged into this whole situation.

The hotel lobby is bustling with loud, largely inebriated people. I don't have a lot of experience with these sorts of things, but it seems like if you fly a bunch of people in and start the first day with an endless supply of free alcohol, there is only one potential outcome.

There are half a dozen other people on the elevator. I can't shake the paranoid feeling that everyone is staring at me and whispering. I know it isn't true, but that knowledge doesn't diminish the feeling. I take the elevator to the twelfth floor and walk back down three flights.

I grab the ninth-floor door and yank. It doesn't budge. It's locked. I try it again, but it hasn't magically become unlocked in the last four seconds. I look at the sign on the door that I hadn't processed before. It says, 'Door does not open from this side, exit only.'

I remember when we came in before, and I realize that Will had propped the door open with an empty beer can. I didn't really take note at the time because of the weird interaction between him and Genevieve. So, I make my way down the stairs, back to the lobby, and take the elevator back up to the ninth floor.

No one notices or cares, of course, but I still feel sheepish and self-conscious as I stand in the corner of the elevator. When I finally return to the room, I realize Genevieve never gave me a key. With a deep sigh, I knock.

Genevieve answers the door. She's wearing a bathrobe and has a towel wrapped around her hair. Her face is covered with a light green, moist-looking muck. Behind her, I can hear the television blaring.

"Hey," she says, non-plussed. "Where you been?"

"Like I said, I needed to go for a walk."

"You left me," she says as the door closes behind me.

"You got in a fistfight with your conference nemesis in the middle of the ballroom. People were recording it, Genevieve. After last week, the last thing I need is to get tagged in some viral 'girls gone wild' video."

"It's #CougarFight #ClawsOut," she says, crossing her arms.

"Really?" I ask.

She only nods.

"Really?"

"Yeah, but don't worry, I don't think you are really in any of the videos. It's mostly just close-ups of me straddling Marsha and repeatedly demanding that she say my name."

I stare at her, blinking incredulously.

"Not my finest hour."

"So, I am sorry. What happened after I left?" I ask. It sounds like things really went sideways.

"Pretty much just that. Then, some hotel staff showed up and pulled us apart. I had to talk to some people, but I know the coordinator pretty well. She smoothed things over for me."

"What happened to Marsha?"

Genevieve shrugs, "Banned from yet another industry venue."

"Wow, no wonder she hates you."

"I know," she says, but she has a sideways grin on her face as she does.

"That is really awful. So they banned her, but you got off scot-free because you know the coordinator? That hardly seems fair."

"Yeah, what can I say? The coordinator owed me big time."

"Oh?" I say. I am feeling disappointed in Genevieve and, frankly, a little scared of her.

"Yeah, my boyfriend and I helped uncover a fake haunting in her house and got the culprit arrested."

I look at her, puzzled for a second. How many boyfriends has she investigated fake hauntings with? Oh...

"Portia is the conference coordinator?"

Genevieve tries to poke her nose to indicate that I am 'on the nose' but misses it, so she ends up rubbing her cheek instead. Apparently, she is a little more intoxicated than I thought.

"I know you've had a few, but can I talk to you about this? I have never seen you like this before, and I don't think I like it."

"What do you mean?"

"I don't know how you went at Marsha. I wasn't a huge fan of hers, but wow, you were mean."

"Marsha and I have history—more than just being banned

from a convention. Remember how I said I used to have a fiance? Well, she's part of why it didn't work out."

"Ah," I say, "And so then you see her hitting on me, and that maybe dug some old emotions up?"

"She was hitting on you?" Genevieve slurs slightly and raises a fist, "I'm gonna go find that skank."

"Woah, slow down there!" I say.

She waves a palm at me dismissively, "I was just kidding. Relax there, buddio."

"After that, show at the mixer..."

"I thought you would be into that. It was like season one, episode six of Craven's Gate," she says, motioning at the television.

I hadn't really been paying attention to the television, but now I see that it is, in fact, playing an episode of Craven's Gate. In the episode, Sofiana throws a ball at Craven's Manor. She meets Gerald for the first time, but he's there with a date, Taylor, I think the character's name was. Sofiana and Taylor get into a fight and throw wine in each other's faces. There are some shocking parallels between the episode and my evening.

"It's pretty trashy," Genevieve says, letting her robe slip off her shoulder. But kinda hot."

"You are pretty drunk," I tell her. "We should just get some sleep."

"Party pooper," she says sullenly, plopping down on the bed. I go to get changed into bedclothes and brush my teeth. By the time I return, she has passed out on the bed.

I sit down and watch the old episode of Craven's Gate until I fall asleep.

CHAPTER 29

Genevieve is still asleep when I wake up. I quietly slip out of bed and get dressed. The room has an extra card key on a little table near the door. I take it so I can let myself back in. When we checked in, we were informed that there is a complimentary buffet on the first floor. I sneak out the door and head downstairs.

The buffet is huge, but there are only a handful of people up and about at this hour. The whole hotel was up late carousing last night. I get two plates of eggs, bacon, biscuits and gravy. I suspect that is what Genevieve is going to want after last night's libations. I walk over to the hot beverage counter. There. A LavaJava 24K sits glaring at me with its baleful red indicator light. I stare it down for a long moment, considering if I want to tangle with this fearsome beast again and choke a decent cup of coffee out of it once and for all. Then I remember, sadly, that I am not drinking coffee anymore.

With my head hung low, I move over to the hot water spigot and pour myself a cup of black tea. The thing with tea is that no matter what other flavors they add or how they try to cover it up, at the end of the day, it tastes like hot water and sticks if it is black tea or hot water and grass if green tea. I add sweetener until I have a mug of sweet, dirty stick water. I gaze into the murky red-brown depths of my tea, and I imagine this must be the color of despair.

With my carefully balanced tray of food, I make my way back up to the hotel room. There is a strong and fairly unpleasant odor when I open the door. It is, I think, the odor of hangover. I didn't notice it before because I had been sleeping in it, but after a little break, it is now overwhelming. Genevieve must have had much more to drink than I thought, which is saying a lot, considering I previously suspected she had imbibed quite a bit. She is going to have a rough day.

I set the food tray on the small breakfast table by a sliding glass door. Beyond the glass door, there is a small balcony. The balcony is too small to do more than stand on and look down at the courtyard below. I open the sliding glass door to let some fresh air in and sit down at the round wooden table to eat.

I haven't eaten half of my breakfast yet when Genevieve groans her way out of bed. Half walks, half crawls her way to the bathroom. I'm just finishing my food when she comes staggering back out wearing a bathrobe and sunglasses.

"Uranaga," she mutters as she shoves two whole slices of bacon in her mouth and drinks some of my tea.

"Good morning to you," I say.

"Was Marsha at the mixer last night?" She mumbles.

"You don't remember?"

"It's hazy. I either had a dream that I got in a fight with her, or I did?"

"You did."

"And Portia was there?"

"I think that happened after I left."

"I really need to stop drinking at these things."

"And Marsha really needs to stay away from you at these things."

"Why? What happened to Marsha?"

"I guess you got her banned from the convention?"

"Again!" Genevieve starts to laugh but then stops, grabs her head, and hunches forward. She looks a little green. "Too loud, Miles."

"That was all you."

"Oh yeah."

"Listen, Genevieve, I think this was a mistake. I think I should go," I say. Maybe now is not really the time, but I want to pull this bandaid off.

"Oh," she says, pushing her sunglasses farther up her nose, "You want to do this now?"

"I just feel like it's better to get it over with."

"Yeah, this probably was a mistake. It's been obvious from the get-go, but I mean, it was still fun. It wasn't ever going to be anything more than that, though. This was just for fun, right?"

"Honestly, I'm not sure this was ever fun."

Her face contorts into an ugly and unhappy knot.

"You know what, Miles? You aren't exactly a ball of sunshine yourself. You are the single, whiniest, neediest person I've ever dated. I know I said that the mannequin thing wasn't that weird, but I lied. That's really, really weird. So, I am glad you finally came out and talked to me about this because, yeah, I think we are through."

Wait, is she breaking up with me?

"Um. I just meant that coming to the conference was a mistake. I am not having fun here, at the conference, and I should go home. Um. Are you breaking up with me?"

"Shit," she says. Then, after a long pause, "Yeah, I guess I am. Listen, Miles, you're cute, and you can be fun, but you are also kind of a mess. We've dealt with flying monkeys, magic heists, and ancient Greek monsters, but I still know basically nothing about you. You are so guarded, and that's okay. That's your business, but it's exhausting. You gotta open up a little, you gotta relax, Miles."

"How is this my fault?" I say. I don't feel it is fair that the lady who gets drunk and causes a scene in the conference can make it seem like I'm the problem. "I don't talk about that stuff because I don't even remember half of it, and the half I do remember, I don't want to. So yeah, it's a little hard to open up to others about stuff I don't even want to think about myself."

I begin to raise my voice a little, not to yelling, but just above normal conversational tones. She winces and puts a hand to her head, "Well," she hisses, "If you want to have a functional human relationship, you better figure that out, Mr. Ward. If that is your real name."

"It's not!" I say as I stand up and start packing my bag. I didn't really unpack much yesterday, so this isn't much of a problem.

"What are you doing?"

"I am packing. That should be obvious. And I might be a little guarded, but you're a narcissistic hedonist. You do whatever feels good at the moment, regardless of the consequences. Or is that just the drugs' fault?" I say, and I immediately regret it. That was just my hurt pride speaking. I want to recant it, take it back, and apologize, but my pride won't let me do that either.

She stops and glares at me through her sunglasses, her mouth slightly agape. "You going through my shit? What the hell, Miles? Enjoy hitchhiking home!"

Genevieve turns and storms into the bathroom, slamming the door behind her. I'm still feeling furious, but mostly with myself. I angrily and sloppily pack my bag and slam the door as I leave the room. The entire trip down the hall, into the elevator, and across the lobby, I half hope Genevieve will come running after me and ask me not to leave. She doesn't.

I find myself sitting on a bench by the valet station in front of the hotel. I start searching for flights I can get today back to California. There are few, and they are all very expensive. The Devora job was supposed to be lucrative, but I spent more money in the end than I made. I made nothing, so the math is easy. My bank account is running dry, and how the publicity I've received from the Devora caper will impact my future business prospects remains to be seen.

When I decide I can't afford a flight today, I start looking for other places to stay until my original flight home. None of the options appeal to me, so I go back to looking at immediate flights. I'm on the verge of despair when a familiar, soft, sing-songy voice says my name.

"Hello Miles, why are you here?"

I look up and see the round, child-like face of Howard, The Hermit.

"Howard?"

"Yes, I am, um, surprised to see you in Atlanta," he says in his odd, sing-songy voice.

"What happened? You just disappeared. And now you are here, at this conference?"

"It became apparent that the, uh, plan was being deviated from and that I would, um, be apprehended, so I ran," he says. "I would ask how you escaped, but that is now a, uh, matter of public record."

"Okay, but how are you here now?"

"My employer, Syzmek Corporation, um, they are revealing a new product here today. I am leading the team that is, uh, securing the technical architecture for that launch. My job is completed. I am going home."

"Oh," I say. Something is itching at the back of my brain. Something that feels wrong here, but I can't quite put my finger on it.

"What are you doing here?" He asks.

"Genevieve and I came to the conference. She was invited. It got weird. I guess we broke up. I am trying to figure out how to get home."

Howard looks thoughtful for a moment. He glances briefly at his phone, then looks back up at me.

"Do you want to come with me on the corporate jet?" Howard asks.

"You fly on a corporate jet?" I ask.

"Most times, I fly coach on a commercial airline, but this time, um, it's a big deal. They have lots of company planes coming and going."

"And you can get me onto the jet?" I ask.

"Let me message my boss and ask," Howard says. He takes out a phone and types into it.

"How are you feeling about that, um, job that we did?" I ask while we wait for a response.

"The outcome was, hmm, satisfactory."

I look puzzled at him. There is no definition of satisfactory I would use to describe that fiasco.

"Satisfactory? Devora came out looking like the victim. I thought you had a grudge."

"Oh," Howard says, "Yes. I am sorry, but I, um, deceived you about that. Hmm, I was, um. A plant, I think that's the right term. When the Hierophant approached me, Devora's security team, um, made a counter-proposal."

"Wow," I say, "Howard, you are more deceptive than I'd have given you credit for."

He nods and looks at his phone. "My boss says that you can come on the jet."

"Great. So, you were working for Devora the whole time?" I ask incredulously. If there was a double agent in the mix, Howard was not the one I would have suspected.

"You were as well," Howard says.

I emit a sound that feels like an awkward bark, but Howard seems to take it as laughter and smiles.

"That's right," I say, "I guess I was."

We sit for a moment in silence. I am not really sure what to say. My head is hazy. It has been since I stopped drinking coffee. My mind keeps returning to the last day with Genevieve and how quickly it went sideways. There is something else nagging at my brain, but with everything else going on, it keeps getting lost in the fog of life.

A black limousine pulls up, and Howard motions me toward it. I climb in, with Howard right behind me. The limo is nice and clean, with black leather seats and a minibar. I notice that the panel on the front of the bar bears the Syzmek corporate logo.

"A company car, very nice, Howard."

"Yes, it is better than taking a taxi cab," Howard says.

"So, if you are here with Syzmek, that must mean you are on the Zinnergy team."

"On the cyber security team ensuring that the Zinnergy systems are not compromised."

"What is Zinnergy?"

"It is a VLSLM capable of generating, copying, and editing manuscripts and printing them."

"VLSLM?"

"Very Large Scale Language Model. The layman's term is AI, but it isn't actually an artificial intelligence. It's more like an extraordinarily complicated Madlib."

"So, what, it writes books?"

"It writes books, newspaper articles, scripts, any and all written media. It then has the capacity to automatically submit the material for copyright and branding and begin publishing. It creates cover art and graphics. Human intervention is no longer needed in the creative process."

I laugh, "I recognize that these systems can technically do that, but there is no way this will replace the human creative process."

"A beta version of the Zinnergy system has written the last twelve of the Craven's Gate franchise romance novels."

I blink, "Really?"

"Yes. They have all been best sellers in their genre."

"Huh," I say. I sit back in my seat and stare out the window, thinking. Howard seems relieved by my silence and the end of the small talk. He sits back and begins tinkering on his laptop.

When we get to the airport, I still have to go through security and answer some additional questions before I can board the plane. Once we've dealt with that, we are escorted to a shuttle that drives us across the tarmac to a small, sleek, black jet. I feel like a rock star as I get out of the shuttle and walk up the staircase onto the plane.

The flight attendant, a pretty young woman in a uniform bearing the Syzmek corporate logo, offers us each a glass of champagne as we get on the plane. Both Howard and I refuse. Howard leads me down to the center of the plane, where there is a small sitting area with comfortable-looking seats, large screens on the wall, a wet bar, and a counter with a tray of snacks.

Howard immediately sits down and opens his laptop. I think I might have socialized him out already. I sit down, buckle myself in, and stare longingly at the carafe of coffee built into the counter across from me. After a moment of longing, I sigh and close my eyes.

I don't fall asleep, but my mind wanders, and I lose time. This seems to be how my uncaffeinated brain works. I get lost in my thoughts and forget where I am and what I am doing. I keep going over the last few days in my head. Wondering if there were decisions I could have made differently. Wondering if I should have seen this coming. Are Genevieve and I done for good? Or was our fight just a consequence of the moment, me still struggling through caffeine withdrawal and her suffering a brutal hangover? Is she sitting back in the hotel room thinking the same thoughts?

"We are closing the doors and will be taking off shortly," I hear the flight attendant say. This is followed by the sound of the doors sealing shut.

"Champagne, Mr. Hale?" I hear the flight attendant say. My eyes fly open.

"Of course!" I say, disgusted, as I see John Hale walking down the aisle toward me, briefcase in one hand, a glass of champagne in the other.

"Miles!" He says cheerfully.

CHAPTER 30

"Is this your boss, Howard?" I demand. Howard looks up from his laptop briefly.

"No, I, um, don't know him," Howard says, examining Hale and looking back at his laptop.

"Miles! Relax. Not everything is a big conspiracy. Sometimes coincidence is just happy coincidence!" Hale says brightly.

I narrow my eyes at him and grunt.

"Okay, this isn't one of those times, not really. I was in town for a conference and was supposed to fly back tomorrow, but then I heard your name come up and thought, 'I'll fly back with old Miles. Give us time to catch up.' So I moved my schedule around to fly back today."

"You work for Syzmek too?"

"I work for Bolton, Berringer, and Belcher. And yes, I know, I keep saying we should rebrand; there hasn't been a Belcher in the firm for twenty years."

"So why are you on a Syzmek corporate jet?"

"Ah, yes, BBnB works for Syzmek. My team works on an

exclusive basis for them, so they let me hitch a ride on the corporate plane. Sometimes it just works out."

He sits down and buckles in. He sips his champagne and closes his eyes for a moment. He looks serene, as if he's just enjoying the moment. This is something I can never do. How can a psychotic asshole like John Hale have a moment of peace when the rest of the world doesn't? We fall silent for a few minutes as the plane taxis and takes off. The ride is bumpier than a larger commercial jet, and I am white-knuckled on the seat. As we get to altitude and begin to level off, I relax just a little.

"Wait," I say as something occurs to me, "If you work exclusively for Syzmek, then why were you there representing Devora? Or Redbrook?"

"Syzmek owns a lot of assets," Hale says, then he chuckles to himself a little, "Well, not owns, owns, you know, a corporation can't own a person, at least not on paper. But there are plenty who owe Syzmek quite a lot and thus are valuable assets to the corporation. We like to keep all the wayward little lambs under one umbrella. It is a relationship you should be very familiar with now as you find yourself under said umbrella."

"So this is all some complicated shakedown? You corner me on a plane to intimidate me and tell me what I am going to do next?"

"Hardly. No, like I said, I saw your name on the roster and thought it would be good to spend a little one-on-one time with you, Miles. You know, catch up. We are so busy, I feel like we never see each other anymore."

"I don't believe you."

Hale shrugs, "Suit yourself, paranoid and guarded as usual, never willing to open up."

"I've been hearing that a lot lately. I'm fine with paranoid and guarded. It's kept me safe so far. It kept me safe from you."

"Well," he says, "if that's what you have to tell yourself to get up in the morning. But let's be honest, if I hand you a parachute and tell you to jump out of this plane, you will. No magic needed. You'd do it because if you didn't, you would be in shackles before your feet hit the tarmac in San Francisco. You'd do it because your chances with a parachute are, I assure you, far better than your chances in prison."

I glower at him, but I have no witty retorts.

"Now, do me a favor, pour me a highball."

I continue to glower at him. He quirks an eyebrow and glances pointedly at the airplane door.

"Fuck you," I say as I get up to pour him the drink. I actually have no idea what goes into a highball, so I pour some stuff into a glass with ice. An ounce of whiskey, a jigger of tequila, dry vermouth, and bitters, with an olive and a maraschino cherry as a garnish.

I hand him the cocktail.

"This is terrible. I think you should take a bartending class or something. I mean, really, this is the worst highball I've ever had. And you put it in a rocks glass. Tut tut," Hale says in a condescending tone.

"I don't know what is in a highball, so I invented a drink. I call it the When Hale Freezes Over."

"Well, ornery as ever," he says, "If you want something done right, I guess you have to do it yourself."

He hands me the rocks glass.

"You drink it," he says, "Then you will at least know what a highball doesn't taste like."

I stare at the drink and put it in the drink tray.

"Drink it, I insist."

This is obviously all a ploy to demonstrate that he has

power over me and make sure that I know my place. Part of me wants to throw the drink in his face and tell him to fuck off. The other part of me knows that he has me over a barrel. It would be easy to have me sent to prison. I do not doubt that what he told me in the emergency room was true.

However, he's just a lawyer, who works for a firm, that works for a company that is pulling his strings. He's a middle-man. He's not calling the shots. He even told me that in the emergency room: we are both pawns. He's just an ambitious pawn. Which means he doesn't have any more agency here than I do. So, the only question is, do I pour the drink on the floor or down the drain? On the floor represents minor damage to Syzmek's property. It demonstrates defiance to Symek. Right now, I need Hale to know I am defying him personally.

I stand up and walk over to the sink, raising the glass over it. Hale quirks an eyebrow and smirks slightly, daring me to pour it out. We briefly make eye contact, and then I throw the drink in his face.

"Oops. Turbulence, sorry!" I say insincerely.

Over Hale's shoulder, I see Howard smirk. Hale's expression is one of near-murderous rage. I see him make a visible effort to control his anger. The flight attendant bustles over.

"I am so sorry, sir," she says, handing him a towel. Hale takes the towel without ever taking his eyes off of me.

"Think nothing of it. My friend here has a case of the butterfingers."

He wipes the alcohol off his face and hair. The flight attendant vanishes into the background. Clearly, she doesn't want to find herself in the middle of this, whatever this is.

"I will freshen up. When I return, we should have a little tete-a-tete, Miles. You are operating under some clear miscomprehension."

"I think I have a pretty good handle on it."

Hale turns and walks away from me. He opens one of the bathroom doors and I can see inside that it looks like a real bathroom, not the tiny little closet on a commercial plane. He closes the door.

"It amused me to see Mister Hale have his drink spilled on him. I don't enjoy his company," Howard says when the door has closed. With his weird sing-song cadence of speech, he sounds a bit like a machine or maybe an extraterrestrial trying to fit in with the human population.

"Yeah, he's the worst."

Howard looks like he is about to say something else, but the bathroom door opens, and he quietly goes back to staring at his laptop.

"Miles, if you wouldn't mind, can I have a conversation with you in the conference room?" Hale says between clenched teeth.

"There's a conference room?"

Hale indicates a door in the back of the plane, past the bathroom doors. I shrug and follow him. The door leads into a small room that is lined with the same small windows and oak paneling as the rest of the plane. However, this space has a table bolted to the floor. It is ostensibly not a large table, but considering the size of the plane, it seems large. There are six cushioned chairs around it, also bolted to the floor, each with its own lap belt. I can see a pull-down screen on the far side and a projector mounted on the ceiling. A pedestal in the middle of the table has cables for attaching a laptop.

Hale sits in a chair, but I notice he doesn't bother buckling himself in. I sit down opposite him and clip the seat belt over my lap very slowly before turning to look at him.

"There is a conference room," I confirm.

"Miles, I have tried to be friendly. I have tried to be frank.

You insult and mistreat me at every turn. Is this the relationship you wish us to have?"

"Hale, let's be clear. We aren't friends. We aren't acquaintances. I hate you. I hate what you did in college. I hate what you did to me, I hate what you did to Shelly, I hate what you did to all of us. You don't seem to be any different now. You are part of a secret death cult, or whatever the Dominium Dolores is. You are a corporate lawyer working for one of the largest corporations in the world. Now that I say it aloud, there must be a link there. So hell, maybe Walt Carmichael is a member of the Dominium, too..." I say, my thoughts spewing out as I have them, "...maybe the richest man in the world is also a member of the Dominium. Fuck. I am screwed, aren't I?"

Hale smiles and nods, "You don't know how much I love these moments with you when you finally see the puzzle pieces and realize that you are just one little blotch of color on one tiny little corner of one little piece."

Walt Carmichael is the boss that Hale mentioned before. The chess player who makes us both pawns.

"What does Walt Carmichael want with me? I mean, I see it now. So many things fall into place, knowing that. JMBaptiste Winery only hired me on Walt Carmichael's recommendation, which dragged me into, well, everything else since. But I'm nobody."

"That is correct, and you should remember that. You are nobody. However, you are a nobody who knows something that the Dominium wants to know. You can walk away, no harm, no foul, if you tell me."

I cannot imagine what one thing might be so important that one of the most powerful men in the world would go through all this trouble to get from me.

"What could I possibly know that Walt Carmichael can't

find out for himself? He could literally buy any information from anyone."

"You know who the Blethspa Amah is," Hale says flatly, making eye contact the entire time.

I want to keep a placid face. I don't want to have a tell. But I can't help but flinch a little. I am surprised by the statement, but I am more surprised that I am surprised. It is so obvious. It's the one thing I know that, to my knowledge, only three other people in the world know, and one of those is a dragon.

"The what?" I say. I know I am not fooling anyone with my cardboard delivery.

"I knew you did. Lamia knew, too. She thought if she could get that from you, it would pave her way in the Dominium."

"You think it will pave your way, too."

"No, I would never stake my livelihood on Miles Ward doing the smart thing," Hale sneers back at me.

"Well, I can't tell you," I say, crossing my arms. I am not going to betray Jeff. I don't know what Hale, Walt Carmichael, and the Dominium Dolores want with him, but even if Jeff weren't my best friend, I wouldn't hand him over. I wouldn't hand anyone over.

Something else occurs to me now. I learned about the Blethspa Amah after being hired for the Syzmek project and the JMBaptiste job. There is something else at play here. I am not sure I can ask about it without showing my cards.

"That is the way out I can offer you, Miles. The alternative is, well, it isn't pretty. There will be tasks. There will be small tasks. There will be big tasks. There will be ugly, unpleasant tasks that make you question your own humanity. You will do them, Miles, because if you don't...well, let's say that your stay in prison will be a joy compared to what else might happen."

"More with the threats. It is getting a little old."

"It is no more a threat than gravity is, my friend."

I shrug and cross my arms on my chest. We sit there in silence for a long time.

"How's Shelly?" He asks. He's goading me. I know he is. "Have you seen her lately?"

I reluctantly shake my head no.

"Did you know that she was released? She's receiving in-home care and is recovering slowly. It's very impressive."

I try to look impassive and unimpressed. I can see what he's getting at.

"How did you do that, if you don't mind my asking? I am betting it was with the help of the Blethspa Amah," he says with a thin veneer of a smile on his face.

I continue to stare at him blankly.

"That's what I thought," he says smugly. "Fine, have it your way, but I will find them, with or without you. I tried Miles. I really tried. There will be a day, hopefully not too soon, when you look back on this conversation and wish you'd played ball. Trust me. None of this is what you think."

"It's not an ancient dragon prophecy about the end of magic?" I ask.

He quirks an eyebrow, "Okay, maybe it is what you think, but I suspect you have only one side of the story."

"Then tell me the other side of the story. Convince me with facts that will sway me more than vague threats."

He shrugs and scratches his chin, "You won't believe me."

"Try me," I challenge him.

Hale sighs. He's clearly ambivalent about this situation. I wonder why.

"They say there are two sides to every story," Hale begins. "This is a fabrication, a commonly accepted untruth. Every story is multifaceted. That sort of binary thinking is always folly. When someone tries to sell you a story with a good side and a bad side, they always try to convince you that theirs is the good side."

"So you're saying that yours is the good side?"

"No, I am saying that there is no 'good' or 'bad'; there are just perspectives. Yes, the Blethspa Amah is prophesied to end magic. But do you really want to live in a world without magic?"

"But it is ending magic by explaining it, by making it mechanical. Right?" I say.

"You don't think that has consequences? Imagine that you have a basket of apples. You could do a lot of things with them. You could eat a crispy, crunchy apple. You could dip them in caramel and make caramel apples. You could make applesauce. The possibilities are endless. Say you decide to make an apple pie with them."

"Okay," I say, not clear why he jumped to fruit suddenly.

"Now you have an apple pie, but where are the apples?"

"In the pie," I say, stating the obvious.

"But are they the same apples? Could you recognize each individual apple? Do they taste the same? Do they have the same character? Are they really the same apples?"

"Yes, they've been altered, but they are still the same apples."

"So you could still caramel dip them and make a caramel apple?"

"Okay, I see what you are getting at. Their potential as apples is changed when you cook them."

"It's the same with magic. Once you explain it, its potential is changed. Limited. When did you last see a magic carpet or flying boom?"

He motions at the airplane we are riding in.

"Magic that has been mechanized, explained, and normalized, you see?"

"Okay, but that's true anytime we do basically anything. We take a breath of air, and that air's potential is changed."

"Yes, but we aren't talking about an apple or air. We are talking about the natural laws that govern how the universe works. You are limiting a universe with unlimited potential."

"I'm getting very confused about what your point is."

"My point is that once the Blethspa Amah defines magic, gives it all boundaries, and codifies a set of rules, the universe goes from an endless, boundless series of potentials to a giant mechanism. The universe no longer has potential. It becomes a device that serves one function."

"So magic goes away, so what? Magic is awful. The world would be much better without people spilling blood to enslave, murder, and control."

"Would it? A world without whimsy, a world without wonder, every day a mechanistic recreation of the last. Does that sound like a world you wish to live in?"

"Okay, so what do you want with the Blethspa Amah?"

"I'm just a pawn. Finding the Blethspa Amah makes me look good to the boss."

"Fine then, what does Walt Carmichael want with the Blethspa Amah?"

"The Dominium Dolores is dedicated to maintaining the integrity of magic and allowing the new, the spontaneous, and wonderful to exist."

"That doesn't sound like the goal of a group that calls themselves the Masters of Pain."

"The world of the Blethspah Amah is a world without pain, suffering, or hurt. That's true. However, it is also a world without love, joy, or creation. It is relativity. You cannot be high if there is no low. You cannot protect the precious without also protecting the vile. You cannot have love without hate. We acknowledge the cost of wonder."

"So you are the good guys."

"I told you, good guys, bad guys, that's a binary tale told by the devious to appeal to your sense of morality. Some wish for a world of magic. Others wish for a blank, mundane, repetitive world without it. We wish to keep magic in the world."

"Because without magic, you would have no power," I say. It's more me thinking aloud than anything I am actually looking for him to confirm.

He grins wickedly, "I doubt that is true, but certainly, it would be a less interesting power."

I nod and think. He evaded my question about what they were going to do with the Blethspa Amah, which is enough of an answer. While there is an internal logic to what he's saying, I still don't believe him.

Do I not believe him because what he's saying doesn't make sense? There is a rationality to it. However, at the end of the day, I think I mostly don't believe him because he's John Hale, a consummate liar, user, and abuser who would betray his own mother if he thought it would get him ahead.

"I can't help you," I say.

The mask of congeniality that he's been wearing breaks. His face contorts into a look of poorly contained rage, red and puffy-looking. I've never seen Hale look like he was going to lose control before. He makes eye contact, and I have a sensation that I have had before. Our eyes are locked in a contest of will. I cannot look away, or I will fail, to some dire consequence.

I turn my head away and break eye contact. "That almost worked on me last time, but it won't again. What is that? Some kind of mesmerism? Are you trying to get into my head?"

He storms past me, leaving me alone in the conference room. I lean back in my chair and sigh a long, heavy sigh.

When I get home, I will visit Goldsmith. He owes me some answers.

After our encounter, I prefer not to leave the conference room and go to the main cabin. I don't really want to sit with Hale for the rest of the flight. I make a brief trip to the main cabin to get my bag, but Hale seems to be in the restroom, so I avoid dealing with him again. I set up my laptop on the conference table and spent the rest of the flight watching movies on it. The flight attendant comes in to give me lunch, but I am undisturbed for the remainder of the flight.

After landing, I sit in the conference room until the flight attendant comes to demand that I deplane. By the time I leave, Hale and Howard are both long gone.

CHAPTER 31

The bumpy road to Goldsmith's seems even more rough and foreboding than ever before. I haven't even bothered to go home. I take my rental car straight through Napa and up into the hills. Previously, I've always had a four-wheel drive car coming up this road. It is much more harrowing in the little sedan. It bounces and bumps over potholes and mounds—the bottom scrapes on rocks. I wonder if the insurance company will ever figure out how they are going to deal with my destroyed Subaru.

I park in front of Goldsmith's and wait for him. It seems to take forever before he comes out. However, instead of standing by his front door and motioning me to enter, he hobbles, cane in hand, to my car. This is different. This is a change, and change with Goldsmith is an ominous portend.

"Young Warder," he says as I roll my window down, "you are no longer welcome here."

"What?" I sputter, "Why not? I have questions. I need help."

"The apostate has claimed you. You have chosen a side," he says.

"I have not chosen a side! I didn't know there were sides until you said I'd chosen one! I can't choose a side if I don't even know there are sides."

"Few choices are made in the light, but we must deal with the consequences regardless."

He starts to hobble back to his cluttered home.

"Well, answer me one last question then," I plead.

He turns and makes eye contact. In his eyes, I see stars born, planets shift, black holes implode, and galaxies die. I see the vastness of the universe and feel very small, alone, and cold in it. Finally, after what is either a second or the entirety of existence, he breaks eye contact and speaks.

"Very well," he says, turning his back to me, "One question, and then you will go and not return."

One last question. I get one last question from Goldsmith. He has been a reliable source of information for me for years. Every time I come upon something magical that I don't quite understand, he's been able to clarify for me. His answers are enigmatic, vague, and deflective, but I always get something out of them. Now I have one last question: I have to make it count. I have like a thousand questions, but I only get one. My mind races through them. What should I ask? Was Hale telling the truth about the Blethspa Amah? What does Goldsmith have to do with Walt Carmichael? I need more answers than I have questions to ask.

"How do I find the answers I need?" I finally ask.

Goldsmith pauses. He is quiet for a long moment. Then he turns back to me. His eyes averted toward the ground, his face furrowed in consideration.

"Your answer is in the cards," Goldsmith says swiftly as he

turns and scuffles his way into his house. The door slams closed behind him.

Somehow, as soon as I asked the question, I knew that would be the answer.

It takes a twenty-point turn to get my beige rental car aimed back down Goldsmith's driveway. I feel impatient to get away from this place. It feels like I am no longer safe here. Like there is a clock ticking down to impending consequence.

I accelerate down the little dirt road, leaving a plume of dust in my wake, banging and clanging away from Goldsmith's. At one point, the car comes down hard, and there is a metallic screeching sound from under it, but it keeps running, so I ignore it. My mind is lost in a spiral of darkening thoughts.

I feel like the whole world has crumbled around me in the past week. Hale bailed me out of prison, and I discovered that Walt Carmichael is probably the head of the Dominium Dolores. I think Genevieve and I broke up. Jeff might be prophecized to end magic and, if Hale is to be believed, make the universe boring. All of that, and the best answers I have, will likely be found in a deck of tarot cards given to me by an undead sorcerer whom I destroyed.

I make it about a mile from Goldsmith's when the check engine light flips on. I ignore it, assuming it will last until I make it home. A couple of miles later, all the lights on the dashboard light up and start flashing and beeping at me. Okay, maybe I can't ignore it.

My revelation, however, is too late. The car stalls, and the engine begins smoking as I pull to the side of the road. I get out and walk a good distance from the car in case it catches fire. A lack of cell service thwarts my attempt to call emergency services. It figures. My week is going to hell, my life is going to hell, and now this. It's like everything is conspiring against me.

I scream and throw my phone at a tree. It shatters and falls to the ground, the screen nothing but a network of fine cracks, the side of the housing bent and broken. It feels cathartic and comforting to see it shatter, but only for a second. Then, the catharsis vanishes like a smoke ring, and regret sweeps in to fill the void.

I pick up my wrecked phone and slip it into my bag—there's no need to litter. I look around the area. A large rock is about twenty feet away, just off the shoulder. I drag my feet to it, sit down, and wait.

Car after car tears down Silverado Trail, all going well over the speed limit. None of them stops. After about ten minutes, I see one start to brake, like they are thinking about stopping to help. However, they are going so fast that they are a hundred yards away by the time they've slowed down any substantial amount; after a moment of ambivalence, they seem to decide that I am not their problem and accelerate back down the road.

About half an hour later, a large SUV bearing the Napa County Sheriff's Department pulls up next to my car. Only a faint trickle of smoke now worms its way out from under the hood, but there is a black sooty ring over the entire front of the vehicle.

A deputy gets out and walks up to me.

"Oh shit, it's you," the deputy says with a tone of exasperation and disappointment in his voice. He's in his thirties, probably, with a thin brown mustache. It is wispy and almost looks like a small, downy caterpillar on his lip.

"I'm sorry," I say, confused. I squint at his badge to catch his name. "Do I know you, Officer Klein?"

"I spent a day sitting outside your ER room."

"Oh," I say sheepishly. I never saw the officers' faces, just the side of their uniforms.

"It just follows you around, doesn't it, Mr. Ward?"

"What's that?"

"Trouble."

I sigh. He's not wrong.

Deputy Klein wanders around my car. He crouches down and looks under it.

"It looks like you tore the oil pan off. Your engine seized. Why did you drive it like that?"

"I guess I didn't notice," I say. It is half true.

"Well, that's going to be an expensive mistake," he says, shaking his head, "I'll call a tow truck."

He doesn't wait for a response but turns and walks back to his SUV, shaking his head incredulously the whole way.

Deputy Klein sits in his vehicle while we wait for the tow truck. I maintain my perch on the rock. My mind has become numb and blank. I want to get home, sleep, and wake up to discover this was all a bad dream.

The tow truck arrives, and the Deputy drives away as soon as my rental car is hooked up. After a long and involved conversation with the tow truck driver, he agrees to drop the car and myself at the rental company.

Hours of grueling paperwork and questions await me. I turn my brain off and go through the motions. Eventually, I find myself being dropped off by a rideshare in front of my apartment. I am now carless, phoneless, and single. Then, in the parking lot, I see Magdalena's car and remember that she said I could drive it and that she owed me a car for getting my old car blown up in a wildfire. At least I'm not car-less.

I slog my way up the stairs to my apartment and open the door.

"Honey, I'm home!" I say into the empty apartment.

"Miles, there is something I have to tell you."

"What's up, Hank?" I ask, tired and sullen. I stand in silence for a minute. "Well?"

"Goddamit! Miles, have I ever told you what a fuck up you are?"

"Every time I walk through the door."

"At least I am consistent."

"At least there is one consistent thing in my life."

"Being a fuck up?"

"That too," I say, walking to my desk. The cardboard box with the Hierophant's final message is before me. I sit at my desk and open it for one more look.

V
THE HIEROPHANT

EPILOGUE

"LISTEN, Genevieve, I think this was a mistake. I should go," Miles says.

"I don't think that's the flex you think it is," I tell him, but he's ignoring me. I know that he isn't ignoring me. He probably isn't ignoring me. It's hard not to feel ignored, though.

"Oh," Genevieve says, pushing her sunglasses farther up her nose, *"You want to do this now?"*

"I just feel like it's better to get it over with."

"Yeah, this probably was a mistake. It's been obvious from the get-go, but I mean, it was still fun. It wasn't ever going to be anything more than that, though. This was just for fun, right?" She quips. Everything about her body language says she's hurt, but Miles doesn't seem to be picking up the queues. He can be very smart sometimes, but he's a real tool when he's not.

"Honestly, I'm not sure this was ever fun," Miles says.

"Oh buddy, you are bad at this," I whisper in his ear. He brushes his ear with his hand, like a fly landed on it. I wonder if he can hear me and is just ignoring me. He usually breaks if he's ignoring me, and I hassle him long enough. But I don't think he is ignoring me. Once more, I am just a fly on the wall.

When people say they wish they could be the fly on the wall, I don't think they know what they are talking about. People's lives are usually pretty boring. Sitting around and watching them all the time is the worst. Every now and then, they get up to something interesting. This moment would probably be interesting if I hadn't seen it coming since the day they met.

Genevieve's face contorts into an ugly and unhappy knot. She has a very pretty face, though I think the living all have pretty faces. Maybe that's something about being dead or whatever I am. There are no faces out here. I'm here, gazing in through eternity and making a running commentary. It's lonely, there isn't much here, wherever I am, and what there is...well, it isn't much company or much to look at. So everything in the living world is beautiful. But the living don't appreciate that.

Sometimes, Miles can hear me, so I follow him around. It's better than just being a fly on the wall until the end of time.

"You know what, Miles? You aren't exactly a ball of sunshine yourself. You are the single, whiniest, neediest person I've ever dated. I know I said that the mannequin thing wasn't that weird, but I lied. That's really, really weird. So, I am glad you finally came out and talked to me about this because, yeah, I think we are through," Genevieve says through clenched teeth.

The kid gloves are coming off. I mean, she's not wrong, but she could be a little nicer about it.

"The mannequin thing is weird! But I'm not a mannequin, you know!" I say. I know she can't hear me, but it feels good to express myself anyway. I express this sentiment a lot: the mannequin and I are not one and the same! But he doesn't hear me whenever I try to talk to him about it. I don't know.

Maybe it violates some law of ghosthood, or whatever this is. Or maybe it's like some mental block for him since he's pretty adamant that ghosts don't exist, even though I've been here most of his life. My least favorite bit of irony.

"Um. I just meant that coming to the conference was a mistake. I am not having fun here, at the conference, and I should go home. Um. Are you breaking up with me?"

"Yes, she's breaking up with you dumbass. What did you expect? You're like fire and gasoline; it only ended one of two ways; at least this way, nothing burns down!"

"Shit, yeah, I guess I am. Listen, Miles, you're cute, and you can be fun," She says, obviously trying to placate his tiny ego.

"Not that cute," I mutter.

"But you are also a mess," she says, not placating as much as I first thought. *We've dealt with flying monkeys, magic heists, and ancient Greek monsters, but I still know basically nothing about you. You are so guarded, and that's okay. That's your business, but it's exhausting. You gotta open up a little, you gotta relax, Miles."*

"How is this my fault?" Miles whines.

"It's a fling, Miles. Get over it," I mutter. This soap opera is getting boring.

"I don't talk about that stuff because I don't remember it! I don't want to remember it! So yeah! It's hard to open up to others about stuff I don't even want to think about myself!" Miles yells. He is such a drama llama.

"Figure it out, Mr. Ward! If that is your real name!" She screams back. She's a drama llama, too. They were made for each other—like fire and gasoline!

"It's not!" He yells back. So, he does remember.

"No! You two, don't break up. You could get married and have kids! They'd be so messed up! Just what the world needs more of!" I say sarcastically. I don't know who I am being sarcastic for. I guess part of me hopes Miles is just ignoring me, and if I am mean enough, I'll get his attention, but it doesn't work.

"What are you doing?" She yells.

I glance over; he's obviously packing his things to leave. We have a classic 'you can't fire me, I quit' situation. He wants to be the one to storm out, and now she's pissed because she wants to throw his stuff out the door into a heap in the hall-way, and he's beating her to the punch. I loved these sorts of scenes back when Miles and I would watch Craven's Gate together. He would never admit it, but he did, too. Maybe this is some kind of roleplaying a fantasy thing?

"I am packing, genius! You'd probably figure that out if you weren't mixing booze with prescription drugs!" Miles says chin thrust out defiantly.

"Went right for the throat there, didn't you?" I say, "You know she keeps a knife in her suitcase, right? Like a big one."

"Have you been going through my shit?" She yells.

"Clearly not very thoroughly, or he'd know about the knife."

"What the hell, Miles? Who the fuck do you think you are? Enjoy hitchhiking home! I hope you choke!"

"You two are way too old for this crap, you know that?" I say, but no one ever listens to me.

Genevieve slams the bathroom door behind her. Miles stands staring at the door, mouth flapping like a dying fish. He has tears in his eyes. He takes his bag and rushes out the door, slamming it behind him.

"I don't think they heard you on the fourth floor, guys," I say to an empty room.

I am about to follow Miles when I hear Genevieve let out a huge sob. I sigh—or at least I make a sighing sound. Sighing isn't really the same when you don't have lungs, a mouth, or any organs, for that matter. It's something I do to try to feel more human, to stay more connected, or something. I go through the door.

Genevieve is lying in a heap at the bottom of the shower. She's crumpled up in her bathrobe, sobbing.

"Don't let him get to you. He's an A..." I start to say, but Genevieve speaks up, finishing my sentence.

"Asshole!" She yells.

"Yeah, he's got intimacy issues; I mean, he's been through some shit. His twin brother died when he was a kid, his mom committed suicide, and his dad was a two-bit con man who dragged him around and never stayed anywhere very long. He never really made any friends as a kid. Human connection is foreign and scary to him," I don't know why I am saying this. I know she can't hear me. I think it's more for me; I need to be able to forgive Miles and look him in the eye again. He's literally the only person I can talk to.

Genevieve lays there sobbing for a bit. I want to be comforting, but I can't. I'm worried she will do something rash and self-destructive, but I don't know what I could do about it if she did. Miles, I have some kind of connection with; I can influence the flow of magic around him, divert it, and use the connection between him and the simulacrum to channel energy. I can even, for the lack of a better word, steer Miles sometimes, though he doesn't know it. With Genevieve, I am helpless to do anything but watch.

A moment later, she jumps violently to her feet. Her robe is hanging half open. She has a look of rage on her face. If Miles were here, I'd make some crass remark to get a rise out of him. I don't really care about naked people or sex or anything. Watching people do basically anything is equally interesting to me. Having someone acknowledge my presence is more validating, and Miles responds more to jibing than anything else, so I've learned what will get a reaction.

"Please don't shank Miles in the lobby. I won't have anyone to talk to," I say, holding my hands up to stop her as she charges out of the bathroom.

"Fuck him," she says, *"Fuck you, Miles!"*

She walks right through me and out of the bathroom. There is no sensation; I don't feel anything, and there is no indication that she feels anything. She is passing through a dream, and I am passing through her. There is no contact or sensation. Miles is the only person I can even kind of feel, a faint and distant warmth.

She grabs her phone out of her purse and sets it on the bed. She then starts rifling frantically through her purse. Finally, she empties it on the bed, creating a heap of things: makeup, loose change, a little coin purse, crumpled-up tissues, random papers, gizmos, and things I can't identify. She finds a little paper rectangle in the mess. I look over her shoulder; a ten-digit number is written in black pen. No name, no other marks. She stabs the ten digits into her phone and holds it to her ear.

Her face is stained with drying tears as she stands in her bathrobe, phone to ear, one bare foot thumping a rhythm on the carpeted floor.

"Hi," she finally says, "It's Genevieve Gale. You want to talk about Miles Ward? Let's talk about Miles Ward."

Well, that's ominous.

About the Author

Justin Godey is an emerging author of modern fantasy, with a touch of supernatural horror thrown in. This is his third book.

Also by Justin Godey

Pinot Noir

Charred-Donnay

Coming Soon: Blood, Wine, Magic: Book 4 - No Rhyme or Riesling